M000166283

ONCE UPON A PAGE

JESSIE CLEVER

SOMEDAY LADY PUBLISHING, LLC.

Copyright © 2017 by Jessica McQuaid

All rights reserved.

Published by Someday Lady Publishing, LLC

No part of this book may be reproduced in any form or by any electronic or mechanical means, including information storage and retrieval systems, without written permission from the author, except for the use of brief quotations in a book review.

This book is a work of fiction. Any references to historical events, real people, or real places are used fictitiously. Other names, characters, places and events are products of the author's imagination, and any resemblances to actual events or places or persons, living or dead, is entirely coincidental.

ISBN-13: 978-0-9984192-5-1

Cover Design by Wicked Smart Designs

For Owen

CHAPTER 1

he day began much as any other day. With murder, of course.
From The Adventures of Miss Melanie Merkett, Private Inquisitor

PENELOPE PAIGET WAS skilled at a great many things. Hiding dead bodies was not one of them.

She had returned to Wickshire Place at half six that morning as was her custom after her regular half day off the previous day. She'd spent her time as she usually did, in the company of Lady Delia Witherspoon, the woman for whom she had served as companion for nearly four years before accepting the position as Lord Wickshire's secretary. Lady Witherspoon continued to enjoy Penelope's company, and as Penelope had no other family in London on whom to call and likewise enjoyed the rather flamboyant observations of Lady Delia, Penelope found herself spending her afternoons off in her former employer's company. It was a pleasant and productive way for Penelope to spend the time as Lady Delia quite enjoyed speaking about Penelope's other professional endeavors—the ones that most of society would think unusual and even unbecoming of a woman of Penelope's refined reputation as the daughter of a well-respected country baron. It was something Penelope enjoyed most about Lady Delia. The woman did not raise an eyebrow at others' unusual proclivities.

It was this fascination with the unusual that had likely secured the position for Penelope at Wickshire Place in the first instance. Lord Wickshire excelled at unusual proclivities. A man who had earned the nickname Poison Peter was not likely to count a snuff box fetish as his most eccentric habit. No, indeed Lord Wickshire did not. He was an academic much like her father had been, and he was prone to eccentric rants on topics of natural history, his true passion running towards that of the chemical arts.

Really, if Penelope were to think of it, it was likely the combination of Lady Delia's desire for eccentric acquaintances acquittances and her father's academic pursuits that had nearly guaranteed Penelope's secretarial position in the Wickshire household. Lady Delia often had Lord Wickshire to tea, and it was through this occurrence that he had learned of Penelope's assistance in her father's endeavors. A woman so skilled at keeping the notes of an academic as well as having intelligence herself was rare indeed, Lord Wickshire had professed, and offered her employment on the spot. With Lady Delia's blessing, of course.

Lady Delia had always said Penelope was far too intelligent to spend her days wasting away as a paid companion even if Lady Delia treasured her company. It wasn't the first time Penelope had heard such, but she had grown better at hiding how such a proclamation irked her. It was with some marked measure of glee that Lady Delia handed Penelope over to Lord Wickshire, claiming he would never be disappointed in Penelope's work.

And he hadn't been. Lord Wickshire, that was. At least, not until that morning.

For as she stood on the threshold of the drawing room of Wickshire Place, the toes of her boots neatly aligning with the edge of the Abusson rug, its vibrant reds, blues, and golds now muted with a peculiar dampness seeping from the dead body lying atop it, Penelope was quite certain she would not succeed at whatever task Lord Wickshire was about that morn.

Penelope stood calmly, her hands folded over her reticule as she took in the sight of the deceased. She had no reason for alarm. That is, she was not frightened by the sight of a dead man. Her own father had conducted autopsies of pigs and cats and dogs. Sometimes even a goat when the opportunity presented itself. She knew very well where meat came from, and how it was that physical anatomy worked. It was nothing more than a bit of natural study. And it wasn't as if there was any messy blood with which to contend. The man was quite intact. Although, if she were being honest, she would have admitted a good splattering of blood would have made the scene far more interesting. As it were, it was just a poor man lying dead on a bit of carpet.

She looked up and about the room. Lord Wickshire enjoyed taking his morning tea in the drawing room where the light was best for reading the day's newspapers. Oddly, however, Lord Wickshire was absent.

Penelope took a small step back, angling the upper part of her body into the corridor where she heard the rustling skirts of Mrs. Watson, Lord Wickshire's appallingly efficient housekeeper.

"Excuse me, Mrs. Watson," Penelope called down the corridor. "Is Lord Wickshire in residence?"

3

Mrs. Watson did not stop in her trajectory down the corridor, the basket at her elbow of burnt candle nubs bouncing against her bony hip. "He is not, Miss Paiget," she said. "He was in the study when I departed yesterday, and that was the last I had seen him."

"Are you aware there is a dead body in the drawing room then?" she called after the retreating figure.

Mrs. Watson did not stop. In fact, she did not even slow her step as she made her way to the back of the townhouse, likely in pursuit of the kitchens. "I do, indeed," she returned. "It's making a terrible mess of the carpet. It's not as if we've nothing to do around here without his lordship making more work for us." The woman opened a door at the end of the hall and disappeared.

Penelope straightened. Everything seemed to be activity as usual then. The poor man on the carpet seemed rather at peace despite Mrs. Watson's declaration of inconvenience to the carpet and the staff. The gentleman was rather young, almost boyish in appearance, with unkempt hair and mismatched patches of stubble along his cheeks as if he were new to shaving. Perhaps he had been. Quite terrible, really.

And the rug was likely a loss now anyway. Mrs. Watson need only worry about removing it from the drawing room and bringing a new one down from the attics.

She leaned back again, her head going around the door-frame to see the clock standing in the hall. It was after seven now. Lord Wickshire usually began his dictation at this hour. Reciting to her any discoveries or ideas he had formed in the late hours he often spent in his laboratories in the extensive basements of the townhouse. He kept his working rooms down there after a terrible occurrence with sulfur when he'd housed his experiments in his second floor study. The fumes had seeped up to the servants' quarters on the fourth floor, much to the glowering disapproval of Mrs. Watson. Lord

Wickshire had vacated immediately for the subterranean comfort of the basements rather than encounter Mrs. Watson in future.

But his dictation, that occurred in the main living areas of the house, usually in the second floor study where he had a desk installed for Penelope. A lovely escritoire of glowing rosewood. It was elegant while at the same time stately. Magical, Penelope would have called it. Perfect for a use of which she did not speak in polite circles.

She straightened once more, her eyes falling to the body, and released a round, deep sigh, her lungs collapsing in repose. There was nothing for it but to wait. At least, that was what she'd planned to do.

Until someone knocked on the door.

She looked over her shoulder at it, just down the corridor from where she stood in the entrance to the drawing room. She peered the other way. Mrs. Watson had either not heard the summons or had deemed Penelope close enough to see to the matter of a visitor. It was likely the second option as it spoke most acutely to efficiency. Something with which Mrs. Watson took uncomfortable pleasure.

Penelope stepped away from the drawing room, her boots loud against the wood floors of the foyer in the quiet solitude of a house just waking. She pulled open the great front door and blinked into the increasing sunshine of what promised to be a beautiful spring day.

Her eyes settled on the gentleman standing on the stoop before her, her gaze falling directly to the bouquet of tulips clasped in his hand. They were purple tulips not yet opened in bloom and streamed with promising bits of white along the edges of the petals. They reminded her of hope and promise, and her fingers twitched against the strings of her reticule at the remembered feel of a quill in her hand.

"Good morning," she said to the bouquet, a smile already

5

coming to her lips before she raised her gaze to the caller. "Oh, bloody hell," she stammered when her eyes fell on Mr. Samuel Black's familiar face. She shook her head quickly at his stricken expression. "Sorry," she said. "Very sorry. It was just that I was not expecting you."

His face crumpled into a frown. "Yes, I'm incredibly sorry about the early hour," he said quickly. "My profession does not relate itself to normal calling hours, and the necessity for an early—"

She cut him off with a waved hand between them. "I meant the year, Mr. Black. Not the hour. Wherever have you been?"

It had been ten years since she had last seen Mr. Samuel Black. In a coffee house in Bloomsbury no less. Samuel Black had roared into her life like a terrible carriage collision. Life altering and quick. There for a moment and then gone, but even after it had all happened, she still couldn't pry her eyes away from the memory.

And there he was. Looking exactly like the memory she couldn't escape.

With that thought came a pain so intense she pressed her hand to her stomach as if it to stop it. The fire sliced through her, freezing the air in her lungs. She swallowed, her fingers twitching against the bodice of her gown.

Everything had been different then. Everything had been different when Samuel made her promise to wait for him.

And she had. Only...not quite.

"About that," he began, but she cut him off with another wave of her hand, thrusting the thing away that had caused her such blinding, momentary pain, thinking for a moment it felt horribly close to fear.

"Please, come in." She backed up to allow him entrance. "It's very rude of me to make you stand on the stoop."

He stepped quickly around her, walking several paces

into the foyer. He looked quite the same. In general appearance that is. His black hair was severely cut, short and precise around his ears and carefully swept away from his face under the brim of his hat. He wore a neatly tailored frock coat, a waistcoat of fine material in a remarkably deep violet that contrasted nicely with the blues of his cravat. His black trousers accented his height as they disappeared into tall boots, giving him a lean appearance. She wondered briefly if all police inspectors kept such a neat and precise appearance.

For she had followed his career. It was hard not to. The way he had stampeded through the House of Lords on the coattails of his grandfather and then his uncle. *The Times* had referred to Samuel as an educated man, well-respected for his studies in civil behavior and government. A real asset as Parliament took up the question of establishing a true police force as the efficacy of the Bow Street Runners had begun to fade.

But even as she recalled these accolades as heralded by the press, she could not remove her eyes from his face.

His face showed the marks of time just as much as she was sure hers did. There were wrinkles where there hadn't been before. Deep sprays of them sprang from his eyes, and defined creases bracketed his mouth. The past ten years had not been kind to Samuel Black. Well, not unkind really. But something had caused him great stress and pain.

She suddenly felt terrible for asking where he had been. Clearly the journey to establishing a police force had brewed with something. Something dark and tense.

"I know I had promised you that I would return someday, Miss Paiget, and I realize that ten years was quite a bit longer than I had planned to take. But the reform acts took longer than I had wished, and the Metropolitan Police—"

"I know." She whispered this, because from what little she

knew of Samuel, she knew he did not accept praise easily, and her admission revealed a great deal more than she had expected to. He would know now that she had been watching him. Watching and waiting. Filled with joy and even pride at every inch of newsprint that vaunted another success in the reform acts.

But that joy had become a little less now with every article. Ever since her own success had become so apparent.

His face changed again now, his frown dipping into something that suggested confusion and even embarrassment.

"You do?" His gaze drifted about her person as if he, too, were taking in the effects of time on her.

She wanted to reach up and tuck her hair more carefully into the chignon huddled under the small brim of her bonnet, the bonnet she had been about to remove when she had been arrested by the sight of the dead body in the drawing room, but she wasn't one to give away any sign of discomfort. It was a weakness heroines did not exhibit.

Mr. Black's gaze lingered a little longer, and she was glad she had selected her newer gown that morning. The one with the dark green flowers in the fabric of the bodice.

"It's hard to miss such an accomplishment when it is the favorited fodder of *The Times*," she said, hoping to lessen his embarrassment.

He looked away briefly as if to gather his thoughts, his gaze moving to his right, sliding over the drawing room door and back to her. "The policing—" he halted, his eyes flying back to the drawing room, his face seizing on a grimace. He looked back at her. "Is that a dead body?" he asked, pointing to the object in question.

"Yes," she said. "It is at that." She stepped up so that she stood far too close to him. She used the excuse of tucking her head around the doorframe of the drawing room to

8

view the deceased, but really, she had just wanted a whiff of him.

Smells were so delicious to describe. It was one of the things she tried to capture most accurately, and Samuel's odor was not disappointing. Vanilla and soap and just a whisper of lemon. She drew a deeper breath and looked back at him, her closer position requiring her to raise her gaze several inches. "Your timing is rather ironic, Mr. Black."

"That would appear so, Miss Paiget."

HIS PLAN HAD BEEN THUS: Appear on the doorstep with a beautiful bouquet of the season's first tulips, apologize profusely for the delay (could one call ten years a delay?), and beg Penelope to allow him in. Into the house? Into her life? He wasn't quite sure on that point. He had only thought as far ahead as getting to her. That had seemed to take him long enough.

Ten years.

It had been ten years since last he had seen her. With her blazing red hair and her glorious freckles. Her intoxicating almond eyes. So many colors of green, he couldn't name just one. Penelope. Penelope Paiget.

Ten years.

He felt the familiar icy clench of dread in his stomach at the first sight of her. The dread that so often haunted him when the possibility of failure loomed in the shadows. For failure lurked with Penelope. Lurked with all the thoughts he'd ever conjured of Penelope over the last ten, difficult years. Even that in itself had been a failure.

Ten years.

How had he let so much time go by?

He hadn't expected her to be the one to open the door,

but perhaps at such an early hour, the other servants were busy preparing the house for the day. He wasn't certain what the home of an eccentric earl required in terms of preparation, but he granted that it must be similar to what every household required. The fires needed to be stoked and perhaps rekindled. The breakfast must be prepared and served. The draperies pulled back and secured.

That had been his favorite duty as a child. His mother always allowed him to help the maids pull back the draperies from their nightly slumber. Every morning he was keen to be the first in a room, the first to grab hold of pulls and swing back the heavy folds of velvet and satin and silk. He had always looked out at the lightening London skyline, wondering what the day might bring.

He had wondered just that the morning Nathan Black had appeared in their lives. He was fairly certain he hadn't been anticipating quite that much when he'd pulled the drapes that long ago morning. But God, he was sure glad it had happened. No, grateful. He was grateful for the sudden appearance of Nathan Black.

He wouldn't be standing in the home of an earl just then, bedecked in a silk waistcoat, fine linen shirtsleeves, and polished boots. He'd be with the other servants. Laying out the fires and beating rugs. That had been his least favorite chore.

But as he stepped into the earl's drawing room it was for entirely different reasons that he was glad Nathan Black had appeared that day.

"I don't assume you know how this body came to be here," he said, stepping carefully around the corpse.

He didn't think Penelope would be upset by his blunt conversation. She had after all been the one to make the first pithy comment about the circumstance. There was a dead body in the home of her employer, and an inspector for the

Metropolitan Police was now standing in the same room as it. That wasn't entirely a favorable situation. But Penelope did not balk, did not make stuttering excuses, did not so much as twitch one of her beautiful, almond-shaped eyes. She took it in stride much as she'd done the first day he had met her when he'd stop a purse snatcher from robbing her employer, Lady Delia Witherspoon.

"It was here when I arrived this morning," she said, following his footsteps carefully.

He noted how she stepped where he stepped, her head slightly bent as if to study his method of observation rather than the room itself. It was unsettling but curious. Perhaps it was a habit developed as a result of her occupation as secretary. Perhaps it helped her to anticipate the needs of her employer and thus serve him more efficiently.

"You do not live on the premises?" he asked, turning to her sharply enough to have her head coming back up to look at him.

"I do," she said. "But yesterday was my half day off, and I typically spend the time with Lady Delia. I'm sure you recall her."

Samuel nodded, Lady Delia fresh on his mind. "I do indeed," he said. He gestured at the body and only then remembered the tulips in his hand.

Penelope stepped forward, reaching for the flowers before he expected her to. Her fingers collided with his, and heat coursed through him, slow and steady and inevitable. There was a pause in which their eyes met, brief but sure, and he wondered if for a moment they both thought the same thing.

I've been waiting for this for so long.

She stepped away as quickly as she had stepped forward, taking the tulips into her arms and backing up, her steps silent until she stepped off the carpet and onto the wooden floors. But her countenance never changed. Her posture never stiffened. She simply stood. Waiting. Ready. Prepared.

He pried his eyes away from her and back to the body before him.

"So you were not in residence when this body may have come to be here?" He stepped as close as he dared to the body, avoiding any obvious evidence he might contaminate.

Penelope shook her head. "I was not, and the other servants were likely not here as well." He cast her a look, and she elaborated. "It's a small staff, and most of them stay with family when time allows."

"How small?"

She gazed at the ceiling as if deciphering the answer from the plaster. "There is Mrs. Watson, the housekeeper, Jacobs, the butler, the upstairs maid and the downstairs maid, two footmen, and the cook." She looked back at him. "And myself, of course."

He bent and pressed two fingers into the carpet where water had clearly saturated the fibers. He pulled back his hand, raising it to his nose, and sniffed.

Penelope stepped forward, the movement clipped as if she hadn't planned to do it. "What is that?" she asked.

He looked at his hand, sniffed his fingers again. "He didn't die here." He stood. "The moisture soaking the carpet has no odor. A body will eliminate its fluids upon death because the muscles containing it are no longer contracted. But the carpet appears to hold only water." He pulled his handkerchief from his pocket and wiped his hands on it. "Did you discover the body or was it another member of the staff?"

She frowned slightly, a delicate line appearing between her brows. "Mrs. Watson is aware of the body, but I wouldn't say she discovered it." She pointed across the room to the fire blazing in the hearth. "Rebecca, the downstairs maid, would have laid the fire at six this morning. She likely also saw the body."

Samuel was alarmed at the lack of alarm he felt over so many persons observing a dead body and not calling a sergeant at once. He had heard of the Earl of Wickshire's eccentricities many times from Lady Pemberly, Margaret Lynwood. Lady Pemberly often worked with the earl on War Office matters, and she had witnessed directly some of the earl's more unusual tendencies. It wouldn't be so outrageous that the staff at Wickshire Place would not have reported the presence of a corpse. They may even have believed the corpse was a part of one of Wickshire's famed experiments after all.

Samuel swallowed against the disturbing thought.

"I will need to speak with both Mrs. Watson and Miss Rebecca..." he indicated with a hand.

The line appeared between Penelope's eyes before she said, "Jarvis."

"Miss Rebecca Jarvis," Samuel finished. "Although this man did not die here, it is possible Mrs. Watson or Miss Jarvis encountered evidence of which they are not aware."

"Of course." She adjusted the parcel of tulips to lay in the crook of one elbow. "Ah, Mr. Black, the odor you speak of—do you mean urine?"

"Yes, quite." He tucked the handkerchief back into his pocket.

Penelope gave an affirmative noise, and he swore he saw her fingers twitch against the bouquet. It was possible he had only imagined it. He had had very little sleep. Another late night in pursuit of ghosts. His current case struck far too close to the very thing he held most precious. His family. He would gladly lose years of sleep if only to keep them safe.

And with that thought was the reminder that it wasn't his family. Not really. He had been swept into the cyclone that was the Black family at the age of nine, and for a very long time had accepted them as his. But not now. Now he felt the truth. Ever since that night. Now he felt the difference, and the dread in his gut churned.

He focused on the body, forcing his wayward thoughts aside and concentrating on the thing that had anchored him for nearly ten years. Police work. It was what drove him. What kept him steady, and he reached for it now.

The man was young. He was well dressed but with enough lack of precision to suggest his appearance was not his first concern. His hair was overly long in a manner that suggested he had missed a trimming and let the style grow too long and not that he'd purposely wished for such length.

"Do you know this man?" he asked, tilting his head toward Penelope.

She was watching him again and not the body, and he wondered briefly what all he gave away. He tried to remember if she had had this overly observant mien before but it had been so long.

She shook her head but didn't say more, her eyes steady on him. Like she was waiting for him to do something.

"Is his lordship home?" he thought to ask then.

But Penelope was quick again with the shake of her head. "He is usually in at this hour, but he appears to be absent. I've already inquired with Mrs. Watson about her knowledge of the dead body, and her answer seemed to suggest she does not know Lord Wickshire's current position."

He liked the sound of her voice. So unassuming. So even. She had a manner of relaying facts as if reading them from a book. He wondered if her voice alone could lull him into a false sense of comfort. Enough so that sleep would finally come.

"Where was Lord Wickshire the last you saw him?"

She indicated the opposite side of the room with a nod of

her head. "In his chair as he usually is. It was raining yesterday. His lordship often reads his journals on rainy afternoons."

"And what time did you depart the residence yesterday?"

She thought for only a moment. "Half past one. I was meeting Lady Delia for tea at her daughter's home in Bloomsbury." Two spots of pink appeared on her cheeks at the mention of Bloomsbury, and he wondered if she were thinking of the day of their excursion to the coffee house.

"I will need to speak with his lordship immediately." He stepped around the body, carefully skirting the perimeter of the rug until he once more stood next to Penelope. "I'll summon a sergeant to take command of the situation here. I'd like to inform my superiors of this and enlist the help of my partner."

Penelope's eyes widened. "You have a partner? How thrilling." She settled one elbow against her bent arm, settling her chin on her fist. "Tell me about him." She stopped, her eyes going even wider as she pointed a finger directly at him. "Or is it a woman?" She screwed up her face as if snared in a thought. "It would be rather extraordinary if it were, so it's likely a man. But not that it couldn't be a woman."

"Penelope," he cut her off.

She looked at him. Her gaze quiet and her lips still as if she had not rambled nonsense at him.

He wanted to kiss her.

Her lips were so close to his. He simply needed to drop his head, allow his mouth to descend on hers and—

The front door opened.

It wasn't just the simple mechanics of a door opening either. It was with a great whoosh of outside air followed by a jumble of frock coat and top hat slanted askew on a head of graying hair.

"Penelope!" came the great bellow from the tumbling mass.

And then all movement ceased. Arrested completely in the silent, penetrating stare of the Earl of Wickshire.

Samuel had seen him before but it had been years previous when he often visited Lady Pemberly's puppies. The Pemberly house was always teeming with puppies, and Samuel had been welcome whenever he pleased to help socialize the hounds. Wickshire often dropped in from time to time, discussing matters that had seemed terribly complex to a younger Samuel.

Peter Grafton, the Earl of Wickshire, was a devilishly handsome man. That's what Samuel's grandmother always said. And although he had aged, he had aged well, and Samuel knew Lady Jane would still say Wickshire was handsome and devilish, but not necessarily in the same order. His graying blonde hair fell in an artful cascade from under his lopsided hat, framing the series of lines that burrowed across his forehead. Creases dripped from the corner of each eye, mirroring those that bracketed his mouth. His straight nose drew one's gaze to aquamarine eyes, and it was all perfectly enclosed by his square chin and firm jaw.

Samuel had become adept at cataloging a man's features after so much time in police work, but it was an older habit instilled in him by his Uncle Alec that had him scanning the man's dress, which was rumpled, creased, and stained with road dust.

"Lord Wickshire—" Samuel began, but Wickshire cut him off.

"You got here awfully fast," he said. "I only just left Maggie."

Samuel moved out of the way as Wickshire swept past him, throwing off his hat and ripping off his coat.

"Maggie is nothing if not efficient." He tugged at his cravat until it, too, fell away.

Samuel looked at Penelope, but she was watching Wickshire, her fingers twitching again. "I do beg your pardon, my lord, but I'm afraid I do not follow," he said.

Wickshire froze once more in the act of unbuttoning his waistcoat. Did the man intend to fully undress in his drawing room with an audience present?

"I have seen you cry at an overly wet kiss from one of Maggie's hounds, dear boy," he said. "I do believe the time to stand on ceremony has passed."

Samuel swallowed and looked at his feet, feeling suddenly a boy of ten once more. "You went to Maggie to send for me?" he asked, looking back up.

Wickshire nodded. "I had thought to enlist the aid of the domestic division of the War Office, but she suggested I would find better fortune with the Metropolitan Police." He let out a stilted laugh. "To think the day has come when the police force is better equipped than the War Office." He shook his head, his mouth slightly open as if in wonderment of his own statement. "Time does march on, doesn't it?"

Samuel looked at Penelope, feeling too much of the truth of that statement. "Yes, it does." He looked quickly away when Penelope met his gaze. "I presume you had Maggie send for me to help you find the murderer of your acquaintance here." Samuel gestured discreetly to the dead body.

Wickshire shook his head. "No, indeed, I did not."

Penelope stiffened beside him, and he felt the brush of tulip petals against his coat.

"I need you to find a professor," Wickshire said and tore off his collar.

17

CHAPTER 2

*S*ometimes the cavalry does not help. Sometimes it only
stirs up the dust.
From *The Adventures of Miss Melanie Merkett, Private
Inquisitor*

THE TULIPS WOULD BE DESTROYED if she did not set them
down. She stepped slightly forward, gesturing with the
beleaguered tulips at the earl.

"He likes to think in his shirtsleeves," she whispered to
Samuel. "He says it removes the restraints from his mind."

"Has he ever..." Samuel's voice faded away as they
watched Wickshire toss his collar over the back of a chair.

Penelope shook her head. "The worst it's ever gotten was
once when he removed his shoes and stockings, but then he
was dealing with rather complicated sums. I don't think
we're in danger of that."

Samuel's face said he did not believe her.

"A professor?" he called across to the earl.

The earl started as if he'd been lost momentarily in his

own thoughts. "Yes, Professor Xavier Mesmer." He pointed to the body. "This chap was his assistant. I can only surmise that with the arrival of the deceased assistant, my friend, the Professor, is in danger."

"Do you have reason to believe that the professor would be in danger other than the appearance of this man?" Samuel asked, also gesturing to the deceased.

Wickshire was quick to nod. "Indeed," he said. "Mesmer presented at the Royal Astronomical Society at this month's meeting. He's a brilliant mind when it comes to telescopes, you know."

Samuel shook his head. "I'm sorry, but I was unaware of that fact."

Wickshire waved off his apology as if it were inconsequential and began to pace the length of the room, his hands bent into the curve of his hips as he processed. "Mesmer was presenting a design that if manufactured would reduce the size of a reflecting telescope." He stopped, twirled and pointed. "But it would maintain the clarity of a reflecting telescope!"

The vehemence with which this was said indicated it was of some import although Penelope had never taken notes on telescopes for Wickshire and was surprised he held so much interest in the subject. But as a man of natural study, she supposed Wickshire enjoyed any such revelation.

"Do you understand what such a consequence would mean?" He threw his arms wide and twirled about again. "If one were to reduce the size of the reflecting mirrors and yet maintain the clarity inherent in the design of said telescope, the technology would become portable!"

Penelope often witnessed this dance from Wickshire. For it was truly a dance. The man became overly excited when speaking of inventions and advancements, but seeing the confusion riddled across Samuel's face, she realized the exhi-

19

bition may be rather odd. But to her, it only infused her with a sense of elation at the unknown. There was so much Wickshire was discovering, so much that would have an impact on real lives. It was all terribly exciting. Looking at Samuel, she wondered if he could say the same about police work.

Her fingers twitched, and she stilled them against the stems of the tulips.

"Ah, by God, man, I knew it," Wickshire said on a muted laugh. "I knew Mesmer was in for it as soon as he opened his mouth. To blatantly project such a thing. To let everyone know of his discovery!" Wickshire threw his hands wide again and spun to face them. "He was ripe for the picking, the stupid sod."

Samuel looked at her, and she leaned in, whispering, "He uses it as a term of endearment."

Samuel nodded and turned back to the earl.

Wickshire had stilled, one hand bent into his hip while the other stroked his chin. His eyes focused out the front windows of the room as the morning traffic increased, clogging the streets. But Penelope knew he saw none of that. She had been with him long enough to understand that moments when he stilled were his most important ones for that was when his body demanded the least from his mind, freeing it to think deeply.

It was only when spots appeared before her eyes that she realized she was holding her breath. She relaxed, filling her lungs, which must have produced a noise because Samuel peered at her. She gave him a hesitant smile and returned her gaze to Wickshire.

"He's gone," Wickshire finally said, his voice soft and lulling. He turned so abruptly Penelope stepped back, her shoulder brushing Samuel's. She looked quickly at him and away before he could see the blush she knew was on her face.

"Mesmer is gone," Wickshire said more forcefully now,

turning about. "I went to his lodgings after this poor chap appeared in my drawing room, but he'd already vanished." Wickshire shook his head. "He could have been gone weeks or days or hours. It is too visceral to nail down."

Samuel stepped forward, raising a hand. "Lord Wickshire, if I may—"

"Peter," Wickshire said. "You must call me Peter. Lords and ladies are only good for a ballroom."

Samuel looked at her, and she shrugged in response.

"Peter," Samuel tried again. "I think it would be best if we start from the beginning. You say that the Professor may have been missing for weeks?"

Wickshire faced them, clapping his hands solidly together. "Mesmer gave his talk nearly a month ago. He's been staying in rooms by the Astronomical Society. Campbell and Willis have been meeting with him." Wickshire paused as if to ascertain Samuel's understanding. "They are officers in the society..." Wickshire trailed off and waved his hand between them as if to clear the subject. "It doesn't matter. Mesmer gave his talk to a full crowd that night, nearly a month ago." He paused again, the hand once more going to his chin, stroking. "It was a Friday evening, an odd time for such an affair but Mesmer had just arrived and Willis and Campbell were eager." Wickshire snapped his fingers close to his chin. "It was the first of the month. That's when it was." He looked to them. "That was almost four weeks ago. So Bobby here would have had time to make it to the Arctic by then and return, but he must have returned by a faster ship because he was still quite frozen when he got here."

A muscle jumped in Samuel's jaw. Penelope stared at it, unable to look away. She wondered when last he had shaved, assuming he had attended to his toilette before coming to call that morning, but there was already a curious haze of stubble there.

"My lord," Penelope called out, her eyes remaining on that ticking muscle. "You're getting ahead of yourself again."

Wickshire looked at her like he'd just lost his puppy. "Oh, blast, I did it again." He struck out a pointed finger at the body. "Robert Egemont. He was studying under Professor Mesmer and served as his assistant."

"And did you say he arrived frozen?" Samuel asked, his tone remarkably calm.

Wickshire nodded. "He did, indeed, which leads me to believe he made it at least to the Arctic. This time of year it will still be intolerably cold there, but he was frozen when I found him, so he must have returned by a faster ship than a research vessel." Wickshire crossed the room, plunging into a pile of newspapers stacked haphazardly beside a chair. He thrust one from the pile and tossed it to Samuel. Penelope peered over his shoulder to see the page. There was a drawing of a ship and the word *Venture* stenciled across its side. "*The Venture* left port on Sunday the third. It's a research vessel being supported by members of the Astronomical Society. It was headed north to capture observations from a higher latitude. Poor Bobby here must have been on it."

Samuel shook the newspaper slightly. "You're certain Mr. Egemont was on board this ship?"

Wickshire shook his head. "Nothing is ever certain, good boy, not even in natural study." He pointed at the paper. "My deductions assert that Egemont was on board that vessel." He crouched down next to the body, using two fingers to outline the figure. "Bobby here appeared in my drawing room yesterday. I had gone down to my laboratories in the base-ment to gather some of my notes, and I had planned to spend the afternoon reviewing them. When I returned to the drawing room, Bobby was here. The servants had all gone for the day, and there was no sign of forced entry although I am very particular about having the home secured." He looked pointedly at Samuel. "I believe you can understand why I would be so particular about such a thing."

Samuel glanced down at her, and she waited, feeling that this moment was of import but not clearly understanding how or why. Obviously Lord Wickshire had a much deeper history with Samuel and his family than she had believed.

"Yes, I can understand that," he said, but he was still looking at her.

"So as to how Bobby entered the home, I cannot say. However, when I examined him at the time, his body was solidly frozen." He moved across the carpet, his fingers going down the length of the arm. "The fingernails had completely turned blue, showing a loss of blood or—"

"Or that the body had been exposed to extreme temperatures."

Wickshire brought the two fingers up to point at Samuel. "Precisely!" He straightened. "*The Venture* was headed north. In the time it left to the time Bobby here arrived, it would have given the vessel enough time to round Greenland."

"Which would have brought them into the Arctic," Samuel interjected.

A slow smile spread across Wickshire's face. "You always were a smart lad, Samuel," he said. "Maggie was right in suggesting I find you." He stepped back. "I can further deduce that while Bobby was on that vessel, Professor Mesmer was not."

"How's that?" Samuel asked.

"Because the professor's dead body is not present, only Bobby's," Wickshire said this as he peered down at poor Mr. Egemont, a hand rubbing at the back of his neck. He raised his eyes to Samuel. "I cannot stress enough how dangerous Professor Mesmer's discovery would be in the wrong hands.

I knew immediately he was a fool to give such a speech in a country constantly at war."

Samuel stiffened. Penelope felt it in the air between them.

"You would suggest the British government is after Mesmer and his technology?"

Wickshire waved a hand. "Of course not," he said. "I would suggest that anyone desperate enough for funds would be after the technology to sell it to a country with a vested interest in having the most elite armed forces in the world." Wickshire's look was cutting, and it was clear to Penelope that he was thinking of the far reaching arms of the great British empire. Arms which did not always carry a hug of sympathy but more often than not a firearm.

"So you believe Professor Mesmer is on the run," Samuel said.

Penelope looked to him, her head bouncing back and forth as she tried to keep up, her mind capturing every nuance between the two men as her fingers twitched uncontrollably.

"Exactly," Wickshire said, moving closer to them. "I believe poor Bobby was a ruse, sent on *The Venture* to lure whoever it is away from Mesmer long enough to allow him to get away."

"So Mesmer is still out there and someone is after him and his technology?" Samuel asked.

Wickshire raised only his eyes again, nodding solemnly.

"Are you able to locate him then?" Samuel asked. "It would be most expedient if you were to contact your associates at the society and determine..." Samuel's voice trailed off as Wickshire was already shaking his head.

"No, no, no," Wickshire said ponderously, stepping once more toward the front windows of the room. He reached one hand out to draw back the gauze of the curtain, and sunshine spilled awkwardly into the drawing room. "I cannot go in search of Professor Mesmer no matter how able I might be."

Samuel took a step closer, following Wickshire's gaze out the window. "And why is that?"

Wickshire turned away from the window, his mouth folded into a sad grimace, the creases around his eyes accentuated. "Because I'm being followed."

* * *

SAMUEL TOOK an involuntary step toward the window and stopped, his boot striking poor Egemont's elbow. He swallowed, his gaze traveling over the dead man.

"Are you certain?" he asked.

Wickshire allowed the curtain to fall back. "Oh, yes, yes," he said in the same ponderous way he had of speaking. "I am quite sure." He turned away from the window and as he had already removed every piece of clothing he could and still be decent, he played with the folds of his cuffs as they dangled around his sinewy forearms. "It's not someone I recognize either, which I find most disconcerting. This would all be markedly easier if I simply recognized the chap." He struck the air with a pointed finger. "Why is it that the villain of this piece cannot simply reveal himself so I may counter his parry with my—" The earl took a quick step forward, and his arm slashed the air in such a precise thrust Samuel's sister, Elizabeth, would envy, having been fencing since the age of three and quite accomplished herself. "Thrust," Wickshire whispered, his arm still poised horizontally to the floor, his imaginary sword struck out over Egemont's body as if protecting the man in death.

Wickshire shook his head, straightened, and dropped his arm. "No, I cannot," he said. "I spotted the tail almost as soon as I left the townhouse yesterday. I took him on a merry chase and still he followed. I can only assume then that poor Bobby was brought here as bait. Whoever it is that is trying to find Mesmer was hoping to spook me. Get me to lead them to Mesmer when I discovered him." He gestured to the body on the rug. "It must be you who takes on the task," he said, his hand going back to the cuff of his shirt. "Maggie agrees with me on this one, and so I cannot doubt it. I trust you will find the good man with alacrity."

Samuel's mind skittered, cluttered with another more pressing and immediate task. Someone was targeting his family, and he didn't know who or what they were after. Two near abductions within hours the previous week. First his sister and then his cousin, the daughter of the Duke of Lofton. His cousin he could understand. The daughter of a duke would be worth a healthy ransom.

His sister though. He loved her dearly. Her intelligence, her kindness, her reason. She wasn't particularly beautiful but neither was she plain. But more, she was only the daughter of what society saw as a genteel farmer. Only someone who knew the Black family secrets would know more. It was this that had the muscles tightening at the back of his neck.

"I am can assure you, my lord, the Metropolitan Police has well educated and qualified men that I can put on the objective of locating Professor Mesmer."

Wickshire spun about. "Most certainly not," he said succinctly. "I will only have you on this case." He strode closer, pointing at Egemont. "One man has already died. Surely you can understand the gravity of the situation. If a foreign power seeks Mesmer's invention for their own gain, the consequences could be deadly. Catastrophic." He was very close now. Samuel could see the faded blue of his eyes. "War, Samuel," Wickshire whispered. "It would mean war."

Wickshire was right. Mesmer could be pursued by a

foreign power. An enemy of the British. It could mean war. Britain was already involved in enough conflicts as it tried to maintain its hold on its empire. If Wickshire were right about the capabilities of Mesmer's invention, the weapon would be a death blow to British military power. And that meant no one else could do it. Samuel straddled an awkward line between domestic police work and foreign espionage. He could not assign away this task to a sergeant on the force. He would need to do this himself.

Awash with resignation, he said, "I'll do it."

Wickshire surprised him with a subdued response. A small nod of his head, his gaze locked on Samuel. "I know," he said and turned away. "You'll leave today. The hour is still early, and you'll make great time on the roads. We have had no significant precipitation for nearly eight days. The thoroughfares will be passable and—"

"I'm sorry," Samuel stepped forward, interrupting. "Where is it I will be going?"

Wickshire turned, a brow raised in question. "Oh, I'm sorry. I'm getting ahead of myself again. You're going to Observatory House. It's in Slough. You can be there by night fall if you leave soon and press hard."

"What is Observatory House?" Samuel asked.

Penelope shuffled beside him, and he realized he'd forgotten she was there. He felt a pang of guilt at that. He had allowed his work in the police force to consume him for longer than he had wished. At least, that was what he told himself. In reality he knew he had no control of his work ethic. It was the first thing that spoke to him, pulled to him, and because of that pull, he lost track of all else. Including his family. Including Penelope. That was how they had gotten so close. That was how they had managed to get to his sister and cousin. It was his fault. He accepted that.

"The Herschel home?" Penelope asked from beside him then.

Wickshire nodded. "Yes, it's the only place where I can think he'd run. He met Herschel some years ago. Before the man died, of course. I would think he would seek aid from them now."

"You mean William Herschel?" Penelope asked. "Mesmer would seek help from John Herschel's son?"

Wickshire nodded, his fingers moving to the other cuff. "Yes, I would think so. It's the only remaining possibility once the rest are discarded for one reason or another."

Penelope turned to Samuel then. "John Herschel was also an astronomer. He made amazing developments in the field of telescopes, and Observatory House was his home in Slough. It houses the largest telescope Herschel ever built."

Samuel looked back at Wickshire. "Mesmer knows the Herschels then? Professional colleagues so to speak?"

Wickshire had his back to them now as his head tilted back, his eyes traveling up the length of the walls clad in red wallpaper scored with gold design. "Yes, precisely. Mesmer was in London more than ten years ago for a meeting of the astronomers' society and met Herschel. They hit it off, what with their common interest in telescopes. Mesmer has stayed acquaintances with Herschel's widow and son. I believe he and the son even continue to correspond on the matter of reflecting mirrors." Wickshire turned, straightened, his arms dropping to his sides. "Some of their correspondence is printed in the society's journal. Most interesting material. It raises an important question—" He stopped. Waved a hand in the air as if to once again clear the room of the aborted thought. "That is not at all relevant right now. Right now you need only know that you're going to Slough. To Observatory House. Mesmer would seek sanctuary there."

Samuel pointed to Egemont. "What about this man? His

death must be properly investigated. It is only right. His family must be notified."

"He has no family," Wickshire said, his face softening. "Egemont was orphaned. Mesmer took him in at a very young age. Mentored him." He looked up, and a sheen covered his eyes. "Bobby would have done anything for Mesmer. And he did."

Samuel stepped back, brushing his arm against Penelope's. Suddenly the tips of her fingers brushed the inside of his palm. He recalled her twitching fingers, and he reached out without thinking, wrapping her hand in his.

"It's good that the two of you get along so well," Wickshire said, blinking rapidly as he turned back to the window. "It will help convince those that are following me that you two have nothing to do with the matter."

"I beg your pardon," Samuel said, the muscles at his neck no longer enough to contain his agitation. The muscle in his jaw jerked furiously, the sense of impending doom tripping up his shoulders.

"You and Miss Paiget," Wickshire said. "She will be accompanying you, of course."

"She will not," Samuel said quickly. But not quickly enough. Under his words, he heard the distinct intake of breath from the woman beside him. A gasp of fear? A gasp of distaste? A gasp of repulsion?

"She will actually," Wickshire said, his voice never increasing as if the subject were already settled. "As my secretary, it is her duty to fulfill any tasks which I see fit. In this instance, I require her to travel with you to Slough. I expect her to take careful notes of the situation and report back to me on the findings. She is already acquainted with the Herschels and will act as an introduction for me." He went back to the stack of newspapers from which he had earlier drawn the illustration of the Venture. "While you and

Miss Paiget go in search of Mesmer, I intend to discover who it is that is behind all of this." He plucked sheets of newsprint from the pile. "Discreetly, of course," he murmured to the sheets in his hand.

Samuel looked at Penelope, tension building in his gut. Her face was like it usually was. Blank and unreadable. It was something he had admired about her. Her stalwartness. Her stoic countenance. Penelope Paiget gave the appearance of capability. But now, he hated it. He couldn't tell what she was thinking. Couldn't tell what she was feeling.

But he knew what he felt. It seared him like nothing else could.

He couldn't do it. He couldn't allow Penelope to accompany him. Her reputation would be damaged beyond repair. He could not, would not, be responsible. The need to keep her safe, to keep her untarnished pulsed through him much as the blood pulsed in his veins.

"I'm sorry, but I simply cannot allow Miss Paiget to accompany such an expedition," Samuel said, stepping toward the door. "I shall assign a trusted inspector to the matter of Egemont's death. The law requires it," he added as Wickshire looked sharply at him. "And I shall deliver regular reports on the progress of finding Professor Mesmer."

"And I am sorry, Mr. Black," Wickshire said, carefully annunciating the mister, "But I must insist on Miss Paiget's involvement in this matter."

Samuel froze at the use of his name, so clearly indicating his position beneath that of a peer of the realm. An earl, no less. He could not refuse Wickshire. That was what Wickshire was saying. He would no doubt go directly to the commissioner, and then Samuel would be in great deeper trouble than he was now.

He looked again at Penelope, and still, her features were clear. Yet he had not been mistaken. She had reacted when

Wickshire had suggested she accompany him. But what her reaction meant, he could not ascertain.

After several moments, her gaze met his as if drawn to him, and in her eyes, he only saw quiet acceptance. To her, she would be completing the task at hand. A duty assigned by her employer. She didn't know of the ramifications. She couldn't know.

"We'll leave at noon," Samuel said.

Wickshire nodded. "I think that will do. But first, we must be sure to lay the foundation of the ruse. You'll need to inform your family members and acquaintances where applicable about the endeavor."

Samuel paused, the sense of dread returning to his shoulders. "Why is this necessary?"

Wickshire selected another newssheet from the pile. "You must perpetuate the myth that you and Penelope are running away to Gretna Green. It is the only possibility for keeping the true nature of your endeavor from being revealed to those who could benefit from it."

Now he was certain Penelope gasped. It was loud and sharp in the sudden stillness of the drawing room. It was that gasp more than Wickshire's dreaded plot that sliced through Samuel. For it was only Penelope who could elicit Samuel's greatest fear.

He tightened his fists, feeling the pulse of the thing he kept pushed so far deep within him, somedays he believed it wasn't there. But then, standing next to Penelope, feeling her outrage, hearing it in her gasp, he couldn't deny it. But he could deny an earl. The cost was simply too great if he did not.

"No," he said. "I'll not endanger Miss Paiget's honor."

CHAPTER 3

od save her from the overzealous whims of honorable men.

From The Adventures of Miss Melanie Merkett, *Private Inquisitor*

"I'LL PROTECT my own honor. Thank you," Penelope said.

Her fingers twitched, but this time it was simply a result of the flash of annoyance that coursed through her at Samuel's concern for her honor. All of the best heroines would, of course, beg for a chance to have their honor so guarded, but not Penelope. Penelope didn't care for such displays of weakness. Her heroine would be bold and courageous. Steady and sure. With no need for a knight to rescue her.

She glanced sideways at Samuel, feeling that tug of apprehension that had plagued her since the moment she had seen him standing on the door step. She pushed it down, calling herself a fool for her traitorous feelings. The muscle in his jaw ticked, and his eyes had gone cold. He didn't look at her, but neither did he look at the earl. He seemed to be studying something inside himself, and this washed away any annoyance she might have been feeling.

Samuel Black had a secret. A secret he was wrestling with at that very moment. A secret that involved protecting her honor.

How delicious.

She stepped in front of him. "I will pack my things immediately for a noon departure. I assume we will want our exit to be observed by the gentleman who has followed you these last few hours?"

Wickshire nodded. "Indeed. It would be best if the entire ton were to know of your retreat to Gretna Green. The more convincing that way."

"Perhaps another visit to Lady Delia would be in order."

Wickshire's brows rose. "What a splendid idea. She is sure to sweep the ton with a splendid tale of unrequited love and adventure." He swept the room with the newssheet in his hand. "Very exciting. Yes, Miss Paiget, I think you must."

She turned about with a nod of dismissal only to run smack into Samuel who had moved directly behind her.

"I'll not let you do this." His voice was low and unrelenting. His eyes were steely but not cold. Determined is the word she would have used. She wondered how grave his secret was.

She reached up a hand, laid it on his forearm. Her touch sparked a response in his eyes, a brief flash of something. She would have called it desire, but it wasn't. Desire would have been a fanciful notion on her part. No, it was something deeper. Something darker. Almost painful to Samuel. She dropped her hand.

"This is a business endeavor, Mr. Black," she said. "I take my occupation seriously, and I will not have your old fashioned notions of propriety impugn my professional reputation."

He stepped back, blinking as her words settled over him. That's right. He hadn't thought of her as a professional woman with employment of her own. Employment she wanted. She shoved that thought aside.

"If you will excuse me, I must pay a call to Lady Delia Witherspoon. I will expect your arrival at noon."

She didn't wait for his response. Too much inside of her was mixed up just then to formulate any kind of response, especially if he were to deny their endeavor once more. She had her own misgivings on the topic of their relationship. She did not need to delve into his secrets as well. But she could be curious about them.

As she had not removed her bonnet or wrap, she strode directly to the door and out into the morning, not bothering to look back. The traffic was thick now as the world had come to life while they had been in concert in the drawing room of Wickshire Place discussing the circumstances of poor dead Bobby Egemont. It was an exceptionally fine spring day, and the earl was likely right that the roads would be good for travel. Yesterday's light rain having little impact.

Lady Delia's residence was not far, and she arrived quickly, the butler admitting her without question.

"Is the lady awake?" she asked Marston, Lady Delia's butler, after slipping into the foyer.

She had known Marston for quite some time as he had been in Lady Delia's employ when Penelope was a companion there. Marston had droopy jowls like a hound dog, his eyes sagging against his cheeks, but he was always quick with a hearty laugh when his employers were not within earshot.

"She is, Miss P.," he said, rocking back on his heels and puffing out his barrel chest. "She's in her rooms with Duncan and Cece. I do not fear I would be presumptuous to assume your visit is a matter of some urgency."

Penelope smiled, shedding her gloves and handing her things to Marston. "It is a matter of quite some urgency, I'm afraid," she said. "I'll see myself up."

Marston bowed mockingly, and she gave him a curtsy in response. It was a game they had between the two of them. In her employ as Lady Delia's companion, Penelope had witnessed some outrageous curtsies by ladies of the ton. Appalling and degrading really. What a lady wouldn't do to appeal to the good graces of Lady Delia. Marston retreated with her things, and Penelope started up the stairs to Lady Delia's rooms.

Penelope went directly to the lady's door, her knock earning a responding chorus of barks from Duncan and Cece. She heard a muffled enter from somewhere within but it was drowned out by the dogs and what was likely a mouthful of chocolate pastry. Penelope strode in and found Lady Delia ensconced in her bed adorned in frippery (the bed and Lady Delia) and surrounded on each side by a large, sprawling poodle. Duncan and Cece bounded up at the sight of her, leaping from the bed only to fall in a graceful sit at a look from Penelope.

"Oh, there are my good comrades," she said, patting each on the head.

Duncan licked at her hand while Cece eyed him for his vulgarity. Penelope only smiled and gave each an additional scratch behind the ear.

"Whatever is the matter, child?" Lady Delia called from the bed, waving a chocolate pastry at her, fine sugar spraying through the air.

"I must go away for a while, Lady Delia, and I require your assistance in perpetuating a ruse."

Lady Delia's eyes rounded nearly as much as her mouth

as she exclaimed, "Oh, how exciting! What is that devil of a man having you do now?"

Penelope went over to the bed and propped herself on the edge of it. Lady Delia had been dear friends with Penelope's mother long ago, and Penelope had always seen the woman as more of an aunt than an employer. It only saddened Penelope to think she knew Lady Delia better than her mother, having lost her mother at a very young age. There were only impressions left for Penelope. Her mother's smile and the sound of her voice, but there was really nothing else. Lady Delia was all Penelope had now.

"I cannot tell you, I'm afraid, other than to say it's a matter of grave importance. I'm going in search of something, but if I reveal what it is, it may put that object in serious peril, and in consequence, the world at large." Penelope knew Lady Delia enjoyed the grand and eccentric and chose her words carefully.

She was rewarded by Lady Delia's wide smile in her round face. "Enchanting, child," she cooed. "What is that I am to say then?" She quirked an eyebrow, and her smile morphed into a grin. "I assume you are going to ask me to gossip, are you not?" She chortled. "You do know how I love a good morsel of gossip."

Penelope reached for the woman's hand, a smile soft on her lips. "I'm running away to Gretna Green with Mr. Samuel Black."

Lady Delia nearly choked on her chocolate pastry. Penelope reached over and gave the woman a hearty slap on her back.

"Oh, dear God, child," she cried. "Mr. Samuel Black?" She tossed aside the chocolate pastry, shaking her hands free of the sugar and reaching for Penelope. "Pen, darling," she said, her eyes shrouded in concern. "Did he finally come? How did he do it?" She tossed back a hand to her forehead. "Lud, darling, how you must be feeling right now."

"He showed up on the door step of Wickshire Place this morning," Penelope said, reaching up to take Lady Delia's hand back into her own, soothing the woman with her touch. "He brought me tulips."

Lady Delia frowned. "He did not immediately declare his undying love for you and propose marriage on the spot? Tulips do not ensure a roof over your head and food on your plate, dear girl."

Penelope shook her head. "Marriage does not guarantee those things either." Her thoughts flitted to her father. The debt he had left in his wake. The reason Penelope had sought employment in the first place. "But the tulips were quite lovely, and circumstances were such that we were unable to resume the conversation we started ten years ago."

Lady Delia's raised eyebrows suggested this was nonsense. "Circumstances?"

"Yes, circumstances," Penelope said. "I must ask you to insinuate to your acquaintances that I have run off with Mr. Black to Gretna Green. Can you do that for me?"

Lady Delia's head ruffled the flounces of the pillows at her back as she said, "Of course, I can do that, but Penelope, dear..." her voice trailed off, but in her eyes, Penelope knew what the woman meant to ask. It was the thing that pulsed inside of her since the moment she had laid eyes on Samuel again. It was the thing that kept her from asking Samuel about his secrets. Because if he told her his, she would have to tell him about hers.

She shook her head before Lady Delia could continue. "I haven't told him."

Lady Delia's eyes fell to the counterpane, her grip slipping from Penelope's. Penelope let her hands fall away, coming to rest in her lap.

Finally, after several moments and a healthy bite of chocolate pastry, Lady Delia looked up. "Any man would be honored to call you his wife, Penelope," she said. "Remember that."

"I know," Penelope said, patting Lady Delia's arm as she stood. "But does he know that?"

Lady Delia brushed crumbs from her hands so she could properly shake a finger at Penelope. "No man is ever aware of what's best for him, Pen," she said. "That's why we must always keep them on the straight and narrow. The dud heads are likely to wander off into their oblivion if it weren't for us women."

Penelope shook her head and reached over to squeeze Lady Delia's hand one more time. "I must go and pack for our expedition. I trust this is enough for you to properly lay the ruse?"

Lady Delia smiled at the anticipation of gossip. "Oh quite," she said. "I hope you do not mind if I embellish a bit?"

Penelope wanted to roll her eyes, but instead, she ticked her fingers against her skirt, committing that turn of phrase to memory. "I would expect no less from you," Penelope said and turned for the door.

Duncan and Cece stood waiting for another scratch as she crossed the room, and she'd reached the door when Lady Delia called out.

"Pen, dear," she said, gesturing with the last bit of chocolate pastry. "You won't do anything Miss Melanie Merkett wouldn't do, of course."

Penelope grinned over her shoulder. "Of course," she said and went through the door.

* * *

"YOU'RE LEAVING me alone with her," the Marquess of Evanshire hissed and pointed through the door as if Lady Emily Black were standing directly on the other side of the wall of Samuel's office.

Samuel followed the pointed finger even though he was quite aware of the fact that Emily was not even in the building. He frowned and returned his gaze to the marquess.

"I realize Lady Emily is not the easiest person with which to converse, but I'm sure in your professional capacity you will see to the matter while I am away," Samuel said, shuffling through the morning's post.

He wanted to ensure he had everything handled while he was gone on this quest for a missing professor. In the five years since the force had formed, he had not taken a single holiday. Had not left the office for greater than a few hours to sleep or bathe. He had done little else than ensure the success of an establishment the greater population looked down on in fear.

He had sent the messenger boys to collect the various parties he would need to establish the ruse Wickshire was eager to impress upon the ton. He had time to square away things at the force and charge the Marquess of Evanshire with a task he knew the man would dread. Any man would dread really.

But after the near abduction of Lady Emily the week before, Samuel had no choice but to leave his best man in charge of the matter.

"What professional capacity would that be?" Evanshire asked now.

This brought Samuel's attention up, and he was met with a single raised eyebrow, the marquess clearly showing his point in his dubious expression.

Samuel felt the tension at the back of his neck grow to excruciating levels. "I am aware that as a marquess you are not technically a member of the Metropolitan Police Force, but as I have expressed in the past, I appreciate your stalwart support of these efforts in Parliament."

Evanshire nodded slightly and said, "And now you are punishing me with the sappy attentions of a debutante?"

Samuel gestured with the post still in his hand. "She's the daughter of a duke. You could do worse."

He didn't miss the grin Evanshire tried to hide at this.

"Very well," he said. "You know I will do everything I can to protect Lady Emily in your absence." He paused, a crease forming in his brow. "But what of the party behind the attempted kidnappings? Should I proceed in the investigation while you are away?"

Samuel shook his head and dropped the post to his desk. "I'm concerned at what we might find in such an investigation, and I do not wish for you to proceed alone," he said, coming around his desk to gather his hat and coat from where he'd shed them earlier. He stepped closer to the marquess, lowered his voice. "You are aware of the Black family's reputation. I can only imagine the levels of criminal activity we should encounter in such an investigation. It would take the worst of traitors to go after a family so loyal to the crown."

Samuel expected a placid agreement from the marquess, as the man did not waste words. But instead, the marquess cast him a curious glance.

"What is it?" Samuel asked.

The marquess shook his head, gathering his own things to leave the office. "It's only that you make it sound like it's not your family," he said.

Samuel had no answer to that and went through the door of his office only to pause and turn. "You're coming with me," he said.

Now both of the marquess's eyebrows rose slowly. "Right

now?" he asked. "Good God, man, I haven't even broken my fast. You should give a man a warning if you're going to thrust such punishment upon him."

Samuel did not hide his own smile then.

They arrived at Lofton House just as a carriage carrying the Pemberly colors pulled to the walk in front of the residence. Samuel approached before the tiger and extended a hand to Lady Margaret Pemberly.

She smiled instantly at the sight of him, her straight white teeth brilliant as ever in the sunshine.

"Samuel!" she said, stepping down. "I am most intrigued by your curious invitation to breakfast this morning."

Samuel began to respond when a mewling noise erupted from the large basket she had wedged in the crook of her elbow. He stepped back, looking down, a frown already forming on his features.

"Puppies, Lady Pemberly?" he asked.

She continued to smile. "They are all of nine weeks old now," she cooed. "I know your aunt Sarah was looking for a companion for the twins now that Ashley is off at school."

Samuel had an instant image of his rambunctious and often mischievous twin cousins stampeding through the house with a pack of puppies. He felt a pang of sympathy for his uncle Alec.

"That sounds most disastrous," the marquess said from behind him.

Lady Pemberly turned her head as if realizing there was someone behind Samuel for the first time. "Oh my, you must be the Marquess of Evanshire."

Samuel stopped the laugh before it erupted from his mouth. Clearly the ladies of the Black family had been conversing over the matter of the Marquess of Evanshire, and really, Samuel could find no blame other than with the marquess himself. It was only in the week previous that the marquess had shown a rather daring display of gallantry to rescue his sister Jane from a near kidnapping. And although the Black family women were familiar with acts of bravery from their men, it was quite another thing for a complete stranger to rescue a member of the family. The marquess clearly only had himself to blame for this focused attention.

The marquess cleared his throat and managed a crisp, "It is indeed."

Samuel took Lady Pemberly's basket, holding it awkwardly as it squirmed with puppies while the marquess offered her his arm to lead her into the house. When Samuel had first met Lady Margaret so many years ago, she had been unusually reserved, but marriage had set well on her. She rather glowed now, as if life had found its way back to her.

She laughed then. "You needn't look so worried," she said to Evanshire now. "My daughter is all of nine years old. You are in no danger from me, as I will not be seeking a match for her for quite some time." She paused as they entered the house, shedding her bonnet and gloves. "Although to be honest, I cannot say the same for her father. He'll likely never allow her a match." She shrugged, took the basket back from Samuel, and made her way up the stairs to the library.

Samuel only shook his head at Evanshire and followed after Lady Margaret.

He should not have been surprised to find them all assembled and ready for his audience. After last week's act of chivalry on the part of the marquess, Samuel wouldn't doubt the Black family ladies would be ready for more adventure. That was really the problem with the lot of them, and why he felt his stomach turn over at the thought of leaving now. Any one of them could take it upon herself to pursue the perpetuator, and he could not think of what the consequences might be in such an act.

"Ladies," he said, entering the library with a small bow.

"This is the Marquess of Evanshire," he said gesturing behind him. Although, from the smiling, wide-eyed looks of the ladies, he was sure they already knew very well who it was.

"Ladies," Evanshire said with a bow.

It was his aunt Sarah who stepped forward first. "Oh, you needn't bother with all that rubbish." She went right up to Evanshire and drew his hands into hers. "We're all working in the same business in one form or another, and really, there is just no time for the polite necessities. You must call me Sarah or it will get just too confusing."

His grandmother stood next. "So lovely to see you again, Evanshire."

Evanshire bowed. "Lady Jane," he said with a soft smile.

Lady Jane dipped her head regally before resuming her seat. "Have you brought more puppies, Maggie?" she asked as Lady Margaret unwrapped her bundle, lifting two squirming masses with oversized ears into her arms.

Sarah jumped forward snatching one against her chest. "Oh, they're perfect, Maggie. Maddie and Michael will utterly terrorize them."

Lady Margaret laughed. "I expect so, but these puppies should most certainly try them."

"One can only hope," Sarah said, sitting with the puppy in her lap.

Samuel looked across the room to where his mother, Eleanora Black, stood quietly by the windows, a small smile at her lips. He went to her, drawing her hands into his own and placing a kiss on her cheek.

"Mother, this is the Marquess of Evanshire," he said, bringing her across the room. "I've asked him to assist me in this matter."

His mother gave no visible reaction to his words, and instead only said, "Indeed," as she greeted the marquess. "I suppose an apology is in order then, Lord Evanshire."

The marquess smiled, sharing a look with Samuel. "Something like that."

"I suppose you're referring to Emily," Sarah muttered from her seat with the puppy.

Samuel turned. "I'm afraid I've been called away on another matter. I leave almost immediately, and I'm unsure of my return. In my absence, the marquess has agreed to monitor the situation."

"You mean he's going to watch us like a nanny watches a brood of unruly children?" Lady Jane piped up.

Samuel would not rise to her bait. "Precisely. And I've told him to watch you with utmost vigor."

"I bet you did," she muttered.

"But there is something else I must ask you to do in my absence," Samuel went on. The words stuck in his throat almost immediately, the image of Penelope as she had left Wickshire Place, brushing so defyingly past him. He swallowed down the fear and pressed on. "I must ask that you spread a rumor about me."

Lady Jane nearly twittered. "Oh, I love spreading rumors. What is it you've done now?"

Samuel watched his mother as he said, "I'm eloping with a woman to Gretna Green."

"Oh, the poor woman," his aunt Sarah said, and Samuel heard a distinct aborted laugh from the marquess behind him.

"Yes, I'm afraid so," Samuel continued. "It is a matter of grave concern, and I've agreed to undertake the endeavor. However, the affair must be carried out in the most clandestine of efforts."

"You saw Peter then," Lady Margaret said softly. "You'll do it?"

Samuel nodded. "I must."

Lady Margaret didn't quite smile, but her expression said

she approved of his decision. "I would like to inform Lord Crawley of the investigation if that is all right," she said.

Samuel nodded, thinking the current agent in charge at the War Office should be notified of such an investigation occurring in the domestic sphere, regardless of its involvement with the Office.

His mother stepped closer to him now. "I will not ask what it is that you're attempting to do as it is likely a delicate matter of which it is better for me to not know the details, but I will ask that you be careful." She put a hand against his arm. "You are still my son after all."

Wrinkles had sprouted across her face sometime in the last few years. Some time when he wasn't looking. He realized there had been far too many times when he hadn't noticed his mother. So consumed he had been with the police force. He regretted that now.

He squeezed her hand as it lay on his arm. "I will be careful, Mum," he said, and a flash of a smile erupted on her face at his words. He soaked in her warmth, holding it close to the pain he carried in his chest.

But only for a second as the moment shattered with a squeal and a thud as someone came into the library.

He turned to see his sister, Jane, standing on the threshold of the library, the books she had likely been carrying in a tattered heap at her feet. The color had completely drained from her face, and her hands shook in midair where they had most certainly been grasping the bundle. Her eyes were riveted to the Marquess of Evanshire.

Samuel forced the smile from his face even as his mother squeezed his arm, glancing knowingly up at him.

Samuel stepped forward before his sister could embarrass herself further, but the marquess beat him to it, bending to snatch up the books and put them back in Jane's arms.

"Miss Black," Evanshire said, smiling quietly. "It's a pleasure to see you again. I wish it were under different circumstances."

If Jane had been flustered before, Samuel feared she would faint dead away at any moment. He shuffled closer, but his mother's hand pulled him back. He looked at her, and she gave a quick shake of her head. He glanced at his grandmother, but she did the same thing to him, her lips a firm line. He stood back, nearly holding his breath as he guessed the rest of their audience did as well. His gut tightened, wrenching against the thought of not helping his sister. But he knew his mother was right. Lady Jane was right. His sister must do this on her own if it were to help grow her courage.

"Circumstances?" Jane asked, her gaze shifting to take in Samuel. "What's happened?"

"I have been called away on another assignment," Samuel said, keeping his voice low and soft as if his very words would spook her. "The marquess has agreed to take on the matter of your attempted kidnapping in my absence."

Jane stilled so much he feared she had stopped breathing. Her already large eyes grew rounder in her face, the fringe of her hair clouding her raised eyebrows.

"Oh," she whispered.

The marquess cleared his throat loudly, shifting his body so as to conceal Jane ever so much behind him. Samuel had always respected the Marquess of Evanshire from the moment the man had pledged his support for the reform acts in Parliament. But now, standing there in the library of Lofton House, his respect grew tenfold.

"You'd best be going, Samuel. You'll need to be on your way," the marquess said.

Samuel nodded, turning to bow to the ladies in departure. He paused as he turned to the exit, taking his mother's arm in his to draw her away from the group. Leaning down he said, "Is Father at the club with Uncle Alec?"

His mother nodded. "Yes, he left early this morning. You know how he enjoys sharing stories with the old lot at the club in the mornings." Her smile was decadent, warm with nostalgia for a time when she herself had participated in missions for the War Office. "Would you like me to tell him what's happened?"

Samuel shook his head. "No, I'll go see him myself. I need to ask a favor of him."

CHAPTER 4

*S*ometimes one must deal with unsavory types. It is a
simple hazard of the profession.
From *The Adventures of Miss Melanie Merkett, Private
Inquisitor*

It was nearly ten o'clock by the time Penelope returned to
Wickshire place. She rushed toward the stoop, her mind busy
cataloging the things she would need to bring with her to
Observatory House, so she didn't see the man until she
nearly fell upon him.

"Oh," she said, crashing into his arm. Strong, thick hands
reached out and grasped her shoulders steadying her. She
looked up, trepidation tripping over her skin. "Sir Cross." She
forced her lips to curve in some semblance of a pleasant
greeting.

Sir Devlin Cross was a braggart and deserved nothing
more than to romp in the mud with pigs. Actually, that was
cruel to the pigs.

"Miss Paiget," he said with a weak bow.

Sir Devlin Cross had become accidentally famous the previous season when he had unknowingly uncovered the reaction of a metallic element that was until then undiscovered. It was believed in the academic community that such a reaction to the mixture of substances may affect the status of weather patterns. Of course, the ton took this to me Sir Devlin Cross was capable of stopping the rain. An absurd and scientifically unsound conclusion. But Sir Devlin Cross's fantastically handsome looks and charming ways were enough to have the ladies of the ton pushing Sir Cross over into idolatry.

Penelope was certain the only thing Sir Cross could stop was his hair from falling out of its exacting style, so much hair paste did he apply to it.

"Isn't it a stunningly gorgeous day?" he cooed, his wide smile spreading over his sickeningly handsome features. "Why, I may not even have need of my discovery today!"

That was the other thing about Sir Cross. If he could, he would slip mention of his discovery into every sentence he produced. Penelope wished she were the sighing sort.

"It is a beautiful day at that," she said, clutching her reticule to her chest as if it might act as a shield. "You are here to see the earl," she added, pasting a smile to her face. A smile she felt wobble even before she managed it. She slipped a foot to the right moving her body as she began the stealth attempt to get around the man to the front door of Wickshire Place.

Sir Cross seemed not to notice. Which was the point.

"Yes, as a matter of fact, I am," he said, rocking back on his heels, chest going up, as he surveyed the sky somewhere behind her. He tossed his ubiquitous walking stick from one hand to the other, the sun glinting off the Poseidon ornament that adorned the top.

She was tempted to turn about and see what it was he

saw, but she knew he only did this for dramatic effect. It was part of his charming ways the ladies of the ton so gushed over. "There was an article in the *Journal of Metal Substances* that I am dying to discuss with him."

Penelope at least blinked at this as she felt the railing of the stoop come up against her back. There was no *Journal of Metal Substances*, but Sir Cross likely thought her ignorant enough to believe there was.

That was another thing about Sir Devlin Cross. For some unknown reason, he had become uncomfortably infatuated with Penelope. She wasn't trying to flatter herself with such a thought. It was common knowledge. A thing which the earl often commiserated over with her. For Sir Cross's infatuation with Penelope meant Wickshire had to endure several inane visits from Sir Cross. Wickshire was never one to rebuff another member of the academic community. He was much too gracious for that. So it was that he sat through calls discussing academic journals which did not exist.

"Indeed," Penelope said, slipping one foot up the stoop. If she could make it to the door, she could at least summon a footman to deal with Sir Cross, plead work that she must attend to, and flee. She need only reach the door.

Sir Cross leaned inappropriately closer, his hand settling on the stone railing of the stairs. He would have caged her in if a wall had been against her back, and she clenched her jaw against demanding he back away. Sir Cross was largely harmless. He was simply an oaf that she had to endure to keep her position and maintain Wickshire's exalted position in academic circles. But still. Sir Cross really needed to be taught better manners.

"I hope you will be joining us for this discussion." His eyes were blue. Brilliantly blue. He had a cleft in his wide chin and bushy black eyebrows. He was too large really. Much too large. Not fat. But big. Penelope couldn't see why the ladies of the ton had marked him as such a favorite. She honestly didn't see that much worth remark in him.

"I'm afraid I have other matters to attend to," she said, slipping a second foot onto the first step.

But then she paused, regarding Sir Cross as she had come nearly nose to nose with him in her heightened position.

Sir Devlin Cross received every invitation to every social function the season would offer. He had the ear of every lady of the ton. If anyone were to successfully spread rumors of her flight to Gretna Green, it would be Sir Devlin Cross.

But was it worth the price? She would be returning to London at some point, and she would need to suffer the consequences such a connection with Cross would entail. She wasn't certain if the cost of making an association with him, that of entrusting her secret to him even if it wasn't really a secret at all, would make up for what she would be forced to endure upon her return.

Worse, he might think her jilted. Cast off. Broken hearted. Would he try to soothe her? Would he play the chivalrous knight and attempt to vanquish her demons?

Oh lud, what an appalling thought.

But poor Bobby Egemont. A young man with such a tragic tale. Spending the last of his days helping the man he admired so much. Penelope couldn't do it. She couldn't let down Wickshire. She couldn't fail Bobby Egemont.

She peered to either side of Cross, her gaze traveling down the street as far as she could without moving her head. She wondered if the tail was there. If the man who had followed Wickshire still lurked. Likely he did. He was waiting for someone to take him to the professor.

Steeling her nerves, she straightened and leaned forward, bringing her body dangerously close to Cross. She saw his reaction. Saw the way his head jerked back the slightest bit at her nearness. Surprise gripping him before he could relish the closeness of her person. What it might suggest.

Swallowing the bile in her throat, she picked up a hand, laid it on his arm. "Can I trust you with a secret, Sir Cross?"

His eyes darkened instantly, and Penelope's fingers twitched. She didn't know eyes could do that, and for a moment, she forgot her repulsion. She would need to recall that later. The way they went from an azure to almost a cerulean. Perhaps she could work that in to—

She shook her head, scattering her wayward thoughts so she could concentrate.

"I mean," she said. "It's just that we've been acquainted for rather a long time, and I had hoped we had developed a friendship of sorts. A confidence that I may rely on."

Cross's lower lip had fallen open, giving him a rather stupefied look. Once more Penelope wished she were the sighing type.

"Of course, Penelope," Cross rushed, his breath smelling of tobacco and stale coffee.

It took much of her reserve not to pull back or least squish up her nose at the odor. It took even more not to reel away from his appalling overstretch of propriety. She had not given him permission to use her given name, but she could very well understand. He thought this interlude was real after all.

She gripped his arm harder. Not out of any effort to appear transfixed, but rather to steady her nerves through force.

"I'm running away," she whispered.

He did not move. He did not blink.

"I'm running away to Gretna Green," she added. Still nothing. "With a man." She was making a muck up of this. "I'm in love, Sir Cross. I'm in love with a wonderful man, and I'm running away to Gretna Green with him." And only belatedly she remembered to add, "Please do not tell anyone."

For several seconds, she thought her volley would go without sounding. Sir Cross stared at her, that lower lip hanging just the smallest of bits. Penelope began to doubt her wild assumption that Cross would be a likely candidate for cementing the rumor of her tryst within the ton when Cross suddenly straightened, grabbing both of her shoulders in his hands.

"Penelope, no!" he cried, his voice soft and breathy, much as she pictured a great Shakespearean actor would assume. "You mustn't. Your reputation. Your—" He stopped so abruptly Penelope felt herself pitch forward with the momentum of it.

Something played out behind his eyes, and Penelope wondered if she had underestimated Sir Cross. He was clearly thinking. Weighing his options. Realizing that if he truly showed concern for her person, he would support her decision. Wouldn't he?

Penelope had very little experience in matters of the heart, and her own current love affair was on rather unstable footing. Not that Samuel realized that. Oh, God. She couldn't think on that now. Sir Cross was gripping her much too tightly.

"I'm in love," Penelope said, hoping she added as much dramatic flounce to her words as Cross did to his. "I'm in love with the most wonderful man, and he's asked me to marry him. We'd like to do so as quickly and quietly as possible." She peered behind her, hoping Cross received her intention. He stared at her. "I do not wish to risk my employ with Wickshire," she whispered.

Cross's eyes widened. "You would still work even after you are wed?" He searched her face. She watched his blue eyes dance about without seeming to find anything of interest. "You shouldn't be working, Penelope. A woman's place is in the home. Bearing children. Seeing to her family's needs."

The bile came up with such force Penelope nearly released it in a stunning spew of revulsion at Sir Devlin Cross. Instead, she merely swallowed.

"We will not be able to afford our life without my salary," Penelope went on, and she saw the hint of suspicion smear across Cross's face. She wondered only for a second how much to reveal, but she knew if this ruse were to work, it must be utterly believable, so she rushed on, "He's only a mister."

Cross released her so quickly, she stumbled into the stonework of the stoop. His mouth was fully open now, his white teeth flashing in the sun. His handsome face twisted into a look of utter regret, his head shaking just the barest of inches.

"Penelope, no," he said, taking a step back. "You mustn't."

She glanced back and forth down the street, suddenly realizing that there was possibly more than the tail watching them. But perhaps that was good. Perhaps it would help the lie if there were witnesses to this interaction. She pulled up her skirts and stepped gallantly off the stoop, raising her chin defiantly.

"I love him," she cried now, and out of the sides of her vision, she saw more than a single head turn in her direction. "I love him, and I will marry him."

Just as gallantly, she spun about and ran up the stairs, her skirts flying immodestly around her. Just at the last possible moment, she remembered to cry, a heart wrenching sob, throwing a beleaguered hand against her forehead, stumbling against the closed door of Wickshire Place. She fumbled with the doorknob more than was necessary, pounding with one hand against the frame.

She wrenched at the knob when she thought she'd been

about it long enough, and turned, resting her back against the door, drawing one last gasping sob. "I love him!" she cried back down at Cross where he stood transfixed on the pavement. "And I will marry him!"

With this she swung about nearly catching her skirts in the door as she snapped it shut. She collapsed against it, her chest heaving for real as she tried to regain her breath. She pulled back, tensing as the sound of clapping reached her ears.

The Earl of Wickshire stood in front of the stained glass pane beside the front door.

"I'm merely paying respect for an outstanding performance," Wickshire said, a half grin on his face.

Penelope frowned at him, and Wickshire stopped, throwing a thumb toward the stained glass instead.

"Do you think you could do that every time he shows up? It might actually make him stay away." He shrugged and wandered off down the hall.

CHAPTER 5

*P*hysical exertion is often necessary in the pursuit of
truth.

*From The Adventures of Miss Melanie Merkett, Private
Inquisitor*

SAMUEL ARRIVED at Wickshire Place seven minutes before
noon. He had secured a rented carriage for their journey to
Slough. His uncle Alec was only too happy to provide a
Lofton carriage, but Samuel thought a rented one would be
more fitting for their ruse. They were, after all, supposedly
eloping to Gretna Green. Such an endeavor suggested a lack
of familial support for the match. A Lofton carriage would
give them away at the outset.

He stepped down from the rented conveyance,
pretending to adjust the sleeves of his coat as he peered one
way and then the other down the street. Pedestrian traffic
was thick at this hour as afternoon calls would soon
commence. Bonneted ladies and the occasional well-tailored

gentleman cluttered the walkways, the air riddled with chatter and the slap and whir of carriage wheels.

Samuel adjusted his hat to better shield his eyes from the full sun as he watched the passersby. He didn't think Wickshire's tail would blatantly step into the fray or attempt to disguise himself amongst the crowd. He was likely posted somewhere just out of sight, but he would have a clear view of Wickshire's front door. He took a couple of steps forward, coming up to the stoop of Wickshire Place. He shifted, drawing out his pocket watch as if to check the time, but the angle afforded him a different view of the street.

A maid opposite swept the steps of another townhouse, a group of three giggling young ladies passed on the walkway beneath her. The door to a townhouse to his left opened and two footmen struggled through with a rolled carpet while a third man in fine dress gestured wildly with cheers of "Steady there!" and "Good man!"

It was then that Samuel spotted him. He lounged against the balustrade of a townhouse stoop on the opposite side of the street. His bent elbow rested on the stonework while he pretended to read the newspaper. Samuel was certain it was not that day's newspaper, and the man had likely gotten it from the rubbish. He had no evidence to support this assumption, but in his experience with such types, the newspaper was always a prop and one often achieved with no cost to the perpetrator. The man's head was bent, but his eyes roved anywhere but at the printed text. Mainly at Samuel and the carriage waiting in front of him on the street.

Samuel replaced his watch without noticing the time and turned as the front door of Wickshire Place opened. Penelope emerged, carrying a small bag in one hand. She peered from side to side as if looking for something, her brow creased in concern. When she seemed satisfied with whatever it was she was searching for, her face cleared, and she started down the steps. She threw him a resplendent smile as she neared him, almost as if she were a child headed out on an adventure in the park. He stared at her, aware his lungs had ceased their movement.

She wore an emerald dress that lit her eyes in a kaleidoscope of green hues. He stared into them, mesmerized by their brilliancy. For a moment, he forgot he was an inspector in the Metropolitan Police. He forgot he was a full grown man raised by a family of spies. He forgot everything as he looked into Penelope's eyes.

Her smile faltered, and he roused himself from the momentary trance. What was it she had been looking for when she opened the door? And why had she looked so concerned?

"Are you all right?" Her brow furrowed again as she placed a hand on his arm.

Her touch seared him more than the casual brush of their fingers had earlier when he'd handed her the tulips. He looked down at that hand, delicate and bright in her white gloves against the navy of his coat. He swallowed.

"I'm fine," he said, returning his gaze to hers. "The tail is behind me," he said. "If you glance to your right, you'll be able to see him."

"The gentleman leaning against the Covington stoop?" she asked.

He had barely seen her eyes move. It was more of a flit of her gaze than anything, her head completely still as if she stared lovingly into the depths of his eyes. He squelched the pulse of heat that erupted in him at the thought of it.

"Yes, him," he answered and drew her hand through his arm to lead her to the carriage but she stopped him, pulling back on her arm.

"Kiss me," she whispered, her gaze intense.

He faltered at her words. He had wanted to kiss her for

more than ten years. The need was primal and raging, and he had wanted to succumb to it the moment she had opened the door that morning. But he couldn't. Not like this. A gentleman did not ravish a lady on the pavement for all of London society to see.

But Samuel wasn't a gentleman. Not in the basic sense of the word.

"I will not," he said, his tone a touch more forceful than he meant it.

"We're eloping," Penelope whispered. "Look like it."

He went to shake his head, disagree, but Penelope reached up, her small hands clasping him about the neck and drew his head down. Her lips were soft, warm, and hesitant. He realized only too late that she was inexperienced. Unsure. Unpracticed. But at the first touch of her lips against his, he lost it. Lost everything. All thought. All concentration. Ten years of longing erupted at the touch of her lips against his, and he lost it all.

His arms moved, sweeping around her, his palms splaying across her back as if he couldn't reach enough of her. Touch enough of her. The muscles of her back tightened beneath his hands, and he drew her in. Not exactly slowly. Not exactly with grace. But with need. Pure, unadulterated need.

Finally, she was pressed against him, the full length of her. Her skirts billowing around his legs, the buckle of the belt at the waist of her gown dug into him. But he pulled harder, bending her into him as her head went back.

And he drank. He drank in her heat. He drank in her taste. He drank in her. Penelope.

The rattle of a carriage and obscene holler of a coachman had him breaking off the kiss only seconds later but it might as well have been hours. Years. He came fully away from her. His arms falling uselessly to his sides. His chest heaved not with the exertion but with exhilaration.

Ten years.

Ten years was a long time to wait.

Penelope stared at him, her almond eyes wide now, wide and...wary. He stilled, his breath catching once again but now for entirely different reasons. She regarded him as a child might a bee who knew the bite of its sting. The exhilaration drained away, allowing dread to pool where only moments before elation had wallowed.

And then as if her expression was not enough, she reached up, the three fingers of her left hand touching her bruised lips. Touching and not touching. As if she feared her fingers might smudge the echo of his kiss.

It undid him. That hesitant touch. That wary gaze. He clenched down on the thing inside him. The thing that he had battled to control from the night he'd first discovered what lurked inside him. The true son of a man who was more beast than human.

He wanted to reach for her. Draw her more gently against him. Cradle her so she knew it was all right. That he would never— That he couldn't—

He didn't do any of those things. Instead he took the two steps to the carriage and opened the door. He didn't reach for her hand. He didn't offer her assistance in climbing aboard. He just stood there. Waited. Gave her the time to collect herself and decide if she would continue on this journey with him.

If she should trust him.

Her expression didn't change but her feet moved, bringing her closer to him. Now he did reach for her, or her bag rather, carefully taking it from her. She paused on the step, turned her head, and regarded him once more.

The wariness had seeped from her gaze, replaced by something else. Something murkier. Something he didn't understand. But then she shook her head as if she were answering an internal question and finished climbing into the carriage. He nodded to the coachman above and turned to climb in himself, casting one last look at the tail across the street.

He was where he had been, but he no longer pretended to read the newspaper. He stared openly at them, clearly having enjoyed the demonstration Penelope had initiated and that Samuel had let go astray.

Samuel retuned the stare, allowing the anger at his slip in countenance to travel the distance between them. He didn't know who the man was. He didn't know who had killed Bobby Egemont. He didn't know if they would find the professor in Slough. But he knew he was going to find out all of those things, and it was this that he hoped to convey in his stare.

The tail straightened, flapped the pages of the newspaper, and folded it over to a new page. Bending his elbow once more, he settled back into his place with one last glance at Samuel.

Samuel didn't wait any longer, climbing into the coach, and drawing the door shut behind him. He heard the slap of the reigns as the carriage jolted into motion.

Penelope sat on the opposite bench, her gaze directed out the window. She had removed her bonnet, and one hand massaged the back of her head where a chignon was pinned against her neck. The gesture was involuntarily, he knew. Her gaze was much too focused on something beyond the carriage for her to realize what she was about. But it wasn't the landscape she watched. Her steady gaze said she searched something within herself.

It was then that he noticed her other hand. Her right hand drummed along the rim of her bonnet now resting in her lap. It was almost as if she held a phantom quill, her fingers moving it in an unseen line across the ridge of the hat.

"Penelope," he said, no longer able to stand the silence.

She jumped, and he regretted his interruption immediately. She didn't deserve this. She didn't deserve to be thrust into such a situation like this with him.

Yes, he planned to marry her. Yes, he planned to make her his wife. But not like this. Not under these circumstances. There would be talk. The foundation they had laid would make sure of it. The Duke of Lofton's nephew had run off with the Earl of Wickshire's secretary. The rumors would spread. The tales would be wicked. And in the end, Penelope's reputation would be a little less.

He would marry her. Of that, he could feel sure. But in the end, would their marriage be a little less as well?

She turned her gaze to him, and he was surprised to see her eyes were still as wide as they had been when she'd first come down the steps of Wickshire Place. It was as if whatever it was she viewed inside her mind required a greater focus. He wondered what it was. He wondered what she saw in there.

"Penelope, I'm sorry for—"

"Don't," she said so quickly his tongue stopped between his teeth on the next word. She shook her head quickly, the chignon rasping against the fabric of the bench behind her head. "Please don't apologize for that kiss."

He wasn't going to apologize for the kiss. He would never do that. He would only apologize for his manner. The manner in which he had delivered the kiss. A gentleman did not do such things to a lady. A gentleman exercised restraint. A gentleman showed care and respect. But that was the very problem of it. Samuel was no gentleman. He was only pretending to be.

"I shouldn't have acted that way," he pressed on ignoring her protest. "I should have acted with greater care."

Penelope was still shaking her head when he finished, but now, the line had appeared between her eyes again, and confusion dotted her gaze.

"It wasn't that, Samuel," she said. "It's just..." She looked down, her fingers twitching madly against her bonnet. "It's just I didn't know a kiss could be so amazing." She shook her head again as if to retract her thoughts. "That's not it," she said. "It's just—" She stared at him as if he could deliver the words that would best fit her thoughts, but he had been rendered utterly speechless at the earnestness with which she spoke. And the words. Her words drove all language from his mind. "It's just I never imagined a kiss could mean so much."

Slough was more than twenty miles from London. By carriage, it may take them as much as two days depending on the condition of the roads and the carriage and the health of the horses. Samuel stared at Penelope, her words ringing in his ears and bouncing about in his chest and his stomach and his heart, and he wondered why in the hell he had agreed to this.

* * *

THEY DIDN'T MAKE it to Slough before nightfall. Samuel knew this was the fates way of testing him. Of that he was certain.

Ten miles outside of London they had encountered cows. A whole herd of them. Plus the farmer who was trying to move them back into the pasture from which they had had escaped. Trying and failing.

"Are those bovine?" Penelope asked, her head nearly going through the window of the carriage.

"It is," Samuel said, staring at the way the soft afternoon

light lit the freckles on her face instead of ascertaining the extent of the problem with the cows.

"Do you think he requires assistance?" Penelope said.

"The farmer?" Samuel straightened as he forced himself to concentrate on the important topic at the moment.

"Yes, he looks to be in a bit of a spot." Penelope turned her head away from the window, her green eyes assessing him.

He scrubbed a hand over his face. "Where is my sister when I need her?" he muttered.

"I beg your pardon?" Penelope asked, one eyebrow going up.

He shook his head. "I'll explain later."

Before she could say anything further, Samuel opened the door and jumped down from the carriage, raising a hand to signal the farmer. He was a short man with bushy gray hair protruding from a worn cap. He waved back before extending his arms as if in apology for the inconvenience, but that there was nothing more to be done than what he was already doing.

Samuel waved him off and waded into the herd of cows. They sauntered up to him, unconcerned with his presence. He had spent a great many hours with cows at his father's farm in Kent, and he knew how curious they could be. He kept his arms raised, however, shielding off their inquisitive noses.

"All right, chaps, back into the hold," he said, walking slowly forward.

One animal began to move as he gestured, and he took that as a small sign of progress. That was until he heard a sputtering holler behind him.

"Here now!" came the call, and Samuel spun around to find Penelope surrounded by cows standing not more than twenty paces behind him.

He wasn't sure why he had expected her to stay in the

carriage as she had made it abundantly clear that morning that she did not require the protective observances of a gentleman. He let his arms fall as he watched her, settling in as he took in her predicament.

She stood with fisted hands to her hips, bent slightly at the waist as she scolded the bovine closest to her. "I've not given you permission to do such to my person."

Samuel had only to wait for a moment to realize what it is the cow had done for it proceeded to do it again. It licked her, a smearing swath of rugged cow tongue straight across Penelope's cheek. He took a step, ready to help her when he stopped, waited.

"I said no," Penelope scolded with a shaking finger in the cow's face now. "You do not have permission to make such advances."

The cow butted her with her nose and let out a wallowing moo. It sounded pitiful, as if it truly understood Penelope's scold.

Penelope stopped shaking her finger, her hand stilling in the air.

"Oh," she said, so softly Samuel almost missed it.

She flattened her hand, reached out, and caressed the cow's bulbous nose. The cow butted her hand in return. Penelope laughed.

Samuel was sure his sisters would say the sound was the tinkling of morning dew on blades of grass in the early dawn or like the water of a brook, clear and cold, tumbling over rocks. It was all of those magical things and more. Penelope's laugh.

He continued to stare at her as she chatted with the cow in front of her and then another as a they began to vie for her attention. The laugh came more frequently now as she stroked one nose and then the next.

Until another cow burped in her face.

Penelope yanked her head away, her nose squishing up as she slapped a hand to her face.

"That is entirely inexcusable, Maeve," she said against her hand.

She'd named the cows.

In the few seconds she had been standing there, she'd given them names. And she conversed with them as if they were old friends.

The pain began in his chest like it usually did, but it grew hotter than he'd ever felt it before. Hot and tight. Grinding inside of him. He pressed a hand to his breastbone as if to quell it although it had never worked before. It likely wouldn't work now.

A cow beside him nudged him curiously. Samuel looked at the animal, at its wide dark eyes. So inquisitive. So curious. He looked back at Penelope. She scratched at another cow's ears, receiving a baleful moo in return, the cow lolling in pleasure against Penelope's upraised arm.

Standing in the heat of the afternoon sun, cows bleating all around him, the farmer cussing behind him, Samuel understood something. He could conquer the thing inside of him. The thing that told him he was just like his real father and not the father who had saved him. The thing that told him he was a beast. The thing that told him he didn't deserve beautiful things. Like Penelope.

He did deserve Penelope. And standing there watching her talk to the cows, he was determined to make it true.

CHAPTER 6

It is imperative to associate with natives if one is to uncover necessary clues.
From The Adventures of Miss Melanie Merkett, Private Inquisitor

IT TOOK ALL of two hours to move the cows back within their pasture and repair the fence they had broken through. By the end of it, Penelope smelled, well, like a barnyard, and her dress was completely sodden three inches up from the hem of her skirts. Not to mention the sweat caused from the exertion that now sucked her bodice to her back and had her hair falling in frizzy strands around her face.

As their carriage pulled away, she leaned out the window, a hand raised in farewell.

"Do be nice to your sisters, Dolly," she called and pretended the responding moo proved Dolly had heard her and understood. Although at this distance, she could no longer make out which one she had called Dolly.

She withdrew from the window, settling back into her

seat despite the damp of sweat against her back. She had never had to wrestle an animal of such size, and she found the whole experience exhilarating. Her fingers twitched, and she longed to pull her writing box from her bag, scratching out the experience she had just had so she wouldn't forget the minutiae of it.

The way the dry grasses of the field crunched under her boots. The sound of the bleating as if one cow spoke to another only to be scolded by a slew of bleating from others. The feel of the sun against her back, so hot and yet so comforting. The way Samuel moved through the herd, confident and yet calm. Never asserting himself with any show of great strength. It was almost as if his greatest weapon was peace. An odd thing for a police inspector.

She watched him on the opposite bench. He'd pushed his hat back, and his dark hair fell against his brow. He regarded the passing farmland out the window, absently rubbing a handkerchief across his brow.

She hadn't expected him to kiss her like that. Of all the times she had imagined being kissed or kissing someone else, she had always thought of the physical aspects of it. She'd never pondered what it would feel like. Oh, not the squishy, rumbling, earth-shattering parts of it. Not the way his lips were soft against hers. Soft and yet demanding. Not the way his hands pressed against her back until she felt molded to him.

It was the other kind of feelings. The ones that tickled at her heart. The way those hands made her feel safe for the first time in a very long time. The way the warmth of his body made her feel wanted. The way the caress of his lips made her feel cherished. It was all those feelings words she hadn't anticipated, and it was those that had so upset her.

She regarded him with what she hoped was a neutral expression. Neutral with perhaps a bit of shared camaraderie as it wasn't everyday one had to assist in the control of bovine. But mostly neutral as she tried to keep her fingers from twitching.

She knew she would have to tell him the truth. Her mind drifted back to their brief time at the coffee house ten years previous. His calm assurance that he would come back to her. She had held onto that declaration. Through the long, quiet nights as a paid companion. Through the endless teas and social calls. She had held that one moment in time so very dear.

Until it had begun to fade.

She knew precisely the moment it had happened, but the memory had already become so unyielding in her mind, almost as if it were manufactured. It was a thing that had happened yes, but it was the momentum behind it that had been lost. The momentum simply vanished when she'd sold her first serial to *Coburn's Weekly*, and suddenly, she'd had a new dream to occupy her thoughts. An immediate dream over which she held the control.

Her mind halted on the word, tripping as if it were a physical hindrance to its processes. She stared at Samuel as he replaced the handkerchief in his pocket. He was so utterly handsome. So solid and sure. Any woman would be proud to call him her husband.

Any woman but her.

"We'll not make it to Slough now," he said, scattering her thoughts.

She glanced at the window, only now taking in the setting sun. "We've squandered away the day, it seems."

Samuel gave a weak laugh. "I hardly think wrestling cows is a waste of the day."

Penelope reached up and slipped the pins from her bonnet, pulling the straw hat from her head and allowing air to sweep over her, instantly cooling. "My father did a great deal of study on the bovines of this region. He was convinced their milk was affected by the types of grass on which they fed." She returned her gaze to the window as the farmlands flittered by. "He never reached a conclusion though. I think it was more the journey to discovery he enjoyed than the results themselves."

"I can understand such a fetish," Samuel said. "You assisted your father quite a lot then?"

"Yes, I did," she said. "After Mama died, there really wasn't much choice in the matter. Father never really truly understood what to do with a girl child, and it was only natural for him to share his interests with me. When he discovered how good I was with a quill and ink, he sent me to transcribe his notes."

Samuel shifted in his seat, unbuttoning his frock coat. Penelope shifted as well, that surge of pure physical reaction pulsing through her once again. She really hadn't expected such a charged reaction to the man, and she wondered how powerful time must have been to erase the memory of that. Time and...other things.

"I take it that is why Wickshire hired you on," Samuel said. "You must know a great deal about the natural arts."

Penelope stilled waiting for Samuel to say more. Waiting for him to say something about her intelligence and how it was wasted on writing letters and transcribing notes. But he didn't say anything more.

"Yes," she finally said. "I know entirely far too much about the chemical attributes of sodium and nitrogen." She said this with a grin that Samuel returned.

She set her bonnet beside her on the bench, pulling her gloves from her hands and stretching her fingers. Only now realizing just how exhausting herding the bovine had been especially in her arms and hands as she had gesticulated wildly to get the creatures to move. In truth, she feared she could fall asleep if the carriage continued to rock so gently. Distracted by her sudden exhaustion, she didn't realize immediately that Samuel had stopped speaking or that a look of concern now creased his brow.

"What is it?" she asked when she finally noticed him staring at her.

He shook his head almost imperceptibly. "Does it interest you?"

The question was unexpected, and Penelope opened her mouth without words emerging. She closed it. Tried to think. But no one had ever questioned her abilities before. It was already quite astounding that a woman in her position, the daughter of a respected member of society while, although only a country baron, of good family and adequate wealth, adequate wealth until his debts had been revealed upon his death, should have gained so much knowledge regarding natural subjects.

"No, it doesn't," she said. The words frightened her. She'd never spoken them aloud although she feared she had felt them for quite some time. It was just what was expected of her. A woman of her experience and in her position. Anyone would have thought she needed the position with Lord Wickshire. It's just anyone didn't know the truth of the matter. "I actually have a great deal more interest in other areas."

"Why have you not explored those interests?"

The question was asked calmly, but in his words, Penelope felt a trap. Surely a gentleman of society would not suggest a lady of employment seeking out her own interests. There were expectations for ladies in Penelope's circumstances. Expectations that Penelope found incredibly dull.

For a moment, the truth came to her lips, ready to spill forward, ready to reveal its ugly self.

"The opportunity hasn't arisen," she lied, her courage faltering at the last moment.

Samuel did not say anything, but Penelope knew he didn't believe her. She could see it in the unspoken question in his eyes. She was saved from having to respond when the carriage came to a stop, the conveyance shaking as the tiger jumped down and opened the door.

Samuel sat forward, pulling his hat back down properly on his head.

"I instructed the coachman to stop at the first posting inn," he said, peering out.

Penelope leaned forward as well. Her nose came dangerously close to Samuel's shoulder, and she smelled sweat. Manly sweat. It was disgusting and delicious at the same time. Her fingers twitched.

The carriage had indeed stopped in front of an inn. The wooden sign over the door proclaiming it the King's Arms. Samuel stepped down, reaching up for Penelope, and she followed him down into the yard of the inn. The sun had nearly set now, and the golds and reds and purples of twilight hung about them. Noise from the inn drifted through the cooling air. Laughter and singing. Penelope's head turned toward the noise and found yellow light filling the windows of the first floor of the inn.

She took an involuntarily step toward the commotion, forgetting Samuel stood beside her until his hand gripped her elbow.

"I'll see to rooms and supper," he said even as he began to move toward the inn.

She didn't hear him. Not really. Her gaze remained focused on the windows, her mind already drawing up what she had imagined a country inn's tavern would look like. Filled with bawdy, working types, filthy and disheveled from a day's toil. Her fingers twitched again.

They entered the inn through a door so narrow and short, Samuel had to duck as he went through, drawing her in behind him. Her head swiveled to the right and the beckoning glow of a similar small door. The noise was louder now. The laughter more intense. She reached out a hand toward it, but instead of drawing closer, she was being pulled away.

It wasn't until Samuel was drawing her up a worn flight of stairs that she came to her senses, pulling on the elbow he still held.

"Where are we going?" she asked, her eyes traveling up the dimly lit stairwell to a flickering sconce above.

"I'm taking you to our room."

Room. Singular. The reality of their situation came crashing down around her like the farmer's fence had earlier despite multiple attempts to repair it. Of course, they would share a room. They were eloping to Gretna Green. That was their story after all. She yanked her elbow free, and in the yellow light of the wall sconce, she thought she saw a flash of hurt in Samuel's eyes, but he quickly hid it.

"Shan't we take supper in the tavern below?"

Samuel's eyes moved down the stairs they had just climbed. "It's too dangerous," he said. "There will be too many people who can report on our actions should anyone follow us."

She followed his gaze, her imaginative thoughts evaporating for a moment. Or at least, changing slightly. "Do you think someone has done so?"

Samuel shook his head, but he took her elbow again. "Likely not, but I won't take the chance." He opened a door along the hall with a key she hadn't seen him procure although somewhere in her brain she recalled hearing the scratchy voice of a woman saying there was only one room left.

Samuel pushed Penelope inside. Pushed because he didn't enter with her.

"I must see to accommodations for the carriage and horses and food for supper," he said. "You'll stay here and keep this door locked." He pointed at the door in question as if Penelope had never seen one before.

And then the blasted man shut said door in her face. Penelope stared at it a full four seconds before drawing a deep breath. A deep breath to help her quell the spark of frustration at the stupid man.

Wrenching open the door and making her way back to the stairs and the tavern below, Penelope wondered if Samuel would ever learn she didn't take well to other people deciding what was best for her.

* * *

THEY WERE SINGING a bawdy song about a wench's hips like fine white lilies when Samuel returned to the inn after seeing the coachman and tiger settled and horses properly cared for in the inn's stables. His father had told him a good man always saw to his horses and his men. At the time, his father was referring to his comrades at the War Office and fellow agents involved in a mission. But Samuel had since related the advice to other aspects of his life.

He was rumpled and dirty from the road and from wrestling the cows. He fingered the muddied edge of his frock coat, wishing not for the first time that his salary as an inspector could afford him such luxuries as a valet. It wasn't that he lived in uncomfortable hardship. His uncle had more than once offered Samuel an allowance from the Lofton coffers, and more than once, Samuel had refused. He would make do with what he earned himself and not rest on the fortunes of others. It was one thing he could do to ensure he was more like Nathan than his true father.

He stepped into the tavern room, his gaze focused on the bar at the back of the room. He'd order a tray be sent up to their rooms. No, room. There had only been one left but not that that had mattered. They were to be eloping after all. One room was all they would need to support their ruse.

A buxom woman was scrubbing down the wooden surface of the bar as he approached, the chorus behind him erupting into a cascading fall of notes, lamenting the wench's departure for Portsmouth.

When the crooning dissolved into a mess of hoots and laughter, Samuel signaled the buxom woman with a single finger. She raised an eyebrow at him, wiping her hands on the rag she'd just used to clean down the bar. Waddling over to him, her stomach pressed into the bar long before her head came close enough for Samuel to speak to her. He would have to shout then.

"A tray of food, please. Whatever it is that you have available for the lady upstairs," he said. He adjusted his coat as if to take a seat at the bar and thought better of it. It still appeared sticky despite the assignations of the buxom woman beyond. "A meat pie, if you have it, and some cheese and bread. She would likely prefer tea as well."

A roar erupted behind him, and he turned slightly, taking in the melee. It seemed all of the patrons of the room were gathered around a single person seated in the middle. He couldn't make out much, but every once in a while a hand appeared as if animated in storytelling. He turned back to the woman at the bar.

"If'n it were me, sir, I would say the lady likes herself a spot of ale," said the woman, gesturing behind him.

Samuel glanced back but only saw the crowd of tavern patrons, eyes riveted to the storyteller, the man's voice muffled and skewed by the various sudden outbursts in reaction to the tale. A man sloshed his tankard of ale here while another called out the impossibility of it from over there. A third man chewed nervously at his nails, spitting out the cast offs every few moments and starting over.

"I beg your pardon?" Samuel said turning back to the woman behind the bar.

He noticed the sheen of sweat along the frizz at her forehead now, the dampness at the edge of her apron. He reached for his coin, thinking a piece may help move the transaction along.

A beefy hand mottled in red patches and creased in cuts settled on his arm. He looked up. The woman leaned across the bar now, a sly smile on her face revealing missing teeth and allowing her odorous breath to escape. Samuel steeled himself from reacting, believing a negative response at that moment would prevent any of them from eating.

"The lady," the woman said now, her voice rising above the scene behind him. "The lady 'as already eaten her fill and is enjoying a spot of ale with the boys now." She released his arm and straightened, rubbing her raw hands in the rag once more.

Samuel blinked at her, her words scuttling through his brain but not finding purchase. That was until the storyteller behind him jumped up on the table, throwing his arms wide at the climactic scene of the story.

Or rather her arms, as it were. Her small, lithe arms. A tankard of ale in one hand. He observed no liquid spilled over its rim at the movement, which indicated it was not full. Its contents having been drunk at some point. Drunk by its possessor most likely.

Anger flashed through him at the sight. Anger at himself. Anger at the earl for putting them in this situation. Anger at the thing inside of him that he tried so hard to suppress.

He needed to keep her safe. He needed to keep her away... away from—

He looked about the room. Every man seated at her feet was caked with mud and grime, the reward for a hard day's work. Some exhibited the clear lack of a razor, grizzled beards and patchy mustaches adorned weathered faces. Some missing teeth or even eyes in one matter. Each wore the garb proclaiming his occupation. The leather apron of a blacksmith. The bloodied sleeves of a butcher.

There they sat. Entranced. Mesmerized. Enthralled by the words of one Miss Penelope Paiget.

She continued to speak, her words spinning the enchantment as the men about her careened to the edges of their stools, leaned against tables, shifted ever closer, as if their proximity would allow her words to reach them sooner.

But he didn't hear her words. He didn't understand what she said. The anger in him boiled too hot, raging until it filled his ears with a tormenting roar. She was his responsibility. He had a duty to protect her. And here she stood, surrounded by all types of society and none of them good.

Him least of all.

Once more she flung her arms wide and up, her voice crescendoing through the tavern room, as she swept her hands forward, bending at the waist. The men about her sprang back and away, shouts echoing through the crowd, gasps lurching across startled lips.

Then everything exploded. Men erupted from their seats, tankards of ale falling away forgotten. Clapping ensued, clapping and cheering, and even a few whistles of appreciation.

It was the whistling that had him moving. He was across the tavern room in less than a breath, stepping up on a bench to seize her arm and yank her down. She looked up startled, the color draining from her face as realization struck. Her green eyes pierced him. What had only seconds before shone with triumph and glee, now stung with apprehension. Worry. Wariness. Again, the wariness.

He didn't let go though. He leaned in, nearly growled. "I told you to stay in the room."

It was all that he got out before hands grabbed at him, wrenching him away and across the room. He spilled backward, landing hard against the grimy floor of the tavern. He looked up as men gathered, looming over him, their backs to Penelope as if shielding her. He realized quite quickly where he had made the mistake.

"Gentlemen," he said from his undignified seat on the floor. "There's been a misunderstanding."

"I'll say there is," snarled one man, shaking a hand—no, there was no hand, only a hook where the hand should have been—at him. "That's no way to treat a lady."

"I realize that," Samuel said, a little startled by the man's words.

"It's right obvious you don't, gent," came another call from somewhere in the back.

He opened his mouth again, but quickly shut it as the men about him pressed in, their faces hardening to stone, their hands clenching to fists.

"Penelope." Samuel called over them, deciding now was not a time to prove his strength as a man.

A flash of red hair broke through the throng, and finally Penelope stood in front of him, her arms up in the universal sign of placation.

"Gentlemen!" she called. "I'm so terribly sorry. I failed to introduce you." She turned and reached down a hand.

He looked up at her and then back at the crowd. She stared at him, nodding her head just the slightest as if to indicate he should accept her help. He did, not caring to waste more time in this situation. They had a task to carry out, and he refused to put Penelope in any greater danger than necessary. He had already failed in so many ways on this journey, and they weren't even a full day into it.

He gained his feet but remained silent. It was a moment before he realized Penelope had not released his hand, and he looked down at it, staring at the connection. Her hand was warm in his. Slight but warm. And steady.

"Gentlemen, this is my husband."

His head snapped up at her words, the anger in him ceasing instantly at the sound of those words spoken from her lips.

Her husband.

He soaked in the sound of it. Something he had always planned on for the entirety of ten years, but not something that was real. It was more of an imagining. A dream. But she had just said it. Spoken it. It wasn't any more real than the fascinations of a tired young man at the start of his career in policing, but it was somehow different when she said it.

The crowd about them gave up a collective grumble of understanding. Feet shuffled as they backed away, giving the pair of them more room in the middle of the tavern.

Penelope shifted beside him, looking up at him through her lashes in a coquettish way. It was so unlike her he only stared.

"He has such great concern for my well-being," she said now, those lashes batting at him absurdly. "I am sure he has come to fetch me for my rest. What a saint you are, darling." She raised her free hand to his cheek, brushing it softly.

Samuel had been in many odd situations in his life as a police inspector, but that moment was absolutely the oddest as the gang of hardened laborers around him sighed at the sight of a woman stroking the cheek of her beloved. He wanted to pull her out of there. Take her away from all of those prying eyes. But he could only see Penelope. Could only feel her touch.

"I must bid you good evening," Penelope said then turning away from him. He felt the loss of her touch, but more, he felt bereft at losing the heat of her gaze. She gave one of those little bows again to an answering chorus of cheers and clapping.

He was so transfixed by it all, he didn't realize she was tugging him from the room. Eventually he moved, unsure rather to look at her or the men waving them off. She dropped his hand as soon as they left the tavern, and this more than anything he had experienced that night drove a slicing pain through him.

He knew they were only acting a part on this journey. He knew the real courtship would begin once they returned to London. He would have time then to worry about his wooing of her. For now, he had only to keep her safe. Untarnished. Protected.

And he was already failing miserably at that.

She entered their room ahead of him, and he pressed in quickly behind her, snapping the door shut and sending the bolt lock home. He rounded on her, but she stopped him with a single, upraised hand.

"I realize you likely have a scolding speech at the ready, Mr. Black. Something about how I am your responsibility and how badly I have behaved in running off like that against your wishes, and how I've put myself in dangerous peril and how can you be expected to act the gentleman when I do such terrible things."

He blinked. "Something like that," he muttered.

"I know," she said, dropping her hand. "I've heard the speech far too many times. You mustn't repeat it now."

He took a step closer to her although it wasn't really necessary. The close confines of the room required them to stand rather awkwardly between the single bed pressed into the corner and the wash stand opposite.

"I fear that perhaps you haven't learned the point of such a speech if you continue to behave in such a manner even having heard the speech." He fisted his hands to his hips much as his mother had done when scolding him as a child. He dropped his hands immediately.

But then Penelope mimicked him, putting her own fists to her hips. "We have more pressing matters to discuss, Samuel," she said, her lips compressing to a fine line.

"Such as?"

She flung out a hand behind her, indicating that single, lumpy bed in the corner. "Sleeping arrangements."

CHAPTER 7

hen circumstances force a difficult situation, one must seek a mutually beneficial compromise.
From *The Adventures of Miss Melanie Merkett, Private Inquisitor*

SHE KNEW the moment Samuel realized the truth of their situation. The color left his face, and the tightness of anger disappeared from his brow.

"I plan to take the floor," he said adroitly, and she waited for him to look down.

There was less than a full stride between the bed and the opposing wall, and that space was occupied by their bags, a wash stand, a scarred wooden chair, and a stove. The stove already hot with fire, pressing in the available space even more.

She knew too when this obstacle was realized as his mouth went slack.

"I see," he murmured now.

Something flashed in his eyes. The same thing she had

seen when they'd stood so close in Wickshire's drawing room. That secret pain that Samuel carried. She edged closer.

"I see no reason why we cannot share the bed." She gestured towards the item in question. "Circumstances being what they are we can only be expected to make the best decisions possible given the situation's restraints." She smiled but even she wasn't convinced. She stared at the bed, her thoughts skittering to other places. Like the fact that if they were married, there wouldn't be issue with sharing the same bed. And if they were married, she'd have to tell Samuel her own secret. She let out a breath and turned back to him.

"Turn around," she said.

He raised an eyebrow at her.

Pursing her lips, she said, "I may be willing to share a bed with you, Mr. Black, but I shan't allow you to watch me undress."

She had only said it to relieve the tension Samuel was obviously feeling, but when she glanced at him, the color had truly gone from his face and the muscle at the side of his jaw ticked.

"Penelope, I wouldn't—"

"I know you wouldn't," she interjected and stopped her words there.

They looked at each other, and something crackled between them. Something Penelope had never experienced before. But it was thick and explosive. She stepped forward but Samuel was already turning away.

"I'll give you some time to ready for bed." He reached for the door. "I'll return momentarily."

Whatever she had thought was there vanished, and she wondered if she had imagined the entire thing when the door closed behind Samuel. She should have been glad her interruption had distracted him from his earlier frustration with her. He likely thought she would be in danger in a room full of those sorts. Men made rough with a day's hard work.

She opened her bag and withdrew her night dress, setting it across the bed as she reached for the buttons of her gown. There was water in a ewer on the washstand. She poured some into the basin and tried as best as she could to wash away the dust of travel. The water was cool against her face, and at its touch, she remember Samuel's kiss. Her fingers lingered against her suddenly hot cheeks. Surely she hadn't imagined that moment of tension between them.

The thought clenched in her stomach.

A knock came at the door as she sat in the bed, braiding her hair over her shoulder. Samuel entered slowly, his head the last thing to enter the room, and even then his eyes remained on the floor.

"Am I that hideous after a day's travel?" she said.

His head jerked up in surprise, and she gave him her widest smile, hoping to banish the taut pull of his shoulders. His eyes froze on her. She was under the counterpane, and she doubted he saw more than the flounces of the collar of her night dress. Her fingers plaited without thought, but suddenly, she was aware of how soft her hair was. Was it that which drew his attention? There was only one candle in the room, and as night grew deeper, she doubted he could see much else.

Finally, he pulled his eyes from her, slipping into the room entirely and bolting the door behind him. He approached the bed, his eyes on the edge of it, and Penelope followed his gaze.

"It won't bite you," she whispered.

"I doubt that entirely," he said, taking a seat on the edge of the bed to draw off his boots.

"Would you like me to face the wall so as not to offend

your delicate sensibilities?" She hoped he heard the smile in her voice even as his back was to her.

"That won't be necessary," he said. He dropped the second boot to the floor and leaned back, stretching his full length across the bed so that his head was at about the place her feet were under the quilt. He remained thoroughly clothed.

She raised an eyebrow. "What is this? A new form of sleeping arrangement?"

He tucked an arm under his head, putting his head on just enough of an incline to see her. His eyes were hooded now, and she wondered if it were sleep or caution that made them so.

"It's all the rage on the Continent."

She knew immediately what game he played. It was the one he had been playing all day. She wondered where he got this unfounded sense of chivalry toward her. Chivalry fell out of necessity the moment her father had died, leaving behind an insurmountable debt that could only be conquered with two working hands. Penelope's two working hands.

She reached beside her, tugging loose the pillow that was not wedged behind her back and threw it at him. It smacked him in the face, and she thought she heard a wry chuckle escape him. He pulled the pillow from his face and stuffed it under his head, keeping his arm bent there as well.

Finishing with her hair, she tossed the braid over her shoulder and nodded to the candle still lit on the washstand opposite.

"Will you be doing the honors or shall I?" She wanted him to rise to her bait, and for the first time, she wondered why. What was it about Samuel that seemed to prick at her like a torn nail? He hadn't been like this ten years ago, but she hadn't been what she was ten years ago either. But something fundamental had changed in Samuel. Something he believed that he hadn't before. Something she suspected was a lie.

He rolled slightly, coming up on one elbow as he leaned over the edge of the bed. With one sharp blow, he extinguished the candle and fell back on the bed. She couldn't see his features now in the nearly complete dark. There was only the impression of a person lying in wait. She knew his eyes were open though as the heat of his stare burned a line up her torso and across her face.

She scrunched down against the pillow at her back, pulled the covers up to her chin. She didn't feel unsafe with Samuel Black. She felt unsure, which was far worse.

"We'll make it to Slough tomorrow and retrieve the professor. We should be back in London by the end of the week." It sounded as though he were reciting from a school book fashioned to teach one letters and sounds.

Penelope realized her left foot was near his shoulder. She shifted, prodded his shoulder through the quilt with her toe. She felt him flinch more than saw it in the darkness.

"I beg your pardon." His voice was rumbly and agitated, a far deal better than the school marm impression of moments before.

"Tell me something about you I don't know," she said.

"I do not care for black pudding."

She snorted a laugh before she could stop herself. Of all the things she expected him to say, that was not one of them. It was an especially absurd statement coming from a police inspector.

"That isn't exactly what I meant."

She felt him shift and thought he may have lifted his head to peer down the length of the bed at her.

"Did you already know I do not care for black pudding?" His tone was nearly playful. Or as playful as Penelope had ever heard it.

She smiled up into the darkness, pleased that perhaps she may have succeeded in easing his tension. Her body sunk further into the mattress, feeling the pull of the day's exertions against her muscles. She lingered in it, enjoying the rewarding sensation of a day spent in physical exercise.

"I did not know such a thing about you," she said.

"Well, then, I fulfilled your request."

She turned her head at his voice, listened carefully through the dark.

"But perhaps you could tell me something else. Something more personal?"

"What is more personal than my distaste for black pudding?"

Yes, his voice grew decidedly sleepy. She smiled harder up at the close ceiling of their small room.

"Perhaps something about your family?"

She feared he may have fallen asleep when he did not respond immediately. She listened, holding very still so she could hear the intake of his breath. She thought she heard him sigh, and then he moved, his body brushing hers ever so slightly. The touch was infinitesimal. She may have even made it up if it weren't for her body's immediate and flaring reaction. It was only a brush of his body against hers and there were three layers of fabric between them. Probably more considering he was still fully dressed.

When she had given up hope of an answer, he said, "My sister is very bossy."

Again, she snorted a laugh. "Is this the same sister who is experienced with bovine?"

"It is."

"How interesting."

Several seconds ticked by, and in the stillness, the sounds from the tavern below filtered up to them. The clink of pottery and cutlery. The scrap of a chair or a table against the planks of the wooden floor.

"Jane." Samuel's voice was thick with sleep now. "Her name is Jane."

Penelope turned the name over in her head. A piece of Samuel she had not known before. "That's a lovely name," she whispered into the darkness.

Again, several moments passed.

"She's named after her grandmother," came a very sleepy reply.

Penelope shifted against the pillow, picking up her head to better see down where she thought Samuel's head was by her feet. "Don't you mean your grandmother?"

No reply came now, but Penelope remained wedged slightly elevated against the pillow, one elbow beneath her as she tried to discern Samuel's face in the darkness. He had rolled over, his head facing away from her now and toward the outer edge of the bed. A door slammed somewhere. The turning wheels of a cart in the yard cut through the night.

Finally, a reply came.

"It's not my family," Samuel said. "I'm only borrowing them."

When he started to snore, Penelope was left to wonder what exactly he meant by that.

* * *

SAMUEL FLED their little room long before Penelope stirred. He had awoken with a jolt just as the sky outside had turned from certain black to the elusive blues of ebony. He hadn't realized he'd fallen asleep. He could only remember closing his eyes briefly and honestly believed seconds had passed. But a glance at the only small window in their room had proved the truth of it.

He'd slept the night away.

He couldn't remember the last time he had done such a

thing. Slept an entire night. In one deep, dreamless go of it. He scrubbed a hand over his face, as if he could physically push the sleep from him, and in the scraping of his palm against the stubble of his chin, became aware of another sound.

Penelope.

Breathing deeply beside him.

He sat up quietly. With such extreme care, the blood pounded at his temples. He mustn't wake her, but something in him begged to get a glimpse of her. To watch her in slumber.

She appeared so still. There was a quality about her that suggested perpetual motion. Something about her constant smile or inquisitive eyes. Something about the way she made him feel present. In sleep, all of this vanished, and he could see her. Penelope.

It was arresting, and something in him quieted.

Peace.

That was what the feeling was. He felt at peace when he watched Penelope sleep.

It was this that drove him from the bed and out the door of their room with as much stealth as possible. He didn't even think to wake her before he left. They would need to leave as soon as possible to make Slough at a decent hour. She struck him as an early riser, and he hoped he was right. He wasn't going to risk going back in there to rouse her.

Risk what exactly?

The thing in him stirred, and he knew just exactly what.

He left the inn to see after the horses, but his hired coachman and tiger were already taking care of the animals and preparing for the day's journey ahead. Samuel found cause to linger though, as the sun seeped its way across the horizon. When he could tarry no more, he returned to the inn and took a seat at a table in the tavern.

It was quiet this morning, only the other guests of the inn taking up seats here and there across the room. A girl brought him a tea service without asking. The pottery was chipped but clean, and the tea was strong. He drank a cup nearly in one swallow, no sugar or cream to dilute its impact. It hit his gut just as Penelope entered the tavern room, and it nearly came all back up and down his front.

She smiled, and there it was. That perpetual motion, returned with stunning ferocity. He felt the pang of remembrance for the sleeping Penelope and the peace she gave him. But even as he felt it, he felt something else. Eagerness. Anticipation. Those were the things the awake Penelope drove in him, and they were things he hadn't felt in a very long time.

"Good morning," she said and took a seat opposite him at the small table.

He reached to pour for her, but she batted his hand away.

"No need to stand on ceremony," she said.

Samuel leaned back as the serving girl returned, placing dishes of eggs and kidneys on the table before them.

"Might you have some marmalade?" Penelope asked. She peered up at the girl with those wide eyes of hers, her expression hanging as if on a precipice and only the girl could save her from falling over the edge.

Samuel wondered how a look could hold such power and if it were only he who felt it. But as the girl's face heated with a blush, he knew he wasn't the only one susceptible to Penelope's powers.

"I can see what we've got, ma'am," the young girl said and bobbed a curtsy as she left the table.

Penelope doctored her tea with sugar and cream before reaching for the eggs. She held a spoon aloft toward him. He lifted his plate so she could serve him over the tea service.

"I take it you slept well," she said. Her tone jarred him as the musical note she'd given to the girl was noticeably missing. Penelope raised her eyes to him, and in them, he saw a mischievous gleam.

It was then he realized he had not spoken since she entered the room. He cleared his throat and shifted in the chair.

"I slept well," he said.

She lifted her head and frowned.

"I slept very well?" It came out as more of a question than he'd intended, but something in him begged him not to fail her.

She frowned harder though and set her fork down on her plate, her eggs untouched.

"Does this situation distress you so?"

The question upset him for it came too close to the thing he restrained inside him. He picked up his fork and stabbed a blot of eggs. "Yes, it does," he said. "Murder and a missing person should distress anyone of common sense." He took a bite of eggs to keep him from having to say more.

Penelope put both of her hands in her lap and sat up straighter, her frown growing fiercer. "That is not at all what I meant, and I believe you know it."

The eggs stuck to his throat, and he grabbed at his tea cup for a ameliorating sip.

"I think—"

"Don't." She cut him off much as she had done in the carriage the day previous.

He set down the cup. "Yes, it does distress me." His words were simple and yet they tore at him.

"I thought as much," she said, but finally, picked up her fork.

The tightness in his chest relented enough to allow him another bite of eggs.

"You said something odd right before you fell asleep last night."

This bite of eggs nearly upset his entire constitution. He drank the rest of the tea in his cup before responding. "Oh? What was that?"

"You said something about your sister and your grandmother. Only that it wasn't your grandmother." She chewed with small, precise bites as if she were contemplating every morsel for texture, color, and taste as if each subsequent bite would hold something new to discover.

"Yes, my sister's grandmother is not my grandmother," he said. He focused his gaze on her mouth and her precise chewing to finish the thought. "We have different fathers. My sisters and I."

The words came much too easily, and his gaze fell to his empty tea cup.

Penelope swallowed and reached for her cup. "Your mother was married previously, then?"

He let her take a sip of the tea before answering.

"No."

The single word hung between them as if a debutante could reach out and swipe at it with her fan.

Penelope's face remained unchanged. Her eyes assessed him, but they always did. Her mouth indicated no such emotion beyond understanding.

"I see," she said. "Do you wish to speak of it?"

"No." This one spoken with a gentleness he hadn't expected. But then, he hadn't expected her not to press him on the matter.

Penelope was dangerously inquisitive, and he was beginning to understand such curiosity often got her into trouble. Trouble she didn't view as such. In fact, he feared she may find it enjoyable.

"All right." She speared a kidney and went on eating as though he had not just revealed his scandalous secret.

Although it wasn't truly a secret. It was just assumed that he was Nathan Black's son and the nephew of the Duke of Lofton. Outside of his family, only Penelope knew otherwise. It was strange to have someone know. If not in its entirety than at least of its existence.

The existence of how Samuel came to be just a little less than the man who had save he and his mother so many years ago.

"I don't like apples."

Samuel's gaze came back into focus and only then did he realize he had drifted momentarily. "I beg your pardon?"

"Here it is, ma'am."

The serving girl was back with a pot that likely contained marmalade.

"Oh, splendid," Penelope said, and although her voice was rich with gratitude, it didn't sound sickly sweet like members of the ton put on around those of the serving class.

Penelope took the pot and immediately scooped up a heap for the toast that had been brought earlier with the tea service. "I don't like apples," she said again.

"I'm not following."

She finished with the marmalade and took a tremendous bite of the toast, the sound of crunching loud in the early quiet of the tavern. A pair of guests seated to their right turned their heads momentarily, but Samuel stared back quickly enough to have them looking away. When he returned his gaze to Penelope, he found she had her eyes closed.

She was smiling.

Not at him. But at the bite of toast and marmalade she had just consumed. It was a few seconds before she opened her eyes, finished off the toast with her precise chewing, and took a swallow of tea.

"Orange marmalade. Quite good." She indicated the pot. "Would you care for some?"

He shook his head.

"Oh, more for me then." She reached for more to slather on her toast. "I don't like apples," she said for the third time. "You told me something I don't know about you, and it is only fair that I tell you something in return." She took another bite of toast although without so much obvious pleasure. "I realize my distaste of apples is not on the same level of profundity as the circumstances of your birth, but I'm afraid I have a rather boring history. My displeasurable relationship with apples is about as revealing as I can do at the moment."

Samuel smiled before he realized he would do so, and the tightness in his chest unwound completely.

"I can relate to your distaste of apples," he said and reached for a piece of toast. "My younger sister has an exuberant fondness for treacle, and while I'm not one to refuse a good treacle, Cook finds an excuse to make it at every meal just to please her." He prodded her hand away from the marmalade. She pursed her lips at him but allowed him to take a scoop for his toast. "My sister can outdo most puppies when it comes to receiving adoration. She just has one of those faces."

"You have another sister?"

Again, with the inquisitive brightness on her face.

"Elizabeth is the younger and Jane is the elder. Both are awful."

Penelope laughed, once more drawing the attention of the other patrons. Only this time, Samuel didn't care.

"I'm sure they say the same about you."

"I'm sure they say worse."

Another laugh and one he found himself joining.

When she finally quieted, she placed the remnant of her toast on her plate, her facing growing sober. "I suppose we have a professor to find."

The weight of their situation returned with crushing clarity.

"I suppose we do." He stood and offered his hand. "Lady wife," he said loudly enough for the other guests to hear.

"Thank you, my dear husband."

Only he could see her small smile as they left.

CHAPTER 8

lways be prepared for the possibility of gunfire.
From The Adventures of Miss Melanie Merkett,
Private Inquisitor

THERE WASN'T a professor at Observatory House in Slough.

There was only an old woman with a deadly musket and extremely poor eyesight.

The journey to Slough had been dreadfully uneventful compared with the previous day's progress and the wayward cows. She had largely read while Samuel stared out the window, an unusual calmness about him that had not been there before. She mulled over his admission of his birth and its questionable circumstances. Not that she found any fault in it. More that it irked her that he did. It was clear that he did in the instance that he wished not to speak of it. She stole glances at him even as she tried to understand what it was she read.

It was good that their journey came to an end as quickly

as it did for she was certain she could no longer feign an interest in the text. And when their arrival was greeted with a volley sent in the air, reading became pitifully dull.

"We come as friends," Samuel called from their hiding place.

They had exited the carriage in the yard of Observatory House as any visitor might when the shot had split the air. She had never seen a human move as quickly as Samuel had, throwing his entire weight against her as they rolled across the ground and behind a thicket of shrubs along the drive. The shrubs were in no way a barrier, but they did conceal their persons from the old woman with the firearm nicely enough. Perhaps without a visible target she would cease her attempts to kill them.

Samuel looked at her now, but Penelope only shrugged. She had met John Herschel, the son of the famed astronomer, a number of times at society meetings Wickshire had asked her to attend as his secretary. But she had never met the elder Herschel or his wife.

"He said you would say that," came the responding cry and the clink of a funnel as the old woman began to prep black powder to pour into the hold.

"Mrs. Herschel," Penelope tried now. "Poison Peter sent us."

Silence fell.

She could hear Samuel's breath, rustling in and out from the exertion of pushing them to the ground and rolling for cover. The birds had started to chirp again, and one of the horses whinnied. She looked around and saw the coachman and tiger of their rented carriage had taken refuge behind one of the carriage wheels. She hoped the horses wouldn't be spooked, or they would be in a certain amount of danger.

"Poison Peter, you say?"

Penelope looked at Samuel as she answered. "Yes, Mrs. Herschel. Lord Wickshire sent us to help the professor. I'm Miss Penelope Paiget, Lord Wickshire's secretary, and this is Mr. Samuel Black, an inspector with the Metropolitan Police Force."

There was a knocking noise as if Mrs. Herschel had dropped the gunpowder funnel.

"Metropolitan what?" Her voice had grown agitated again. "I'll not be having a policing body on my land. We're good people, and we don't need—"

"Mrs. Herschel," Penelope called over the old woman. "We must find the professor before it's too late. Will you help us?"

More silence.

When it began to ring in her ears, Samuel moved. He stood before she realized what he was about, taking two steps away from the shield of shrubbery.

"Mrs. Herschel." His tone was so calm Penelope wondered if he'd practiced at it. Calm in the face of danger. Or perhaps it was something he had learned after ten years on the police force. He raised his hands to show he was unarmed.

Penelope's thoughts stilled. Was he unarmed? Good lord. What if he wasn't? She hadn't even thought to question it until that moment. Her fingers twitched.

"Mrs. Herschel, I assure you the members of the Metropolitan Police Force only wish to assist you. We mean no invasion into your private matters. I am here at the special request of Lord Wickshire to help in the protection of Professor Mesmer."

Penelope studied his face, noting the openness of his gaze, the softness of his expression and felt a rush of pride at his obvious capability at doing such tense work.

Samuel took a step forward. Penelope had seen very little of the house itself as they had approached in the carriage, the view being largely obscured by the mature elm trees that lined the drive. The modest brick main house of the estate was nestled back behind an unusual barricade of tall shrubs marching along either side of the front door. Beyond the house, Penelope had glimpsed the very end of Herschel's famed telescope.

Samuel moved again now. Edging ever closer to that barricade of shrubs. His arms steady and his face relaxed.

"Mrs. Herschel, I would ask that you not shoot me," he said, stirring a traitorous laugh inside Penelope. "My mother would be very sore at you for it."

Something rustled behind the shrubs, as if Mrs. Herschel were listening with greater care.

"Your mother?"

Samuel dropped his arms. "Yes, my mother. She has acquired many a worry line over my chosen occupation." He smiled then, but he had moved so far forward, Penelope only caught the side of it. He looked nearly boyish in that moment. "My mother wished I had pursued a more ordinary occupation." He took a step in between words and was nearly out of Penelope's sight now. "I showed great promise in school, but alas, I was called to the duty of my family's legacy."

Now there was a great deal of rustling, and Mrs. Herschel's voice was starkly clear as if she had moved from behind the barricade. "What legacy is that?"

"My family has pledged a great deal of loyalty to the War Office, serving His Majesty during the wars on the Continent."

"And you've chosen to protect those at home, is it?"

Samuel gave a self-deprecating laugh. "It appears so."

"Your poor mother." This was softer. Almost a mutter. "What was it you studied at school?"

"Greek."

Mrs. Herschel gave a short bark of laughter. "What would you have done with that?"

"I assisted my professors in translating ancient texts. Specifically ones that were thought to be biblical."

"Good God," came Mrs. Herschel's reply.

Penelope stifled a laugh, her fingers twitching furiously.

"Mrs. Herschel, my companion is still sitting on the ground behind your beautiful shrubbery here. Might I assist her in standing without worry over you ending her life?"

There was a rustling and great woosh of air as if on a sigh. "I suppose."

Samuel stepped back into her line of vision and reached out a hand for her even as he kept his eyes trained on where Mrs. Herschel likely stood. He pulled her up but didn't release her hand.

"Mrs. Herschel, this is Miss Penelope Paiget. Lord Wickshire's secretary as she previously relayed."

Mrs. Herschel was a stout woman. Her white hair fluffed from beneath the cap on her head, a cap that had been sent slightly askew from all her exertion with the musket. She had squinty eyes and a hooked nose over thin lips. Her dress was two decades out of fashion with a high waist under a wrap that had frayed at its edges.

The musket, however, was not a musket at all but a rifle. A Baker rifle. Lord Wickshire had been commissioned by the War Office to test the stability of a new gunpowder and as part of the experiment was required to utilize some of the military's latest firearms. A special delivery of Baker rifles had been sent to Wickshire Place from the factory in Enfield. Why would Mrs. Herschel have such a weapon when a simple musket was more common for country folk?

Penelope squeezed Samuel's hand as if to convey the import of this, but his gaze was focused on Mrs. Herschel.

"My God, child." Penelope looked up sharply from the rifle in Mrs. Herschel's hands to the woman herself. Her sagging face had tightened, her squinty eyes going wide. "You're the exact image of your mother."

Penelope froze, her thoughts of the curious rifle fleeing as her mind attempted to grapple with what Mrs. Herschel had just said.

"I'm sorry?"

Mrs. Herschel lowered the rifle further, taking a limping step forward. Right leg. Mrs. Herschel had a limp through her right leg.

"You said your name was Paiget, right?" Another limping step toward them. "You must be the daughter of Mr. Arthur Paiget. There's only one woman in my acquaintance who had hair the color of fire like yours and that was Melanie Paiget, God rest her soul." Mrs. Herschel had stopped limping toward them, as she regarded Penelope carefully. "That is your parentage, isn't it, child?"

Penelope swallowed, suddenly aware of the heat of the afternoon. "Yes, it is."

Mrs. Herschel's thin lips perked up into a sort of smile. "You look just like her. Did you know that?"

"No, I was not aware." Penelope had only one likeness of her mother. A small portrait painted when her mother was only eighteen. The artist had been of a lesser talent, and the portrait looked like any young girl at eighteen. Pale skin, promising eyes, and good posture. The artist had painted her mother with brown hair. "Are you certain my mother had hair like mine?" Penelope reached up, carefully touching the chignon at the nape of her neck.

Mrs. Herschel nodded, one hand wrapping around the barrel of her rifle. "Oh yes, indeed. Your mother and father would often stop here at Observatory House if they were ever passing through." She pointed a crooked finger at them.

"Although the last visit we had from them, you were not yet here." The smile grew wider now, and Penelope saw a beauty mark on the woman's wrinkled right cheek. "It appears you've grown up just like your parents then. Secretary to Poison Peter? Lark. Your father must be so proud."

"My father is no longer with us, I'm afraid." She stopped there, startled by a sudden pressure from Samuel's fingers on hers.

Mrs. Herschel's smile faded. "I was afraid of such. All of the good ones have left us." She limped in a circle, turning back to the house. "Come along, children," she called after them. "I'll not tell you how to find the professor whilst standing in my front yard." More limping steps. "It's past time for tea, and you've kept me from it long enough."

Mrs. Herschel limped behind the barricade of tall shrubs at the front door and disappeared into the house. Penelope made to follow, but Samuel stopped her with a tug at her hand.

"Are you all right?" His eyes were dark with concern.

"Of course," Penelope replied, but his expression didn't clear. If anything, she began to see the tension she thought had dissipated reappear along the tight lines of his shoulders. She squeezed his hand. "I'm fine, Samuel," she said. "It was nothing more than a little gunfire."

His expression turned deadly. "A little gunfire."

Her fingers twitched in his grip before she could stop them. There was something about his eyes just then that she wished to remember. She pressed it into her memory as it would be ages before she could get to her writing box to write it down. Mrs. Herschel demanded tea after all.

She turned the twitch of her fingers into a tug and pulled Samuel toward the door of the house.

"You really must learn that I'm made of sturdier stuff, Mr. Black," she said with a smile she hoped would ease his worry.

It did not.

"That is precisely what concerns me, Miss Paiget."

She tugged harder on his hand. "Come then. If we keep Mrs. Herschel from her tea any longer, she may return with that rifle of hers and this time, I don't think she'll fire it into the air."

* * *

THE RIFLE RESTED against the sideboard in the dining room where they took tea with Mrs. Herschel. Samuel eyed it as Mrs. Herschel poured.

"I do beg your pardon for serving tea in the dining room." Mrs. Herschel set a plate of lemon squares on the table. The china plate was chipped on one side and its floral pattern was quite faded. "I'm still about going through William's things, you see." She paused and looked at him. "That was my late husband, you understand." She pushed the plate of squares toward Penelope as she took a seat opposite them. "The process has quite taken over the other rooms of the house. I never expected it to be such an endeavor, but I suppose the man did enjoy his trinkets."

"I'm very sorry for your loss, Mrs. Herschel," Samuel said.

The old woman paused in the act of adding sugar to her tea. "Oh, no need for that, child. William's been gone more than ten years now."

He glanced sideways at Penelope, who returned the look as she poured milk into her tea.

"But the effects of my husband are neither here nor there now, darlings," Mrs. Herschel said. "You must tell me what this is all about. Professor Mesmer was very limited in his tellings on the subject."

Penelope spoke first. "I'm afraid the professor is in serious danger, Mrs. Herschel."

Mrs. Herschel waved a lemon square at Penelope. "Please, call me Mary, dear. It's been more than fifty years but when I hear someone say Mrs. Herschel, I look around for William's mother."

"Mary, then." Penelope smiled. "It seems the professor has developed a technology that could prove valuable in the course of a military confrontation."

"Weapons?" Mrs. Herschel asked, dropping her lemon square to her plate. "I wouldn't have thought Xavier capable of such—"

"No, nothing of the sort," Penelope interrupted. "Telescope technology."

"Why would that be of such use to the military?" She turned to Samuel. "Are we at war with men from the outer universe?"

She reminded Samuel of Lady Jane, and he smiled before answering. "No, it's rather the telescope technology Professor Mesmer is said to have discovered would allow a military contingent to see a great distance. This in turn would give such a power the advantage at reconnaissance regarding an enemy force."

"There were an awful lot of titillating words in what you just said, young man. I suppose what you mean is that should an army have Xavier's telescope they would have the ability to spy at a greater distance on their enemies?"

"Yes, precisely."

"Mmm." She picked up her lemon square once more. "And who is it that is after Xavier for his innovation?"

"We don't know. That is why Lord Wickshire sent for me."

Mrs. Herschel raised her eyebrows. "Poison Peter believes you to be capable of handling such a dangerous sort?"

Samuel glanced at Penelope, who chewed at her lemon square in that exacting way she had. Her other hand was in her lap though, and her fingers twitched madly at her napkin.

"Yes, this is exactly what the Metropolitan Police Force is trained to do, Mrs. Herschel."

"Well, I'm sorry to disappoint you," she said. "But Xavier has already gone on."

"Did he reveal his intended destination to you?" Samuel asked.

Mrs. Herschel dipped a finger into her tea then as if testing its temperature. She must have found it to her liking because she picked up the cup and took a sip.

"Mmm," she began. "Yes, Xavier is headed to John, of course." She took another sip of tea with a great smack of her lips. "He's in Edinburgh now, you know. I believe he's putting together an expedition. Going somewhere warm this time. South Africa, perhaps?"

Samuel shot a glance at Penelope who stared at Mrs. Herschel, her tea cup raised in an aborted sip.

"South Africa?" South Africa was very far away, and Samuel had no intention of going there with Penelope. Not even a damned earl could make him.

"South Africa. I'm sure of it. Xavier was hoping to catch him before he embarked. Whomever it is that is after his innovation must truly be frightening." Mrs. Herschel leaned in. "Xavier is such a nice boy. I've never seen him looking quite so haggard."

"Do you really believe he's headed to Edinburgh to join John's expedition?"

Mrs. Herschel's eye twitched as if she were insulted to be questioned as such. "Of course, I'm sure. He said so himself not last evening at this very table. He left this morning."

"Did he hire a carriage or does he have means of travel of his own?" Samuel asked.

Mrs. Herschel shook her head. "Post. He's traveling by the mail coach."

Samuel looked at Penelope again. Traveling by mail coach was haphazard at best. Mail coaches were prone to be stopped by highwayman, flooded roads, and wandering gypsies.

"Can you provide us with a letter of introduction to your son, then?" Penelope asked.

Mrs. Herschel pawed at her mouth with her napkin. "Of course, I can. Do you intend to follow Xavier then?"

Samuel frowned despite his police training to remain stoic. "It's our only option. Professor Mesmer is in grave danger as I said. We cannot give up on our pursuit at the first challenge."

"Are the Metropolitan Police so persistent?" That eye twitched again.

Samuel's frown intensified. "Of course. It's what the policing force is trained to do. Persist until a desirable result is met."

The old woman did not look convinced. "I don't see why such things are necessary. Don't we have the Bow Street Runners to protect the citizens of London?" She gestured wildly with her lemon square, sending a puff of sugar into the air. "And out here, we really only have need of the local constable. Surely, such an association as a policing force would be silly. Are they going to keep John Roberts' donkeys from eating my lilacs? I don't think so."

"Do you stave off those donkeys with your Baker rifle, Mrs. Herschel?"

The woman stopped chewing, her eyes narrowing at him. "You know your artillery, Mr. Black."

"I do."

She set down the square and dusted her hands on her napkin. "I rather enjoy a good bit of gun sport, young man, and the British government was only too happy to allow me to test their newest arms."

"Why is that precisely?" Penelope asked.

Mrs. Herschel smiled. "Because William did them more than a favor now and then in his time." Her expression told him she wasn't likely to say more, and then she changed the subject entirely. "I suppose you both are weary from your journey and would like a lie down before supper. We keep country hours here, so don't think I'll be serving you late into the night. I have better things to do with my time." She pushed back from the table and with a great shove to one side of her chair, gained her feet. "I've just received the new Melanie Merkett novel in the post. Do you read Miss Merkett's adventures, Penelope, dear?"

Penelope's hand stilled against her napkin so quickly Samuel was able to catch it out of the corner of his eye. He turned his head just in time to see the same hand clench into a fist against the napkin. He raised his gaze. All motion around her had ceased, and once again, he was reminded of how she looked when she slept. Only this wasn't peace he saw in her stillness. This was fright.

"Miss Merkett?" Penelope asked.

Mrs. Herschel grinned. "I do love her adventures. Quite bold, she is. I'm sure I have another one about here I could lend to you. I don't often get to keep them long. The ladies of my archery club like to share them around. I'll see to having your rooms readied."

With that, Mrs. Herschel limped away.

Samuel turned to Penelope. "Miss Merkett novels?"

Penelope wouldn't look at him, and her tea cup rattled as she tried to pick it up. She aborted the attempt. "I believe I have heard of them. In passing, of course. There are not exactly on Lord Wickshire's list of favored publications." Her smile was weak. "I think I'll take a turn about the yard. My legs are rather stiff from traveling so much today."

She rose and discarded her napkin on the table as she swept from the room. Samuel watched her back, noting the small patch of pale skin between the blaze of her chignon and the collar of her dress, and wondered why Penelope would be so bothered by a novel.

CHAPTER 9

I *f one is to gain the trust of a possible source, one must
be prepared to indulge in local custom.*
*From The Adventures of Miss Melanie Merkett, Private
Inquisitor*

DINNER WAS INDEED a country affair of cold pork and beans.
It was apparent Mrs. Herschel had but one servant, a Mrs.
Dansbury, who performed all necessary tasks Mrs. Herschel
could not perform herself. Maid, footman, housekeeper, and
cook with the last task clearly not her specialty.

It was Mrs. Dansbury who had shown them to their
rooms earlier in the evening. Two small quarters, which
faced the front of the house. They would have the sun in the
morning, but Penelope doubted they would still be in residence at the time to see it. She was sure Samuel planned to
start for the next leg of their journey by then.

Mrs. Herschel had been telling the truth when she said
she had better things to do than to attend them for immediately following the dessert course, a runny dish that Penelope

thought may been an attempt at a treacle, the old woman had excused herself with a conspiratorial wink at her. No doubt the woman was off to ensconce herself with a Miss Merkett novel.

She felt an odd bubble of pride in her chest at the thought.

"Penelope."

She did not miss the stern undertones in Samuel's voice. She had been avoiding him since tea, but this time he did not let her slip from the dining room.

She froze with a hand on the back of her chair as she had been about to stand. Her gaze slid across the table toward him, but she did not speak.

"My grandmother, Lady Jane, that is, is rather found of a good novel now and then. I wonder if she's familiar with Miss Merkett."

Samuel had freshened up at some point. The road dust no longer clung to the shadow of beard along his jaw, and his cravat was neatly tied. He looked quite handsome.

She finished standing. "Do her tastes run to novel reading?"

"I just said as much."

Oh, lud. He had. She straightened her skirts along the belt at her waist. "Well, then perhaps she is familiar with the author. I've heard some talk about her novels in various circles."

"You said this afternoon that Lord Wickshire wasn't fond of such reading. How is it that you've heard of Miss Merkett?" He stood, dropping his napkin to the table as he strode around the table toward her.

His movements were exact, and he never removed his eyes from her face. She wanted to swallow, but instead, she held herself very still.

"Yes, of course, Lord Wickshire would not be so found of

such novel reading, but I was speaking of the other ladies in employ at Wickshire Place. And Lady Delia, of course."

She had said *of course* twice in that sentence. Perhaps he wouldn't notice.

"What is it about Miss Merkett's novels that has you so upset?"

He was close enough now that she could see the gold specks in his irises. She could stare at those little spots of color forever if he allowed it.

"Penelope."

But he wouldn't.

She tried a smile, but her lips trembled. "I don't know what you mean." She tried a laugh next but it came out in a twitter. "What is there to be upset about when it comes to silly novel reading?"

"You find novel reading silly?" Samuel laid one hand on the back of Penelope's chair, his fingers close to hers as she still clung to the piece of furniture.

"No, it's not that." Her words were coming entirely too fast. "Novel reading is fine for those with the opportunity to stretch their minds so. It's a wonderful activity for the brain." She was making no sense at all.

Samuel slid his hand along the back of the chair until his fingers enclosed hers. He didn't say anything. He just let his hand rest there. His touch was cool but not overly so. His long fingers slid carefully around hers to cup her hand in a sort of cocoon. She stared at the connection, her brain fishing for something to say. Anything that made her sound a little less daft.

"Penelope, it's all right if you enjoy Miss Merkett's novels."

She looked up, her gaze once more finding the gold specks in Samuel's eyes. Yes. Yes, that sounded quite innocuous. She smiled, the expression coming easier now.

"Yes, right, of course." She did swallow now, willing her

heart to stop racing. "I suppose it is all right if I should enjoy such a novel now and then."

A line appeared between Samuel's eyebrows. "Is that what upsets you so about the novels? That a woman in your profession shouldn't take to novel reading?"

This had her stilling completely. Even her heart slowed to a normal pace.

"What do you mean? A woman in my profession?"

"As a secretary to a peer," Samuel went on.

Penelope waited, sure there was more to come about how a woman like her had so much potential. She waited, calculating her response. She did like Samuel. Quite a bit, actually. But if he were to suggest that she was somehow less because of her chosen direction in life, she would need to say something or else—

"I think it's a good way for a secretary to stretch her mental capacities through imaginative text." Samuel removed his hand, folding his arms across his chest as he relaxed in front of her. "I've enjoyed a novel or two after closing an excessively difficult case. It's freeing for the mental faculties, I think." He paused, considered something as his eyes studied the carpet. "Do you think there's actually something to that? Novel reading as a leisurely activity to stimulate the cognizant mind?" He regarded her with a curious expression as if he truly wished for her answer.

She had absolutely nothing to say in response. He continuously denied her the use of her canned responses by not behaving as all the others did. What a vexing man.

"If I were to speak the truth on the matter, I think novel reading is most necessary for a healthy mind."

A slow smile came to Samuel's face. "That's an interesting way to put it, Penelope." He considered this, his gaze once more dropping to the carpet. "A healthy mind." He said the words in a savoring way as one might speak the name of a lover.

In that moment, Penelope felt more highly regarded than any of the times praise had been showered upon her for her secretarial abilities.

"I think I will need to discover this Miss Merkett for myself."

The moment of pride vanished.

"What for?" The words came too quickly for her to stop them.

Samuel laughed softly. "Because clearly everyone else seems to take pleasure in them. So should I."

Something coiled, hot and tight, in her stomach when he said the word pleasure. She shook the sensation loose.

"Oh, I'm sure you have much better things to read to occupy your time."

"Like Marshall's latest essays on the social ideals of an urban center?"

"I don't even understand what you just said."

Samuel smiled. "Neither do I, but not only must I read it, I must speak intelligently on it to the commissioner in two weeks' time."

The tension in Penelope softened. "Then I suppose you don't have time for Miss Merkett."

"I suppose I don't."

In the following silence, Penelope realized they would be retiring to separate rooms. They had only spent a single night together, fitted together as they were in the small bed at the inn. But even so, she was saddened by the thought of an empty bed. If she were a distressed damsel sort, she would manufacture a reason to share quarters with him again. But that wouldn't do as they were Mrs. Herschel's guests. Propriety demanded a certain standard. Penelope never did like social standards.

Samuel dropped his arms suddenly, gesturing to the door. "May I walk you to your room?"

Mrs. Herschel's home was not overly large, and she was in no danger of becoming lost on the way to her room. But she suddenly wanted a few extra moments with Samuel.

She smiled and nodded. "I think that would be entirely proper of you, Mr. Black."

He returned her smile and offered his arm.

"Are all Metropolitan Police members as courteous as you?"

"I'm afraid they are not, Miss Paiget."

They gained the stairs, each one creaking under their weight, the sound echoing into the stillness of a house ready for bed.

Penelope stopped at the landing of the upper floor, pulling slightly on Samuel's arm.

When he looked at her, she asked, "Do you enjoy it? The policing work?" She watched his face, a macabre of shadows created by the one wall sconce lit in the upper corridor. "You seemed to have so much hope for it when last I saw you."

A shadow that had nothing to do with the wall sconce passed over his face.

"Yes, I do enjoy it for all that you can enjoy such work, but..." His voice trailed off. She watched him gather his words, his eyes dropping again as she was understanding he did when he truly thought something through. "I just expected more," he finally said, his eyes going directly to hers.

"What more did you expect?"

He shook his head. "I don't know. And it's that that bothers me most."

Penelope could understand. Every time she put quill to paper, she understood. One couldn't desire the thing they couldn't name until starting on a journey they hadn't expected to attempt.

"I'm sure you'll figure it out one day," she said, although she didn't feel any truth in her words.

Samuel seemed to understand this as he accepted her words with a slight frown and shake of his head. He turned them down the corridor, pausing in front of Penelope's door.

"I must bid you good evening," he said, giving her a small, ridiculous bow.

She wanted to say something pithy and smart in reply. She wanted to smile and laugh at his silly behavior. But more than either of those things, she wanted to kiss him good night.

So she did that instead.

She moved her body forward, her lips coming against his in a soft meeting of air and warmth and skin. She tasted his surprise, felt the slight jerk as he realized what she was about. But he didn't pull away. He didn't push her back. He stayed perfectly still and allowed her to kiss him.

She was no experienced lover. She was hardly brave enough to kiss him in the first instance. But always in the back of her mind, she remembered the way he had kissed her on the pavement in front of Wickshire Place. It was that rush of sensation she wanted to recapture. That unexpected surge of simple feeling.

Feeling.

She had spent much of her life alone. Isolated. Without human connection. She'd had her employers, of course, but that wasn't the same thing. The more she prodded the depth of human emotion in her writing, the more she realized she missed being touched.

And when Samuel had first kissed her that realization had come to an explosive point, shattering inside of her to run like molten lava through her conscience.

She wanted to be touched, and she wanted Samuel to touch her.

She pulled back, allowing her lips to trail across his until the last possible moment when she had to step back or risk falling over. His eyes were open, and they watched her. His gaze moving about her face in careful consideration.

She felt the first prickles of regret when he reached for her. Putting a hand to either side of her face, he tilted her head back, the tips of his fingers sliding into her hair as his grip tightened and his mouth descended on hers.

Electric heat sparked through her and once more she was standing on the pavement in front of Wickshire Place, coming alive from a death she didn't realize she had been living. Their bodies never touched. Only their lips. And at that one point, Samuel poured his heat into her. She flared with it, reaching toward him without moving. Without so much as drawing breath.

As quickly as he came, he left, wrenching his lips from hers and stepping back. When she opened her eyes, she found him staring, his eyes hooded and watchful as if he didn't trust her reaction. But she found she did not have the energy for a reaction nor the idea of what a proper one would be.

She reached up a hand, touched his cheek with the barest caress. The hooded expression vanished as his features softened. Finally, his lips tipped into a soft smile.

"Good night, Samuel," she said and slipped into her room before Samuel could ruin the moment.

CHAPTER 10

*S*etbacks *should be expected in the course of one's investigation.*
From *The Adventures of Miss Melanie Merkett, Private Inquisitor*

IF SAMUEL SAT any further away from her, he'd be in another carriage.

Perhaps it hadn't been wise to take such liberties with his person the previous night. It clearly had an adverse effect on the man.

They had left Mrs. Herschel and Observatory House when the blackbirds had begun their morning song. She had just turned to the carriage when she saw Samuel give the old woman a letter to post. It was an odd thing as Penelope was the one to be taking notes of their progress, and Wickshire had asked that she not attempt to contact him on their journey until there was a development. Too much was at stake to have their endeavor traced back to him with a careless note. It may have been nothing more than police business, and she had dismissed it.

Well, she didn't. Of course not. But she did not allow it to ruminate in her mind over much.

It wasn't as if she were completely without blame for harboring secrets.

The carriage rocked pleasantly, and she fancied a small nap before the day was out. The bed in her room at Observatory House had obviously not been slept in since King George III had been sitting on the throne, and her muscles attested to the fact. The cushioned seat of the carriage and the gentle sway of motion was enough to have her slipping right off.

If Samuel would only stop brooding.

"Have I offended you in some way?"

His head snapped up at her words, his gaze darting away from the window when he had been scrutinizing anything but her.

"I beg your pardon." His tone suggested he was in no way perturbed by her presence, but that was even worse than the possibility she had offended him.

"You haven't even asked how I slept." He made no outward sign that he even heard her. "That seems unusual for a man of your careful consideration."

Now he raised a single eyebrow. "Careful consideration?"

"Yes, you're very good at understanding the needs of others and expressing your concern for their persons. But this morning something has you quite upset. Is it because Professor Mesmer has already moved on or is it because I accosted you outside my room last night?"

His face lost what little color she could discern, and he pinched his lips before saying, "I hardly think it's the latter."

"Well, that's good then. Because I plan to do it again, and I wouldn't want to upset your sensitivities."

His lips parted slightly, but no sound emerged. He simply continued to stare at her.

"So it's the professor then, is it?" she went on. "Are you worried we won't catch him in time?"

"That is a significant concern."

"South Africa is a terribly long way away," she conceded. "But we mustn't be far behind him. Especially if he continues on the mail coach."

Samuel leaned forward, his eyes traveling to the sky beyond the window. "If this weather holds."

"What do you mean?" The sun had been shining when they'd bid Mrs. Herschel good bye. She leaned forward as well, catching a whiff of the soap Samuel had likely used in his morning toilette. Her eyes wandered to his clean jaw, and she forgot why it was she was so close to him.

"It looks like the sky might open at any minute."

Rain. Right. She forced her gaze away from him and out the window. Thick, cumulus clouds were bunched up along the horizon, rolling over one another in some odd race to an unseen finish line.

"I'm sure nothing will come of it."

As soon as the words left her lips, a single fat drop of rain struck the glass of the window.

"It's nothing more than a passing shower."

The single drop was joined by another.

"It will be over in seconds. You'll see."

The deluge hit them with such force Penelope shot back in her seat away from the window and the sudden crash of rain. She looked at Samuel who only frowned at her. The carriage rocked forward despite the downpour, and in that Penelope drew comfort. As long as they kept up a steady pace, they were sure to reach the professor in time.

She smiled at Samuel, but it was nothing more than a soft

tilt of her lips because his eyes did that hooded thing they did when he was annoyed.

"We'll make it," she said, but her words were as effective as her near smile.

They went on like that, the carriage rocking forward through the downpour, the noise so great conversation was held to a minimum. As in, not at all. Penelope didn't mind. Her one foray into conversation had not been successful this morning, and if she were learning anything about Samuel, it's that he refrained from speech when he really had nothing to say. There was no point in prodding him on the matter. He was concerned about catching the professor. She would leave it at that.

But her fingers twitched against her skirts.

She couldn't help it. He was all brooding and masculine sitting there across from her, and she wished to capture it. Her fingers twitched more.

The coach dipped unusually low, and her bag, which had been nestled against her feet, tipped over, the top part falling against her boots. She looked down at the handle of the bag now dripping over the toe of her boot.

She glanced at Samuel from under her eyelashes before bending down and reaching for her bag. She snapped up her writing box from its depths. She pulled back the first opening to reveal the pen tray and ink wells. She rummaged about the pen tray until she found a suitably sharpened pencil, kept in her writing box for just such an occasion when opening an inkwell would be unwise. She then rummaged in the blue leather pockets along the lid of the box until she found a reasonably clean scrap of paper.

She wasn't sure how much time had passed before she became aware of just how loud the scratching of her pencil against the paper sounded in the small confines of the coach.

She chanced a glance at Samuel to see if he had noticed. She flinched slightly as she found him staring at her.

"Just making a note," she said.

"Wickshire requires a thorough and accurate account of the proceedings then?"

Penelope stared at what she had written so far, certain words jumping off the page at her.

Warm brown eyes.

Tense jaw line.

Thinned lips.

"Yes, very accurate."

"You must be good at setting down the details of events."

His kisses are better than trifle.

"Yes, you could say that, I suppose," she said, although she couldn't lift her eyes from the page.

"Did you do much dictation for your father?"

She did look up at that. "Oh yes, a great deal. Although Father tended to care more for biological experiments. He was always traipsing off to neighboring farms. Asking to see their goats." She thought a moment. "It was a good thing the neighbors knew him so well or they would think he had gone daft."

"Is that why he gave you that box?"

She looked down at the writing box on her lap, the green velvet of the sloped writing surface worn nearly pale with age.

"How do you know he gave it to me?" She wasn't surprised that he had known. More that she was curious to learn how he had figured it.

"It's an older writing box. The brass filigree and inlaid handles something of an earlier period. Perhaps ten or even twenty years ago. That would make it possible for your father to have given it to you." He relayed his deductions with little feeling, and a pang of something— loss? disappoint-ment?— struck Penelope in the gut.

"It was my mother's," she said, pushing aside the unusual feeling to admire his skill at deduction.

"Ah," he said, and a smile finally came to his lips, but it vanished quickly. "Do you remember much of your mother?"

She shook her head. "Not much. Just pieces of her really. But I don't trust them. Time has a way of glossing over things. Making them shiny with distance."

The line appeared between Samuel's brows, and Penelope stiffened. Her statement had been innocuous at best and should have had no effect upon Samuel besides casual cama-raderie. Instead, her words troubled him.

"Have you lost someone?" she asked. "Your father, perhaps?"

She recalled what he had said, or rather, what he hadn't said about his family. About he and his sisters having a different father. Although she was curious, she knew when it was best to control the urge to pry. However, if she had inad-vertently caused him pain, she wanted to make amends for it.

But as soon as the words were said, Samuel's face fell into a mask of stony anger. He opened his mouth, and Penelope readied herself to receive his reaction but no reaction came.

Instead the carriage tipped over.

Well, not entirely. But enough that it tossed her across the distance of the coach, throwing her into Samuel's ready arms. How he had such reflexes, she couldn't imagine, but she did take a moment to admire them. The coach tittered to the left now, the front corner where Samuel had been sitting now hanging as if the entire conveyance were held up by that single point of the construction.

She and Samuel were quite literally on the floor, her mother's writing desk pressed in a mess against her chest, her back pressed to Samuel's front.

"I think we've gone off course," she said.

She tilted her head to the side to glance at Samuel over her shoulder. His eyes were nearly closed, and his face dipped low against the curve of her neck. A thrill shot through her, so intense the air froze in her lungs. He was smelling her. Just as she stole whiffs of him. Her stomach clenched.

"We have indeed," he said, but he wasn't looking at her. His gaze remained riveted on that vulnerable part of her neck.

"We should probably see what's happened."

"We should."

Neither of them moved until a banging came at the door. With Samuel's help, she pushed herself up on the bench, sliding along its surface to rest against the wall. It was the coachman, soaked through, a steady rivulet creating a waterfall over the broken bent of his nose.

"Road's washed out," he called over the din of the rain. "We're stuck mighty fine, we are."

"What's to be done?" Samuel called back.

"I've got the boy unhitching the horses now. You and the lady will need to ride on to the next town and send back help to free the carriage. There's no seeing to it now. Not the way the road's turned to mud."

They would need to ride the horses. Through the downpour. Penelope shivered in anticipation.

Samuel looked at her with anything but anticipation, however.

"No." The single word might as well have been a boulder cast into her pond of dreams, breaking the surface and scattering anything below. "I'll ride on ahead and bring help."

The coachman thrust his head further inside. "You're not understanding me. We'll not be able to pull the coach free.

Not until the road dries up. You'll need to press on with the horses."

Penelope watched Samuel's jaw, entirely sure it would pop off at any moment.

"Fine." This word was no loftier than the *no* had been previously.

Penelope smiled.

"Splendid." She set the writing box on her lap, thrusting her pencil back into the box and snapping the lid closed. "We'll begin at once then?"

Samuel glowered at her, and the coachman dropped out of the open door. She looked at the mirror of rain framed by the now open door.

"Would you like to go first?" She gestured with a smile at Samuel.

"Has this ever happened to Miss Merkett?" he asked.

"No. Well, at least not yet anyway," she returned and wrapped both arms around her bag, ready to jump out into the storm.

* * *

IF PENELOPE'S arse rubbed against him one more time, he was going to literally die on horseback in the middle of a rain storm somewhere near Oxford.

The dire state of the road had forced them off their route, diverting much further west than they needed to be had the road been passable. The second horse throwing a shoe was the final straw so to speak, and now Samuel was doomed to an indeterminable, wet ride across the English countryside with Penelope's shapely derriere pressed to his groin.

Somewhere a deity was laughing.

There should be nothing untoward about the situation they found themselves in. The rain had made the road impassable. Their carriage had become stuck. Taking the only measure open to them, they had escaped the situation on horseback. It was all logical and prudent. Or it would have been to anyone but Samuel.

As Penelope shifted with the canter of the horse, he clenched in response, forcing his mind to focus on the road ahead. The going was treacherous at best and should have been enough to distract him. The rain smothered them, cold and piercing, slicing through their outer garments within moments. Now he was sure Penelope was just as numb as he was.

He estimated they had traveled greater than five miles like that and had passed nothing. He suddenly wished for the cows from the first day on their voyage while he cursed them at the same time. Now they would never catch the professor in time. He had likely made it past that part of road before it had given out under the incessant deluge. He would make Edinburgh and depart for South Africa with John Herschel while Samuel's socks were still drying.

"Does that appear to be a light?" Penelope's voice was muffled through the rain and the makeshift hood he had created out of a pair of trousers he'd had in his case.

His eyes scanned the length of the road in front of them, but the rain was relentless.

"Where?" he called over the noise.

She lifted a hand and pointed much further to the right than he had been looking. A band of trees created a barrier nearly perpendicular to the road, stretching back through empty fields. Only as he studied the outcropping did Samuel realize the growth was unnatural. It was perfectly straight as if someone had planted it. He strained to see through the curtain of water, and he thought just for a moment he saw a flicker of light.

He turned his head, scanning the fields on either side of

the road. The land was relatively flat here, and fields spread out on either side of the thoroughfare like melting butter running over a crust of toast. It would only make sense that a barrier of trees had been planted to stop the oncoming wind for there was nothing else in the vicinity to suggest a windbreak.

He urged the horse forward toward the place where he thought he saw the light, and in moments, they had left the road. The animal faltered only the slightest bit as her hooves left solid road. Well, at least more solid than the ground of the field proved to be. Samuel hurried the horse along, fearing the animal may get caught in deep mud. With two riders, it was unusually heavy, and he dreaded causing the horse undue pain by getting her stuck.

Finally, they rounded the barrier of the trees, and Samuel caught sight of the barn first. It sagged under the rain as if the next rain drop would bring the whole thing down to the chicken yard. The chicken yard was no better. The tin roof over what was likely the coop dipped far too low on one side, and the ramp into the house was broken through in two spots. Beyond both of these stood a house. Or what Samuel thought was the house. The barn was in better shape.

He nudged the horse toward it though, slowing the animal to a walk before slipping from the saddle as they drew near. He reached up for Penelope, and she came down into his arms much too easily. Rivulets dripped along the brim of her bonnet as it peeked out from beneath the edge of her makeshift hood. She smiled up at him, and he forget to let go of her arms.

They stood like that in the rain for several seconds before the sound of a gun cocking broke Samuel out of his trance. He spun around, his body stepping in front of Penelope without conscious thought.

"What do you want?"

It was a woman. A very young, pretty woman. She stood on the sagging porch of the small house, silhouetted by the orange light of the open door. She had brown hair that fell in odd clusters about her ears and over her forehead as if something had tugged the strands from their coiffure. Her hands were steady though as they held the rifle pointed at Samuel's chest, and her legs were strong as they braced themselves in a pair of boots that had obviously once belonged to a man.

It was the second time he had faced a woman with a rifle in as many days, and he suddenly longed for a good, dark rookery of London.

"We mean you no harm," he said, and Penelope gave an aggrieved sigh behind him.

"That's what anyone who meant harm would say," she hissed behind him.

He frowned, and the woman raised the rifle higher. He forced a calm smile. "I am Samuel Black, a detective inspector with London's Metropolitan Police Force. My—" His tongue stuck in his throat as he'd nearly said colleague. But that wasn't the ruse, was it? "My wife and I were headed north when our carriage became stuck on the road. Our coachman sent us on with the one good horse. We only seek shelter from the storm."

The rifle came up higher. "How is that I'm supposed to trust you? I don't know you."

Samuel raised his hands. "I know—"

"Mama."

The voice was small, and Samuel was nearly certain that he'd made it up out of the senseless noise of the rain. But then a small face appeared, slipping out beside the ratty skirts of the woman. It was a girl with the same thin lips and straight nose as the woman with the rifle, presumably her mother. The girl was painfully thin, and her hands were brown and raw as if she'd been scrubbing.

Samuel recognized those hands. He recognized them because his own hands had looked just like that until he was nine years old, and Nathan Black had come to save them. He dropped his own hands now and reached behind him, pulling Penelope with him up onto the porch of the sorry, old house.

The woman backed up, jarring her shoulder against the doorframe and sending the barrel of the rifle askew. In that moment, Samuel could have snatched the weapon from her, but he didn't. He helped Penelope up the porch steps and reached up to untangle the trousers from her bonnet. When the garment came free, he tossed them aside before reaching into his coat to extract his handkerchief, which was remarkably still dry. Softly, he patted the rain from Penelope's face, taking extra care around her big, almond-shaped eyes.

"Thank you," she said when he finished, smiling up at him in that peaceful way she had. She turned to the woman with the rifle. "I'm terribly sorry to come upon you like this," she said. "My husband and I do apologize, and we don't wish to impose." Her gaze dropped to the little girl. "I'm sure you have enough on your mind without two strangers showing up on your doorstep. What a terrible inconvenience." She reached out and put a hand on Samuel's arm. "We would really just appreciate getting our horse out of the rain. The poor animal has been so good in getting us through the mud. We don't want her to experience ill health because we pushed her too hard."

The barrel of the rifle sagged as the woman darted her gaze between them both.

Penelope bent forward, putting her hands to her knees. "And I bet all this rain has kept you stuck inside today. You must be terribly bored," she said to the little girl. She was rewarded with a tentative smile.

The woman lowered the rifle. "You can stay in the barn

until the rain stops. You can see yourselves inside." She gestured with the firearm toward the sagging edifice.

Samuel nodded. "We thank you very much for your kindness."

The woman began to back up, one hand going to the young girl's shoulders. As the glow from the open door fell across her features, Samuel realized the young woman was likely not much older than his sister, Jane. His stomach clenched at the thought of a woman so young left with so much responsibility. He paused at the edge of the porch.

"I don't mean to be forward, but the rain appears to be staying around for a time. Is there anything that you require that I may be able to assist you with?" He smiled, hoping to illicit the same reaction Penelope had with the young girl. "I spent many years on my father's farm mending fences. I'm rather accomplished with an awl and axe."

The woman's colorless eyes darted to the right, likely taking in Penelope who had moved back out into the rain to lead the horse toward the barn. When her gaze returned to him, it was a little steadier. "Thank you for your kind offer," she said, her voice losing the stiffness from earlier. "I will think on it."

Samuel touched the brim of his hat. "Thank you, ma'am."

He hadn't taken a step before the woman halted him with a call.

"Wait," she said, stepping out onto the porch with him, the rifle moving aside into the cradle of her arms. "There are grooms' quarters at the back of the barn. You'll find a stove there and some reasonably comfortable cots." She looked down at her feet, shuffling them in the oversize boots. "Or they were once. You and your wife can stay there tonight if the rain doesn't stop."

He smiled and nodded again. "Your kindness is much appreciated. Thank you, ma'am."

She stepped back toward the door without another word, and Samuel headed out into the rain, catching up with Penelope as she pulled at the stout doors of the barn. Because the entire building sank toward the middle, the doors would not give without a fight. It took both of them to wedge one of them open enough to get the poor horse inside. As they slipped out of the rain, the horse stomped its feet and blew a force of air, whinnying and flaring its nostrils. Samuel bent to removing the saddle and their bags the coachman had secured to it.

Once it was off, Penelope stepped up, wiping the animal down with a blanket she had found in one of the stalls. The blanket wasn't clean, but it was better than the horse being wet and cold. Samuel found some dry hay and led the horse into a stall before joining Penelope at the open door where she stood gazing out into the rain at the house with the single light in the first floor window.

He put a hand to her shoulder, and she jumped as if he'd startled her from deep thoughts. She smiled and shook her head.

"Wool gathering," she said with a laugh, but her fingers twitched where she had her arms folded across her chest.

He didn't believe her, but he didn't want to pry right then. He was still unsettled from her kiss the night before and from the uncomfortable ride through the rain. His resolve to keep her as innocent as possible was weakening with every mile into their journey. Now he stared at her as the flat light from outside struck the wet sheen of her cheeks, highlighting the dusting of freckles under her eyes and along her straight nose.

"There are grooms' quarters somewhere in the back," he said. "The woman said we'll find a stove there and somewhere to sleep if the rain doesn't let up."

Penelope's lips thinned. "We'll not catch the professor now," she said, echoing his thoughts from earlier.

He shook the rain from the arms of his coat. "It doesn't seem likely."

"But I suppose we must press on," she said and turned from the open door.

He thought about the grooms' quarters and what they would find in them. Yes, they must press on, but he didn't think that's what Penelope had in mind.

CHAPTER 11

It is necessary to ascertain one's motives before accepting the allegiance of an ally.
From The Adventures of Miss Melanie Merkett, Private Inquisitor

"I WOULD LIKE TO UNDRESS."

She wasn't sure why such a look of shock sprang to Samuel's face at her words. Did he truly expect her to remain in her wet garments for the foreseeable future? But there was something else about his face. Resignation perhaps.

Her hands stilled along her belt as she took him in. There was something that bothered Samuel when it came to more intimate moments. She wondered what it was that bothered him. His quest to see her virtue remain intact. Her reputation unblemished. Or did it go deeper than that? Was there something in the act itself, of the intimacies shared between husband and wife, that made him upset?

She regarded him as he laid the fire in the small stove they had found in the grooms' quarters at the back of the barn. He was just as soaked through as she was but instead of seeing after his own comfort first he had found some kindling and poked around the stove until a warm flame began. Already Penelope could sense the chill retreating enough that she had wished to remove her clothing.

The canvas exterior of her bag had protected its contents remarkably well, and she at least had a dry night dress she could don. She had even spied a nice length of rope she could stretch across the quarters to hang their things on. The room contained little else besides the stove and two small cots pushed to one end. As her gaze moved from Samuel crouched at the stove to the two cots, her stomach rumbled in protest.

Samuel glanced up at her. "I'm sorry I haven't any food."

She shook her head, sliding the length of belt through the buckle. "It's all right. A little hunger is always good for building one's constitution."

That sounded entirely made up, and Samuel's expression suggested he agreed with that thought.

He straightened then, brushing his hands against the thighs of his sodden trousers. "I'll step out while you change," he said, his voice more gravelly than usual.

She thought he was likely feeling the effects of the day as well and studied him as he walked by her toward the door of the quarters. He moved effortlessly as she had determined was his custom. Smooth and gracefully. He closed the door softly behind him, and Penelope bent to pull her nightdress from her bag. A thump had her looking down as she took in her writing box, hastily closed and returned to her bag before they'd jumped out into the rain.

She shook her head at it. Even Miss Merkett could not have designed a greater obstacle to their journey. Penelope had never before been the victim of a stuck carriage. It had been quite a delicious episode, and she hoped she'd have time that evening to put it down in words lest she forget it.

The buttons of her dress proved to be another obstacle entirely. After a struggle that would have made Wellington proud, Penelope finally gave up in defeat and opened the door.

"I require assistance," she said into the space beyond.

Samuel stood some distance away, peering through the murky glass of a small window. Only his eyes moved toward her, but she could sense his body stiffening in preparation for flight.

"It's only my buttons, you see. The rain has made the fabric disagreeable."

She saw the moment chivalry won over whatever it was that kept him so tightly clenched when intimacy raised its monstrous head. He turned toward her, his movements just as easy, belying the tensions she saw coiling in his shoulders.

She backed into the room and presented him with her back, lifting the pieces of her hair that had escaped her chignon through the day's ordeal. His footsteps shuffled along the dirt-covered floorboards behind her until she felt his fingers at her back. Or rather the pull of the fabric as his fingers went to work on her buttons. He was dreadfully careful to not touch her directly.

In that second, Penelope had a terrible idea.

She blinked, taking in the two sagging cots at the opposite end of the room. Felt the tug of fabric at her back and the loosening of her bodice as the dress came away. The moment Samuel's fingers left her back, Penelope turned, reached up and snagged the bodice of her gown. The garment, heavy with rain, slid from her body in a great clomp as it hit the floor.

She stood only in her chemise and corset facing Samuel. Her chemise was very wet, very transparent, and her corset boosted her bosom as if to display her womanly curves just for him. He was half-turned as if he'd been going for the door. One arm was even raised as if reaching for the handle. Now he stood frozen, his eyes narrow slits in a face gone to stone.

But his eyes.

In his eyes, she found what she sought. Heat. Pure, lustful heat. The same heat she had felt in his kiss that day on the pavement, the same that had seared her the night before in the corridor. The heat he purposefully kept from her.

She waited, the breath faltering in her lungs. Part of her expected him to turn to the door, complete the movement he had started, and escape the room. Avoiding the confrontation with the intimacy he seemed to evade.

But the other part of her, the part of her that had her reaching for the ties of her corset, that part dared him to stay. To turn back, towards her, and this thing that remained unfinished between them. The ties fell away, and she pulled the corset free, her eyes never leaving his. She saw the flash of heat, the spark that ignited when the corset joined her gown on the floor. Then she reached for her chemise.

She wasn't sure what made her do it. What this thing was that propelled her forward. She had never been so bold with a man, but if she were honest, she had never found one that fired the burning pulse low in her stomach. No one except Samuel.

She slipped one capped sleeve from her shoulder and then the other. The wet material clung to her arms, and she eased it down.

"Penelope."

The word was so low she almost didn't hear it. Her hand stilled on the sleeve of her chemise. Her skin was cold from the damp, and gooseflesh spread over her. She lifted her eyes to Samuel's face, saw his eyes were wider now, drinking her in. But he still hadn't moved, neither away nor toward her. She kept her hand on the sleeve of the chemise. Just a little further, and she'd be bared to him.

Samuel moved his chin as if her were going to stop her with a shake of his head. She ripped the chemise from her torso. It caught on the flare of her hips, but she was exposed from the waist up. Her nipples dimpled as the cold air assaulted them, and she fisted her hands in the chemise to keep from raising her arms to cover herself. She stared at Samuel, but his eyes never moved lower. They stayed riveted to her face.

The steel inside him kept his eyes there, never lingering to her naked body. She could sense the control in him. Sense it thriving as she pushed him further. This wasn't working. His restraint was too great.

She released her grip on the chemise and spread her opened palms against the flatness of her belly. She inched them higher, her fingers gliding over the gooseflesh until slipping into the meager warmth of the underside of her breasts.

"Penelope." He spoke her name again, but this time it was not so low. This time it held fire behind it.

She slid her hands higher, the tips of her fingers brushing her taut nipples.

She didn't see him move, but suddenly he was there, pulling her hands from her chest as he stepped into her arms. His mouth crushed hers, searing her with his heat. Her hands scrambled for purchase along the wet lengths of his coat. She caught him about the shoulders as he plunged his hands down the plane of her back. His broad palms and callused fingers scorching her flesh with unexpected heat.

She jolted against him, her hips driving into him. He groaned, the sound intense against her lips, and his hands dropped further, snagged the chemise at her waist and thrust it over the roundness of her hips. She heard the plop as it hit the floor, and then his hands were on her buttocks, scooping her up and pressing her fully against him.

She shivered, her hips squirming in his grip as she tried to get closer to him. He obliged, lifting her completely off the ground as his arms went around her. The scrape of a wool blanket met her back, and she realized he had lain her down on one of the cots. The position gave her freedom to shift her arms. She pushed them into his coat, driving the garment off. She scrambled for his cravat next even as she wrenched his shirt from his trousers.

Bare flesh.

Her hand met the smooth flesh of his back. He was so hot. She hadn't expected such heat, and she wanted more of it. She wanted to curl into it, absorb it, covet it.

He shifted, his lips brushing her cheeks, her closed eyelids. He seared a path along her jaw until he sucked an ear lobe into his mouth. She jerked, the sensations so focused, so new. The pulse in her belly echoed through her body. She arched into him, and he shifted further down, his lips finding her collarbone, the valley between her breasts.

"Please, Samuel." She'd never whimpered before, but she couldn't draw enough air for proper speech.

But then he was gone. All of his heat. All of his weight. Where she had just soaked into his nearness there was nothing but air. Her eyes flew open but not before the scrape of the wool blanket encased her, scratching her flesh as she jerked away from it.

Samuel was already standing, already striding to the door, his clothes in half-dressed tatters about him.

"Samuel!" She sounded like a mad fish monger in the small confines of the grooms' quarters, but Samuel stopped, arrested with just the sound of her voice. "Samuel." She said it more softly now. Calmer. Coaxing.

But he didn't turn. He didn't look at her. Although he clearly tried to regain his restraint, she saw the heave of his body as he sucked in air. She knew he was affected just as much as she had been. And yet, he had stopped.

"Samuel," she said, "Are you a virgin?"

* * *

ONCE HE HAD BEEN SENT on a mission for the War Office when he was still a young boy. As the son of a servant, he had been skilled in moving about the hustle below stairs without being detected. As such, it made him a good mole. But in this case, he had found himself trapped in the larder behind a smelly wheel of cheese while a footman had his way with a downstairs maid. The maid seemed to quite enjoy the footman's attentions, and Samuel had been stuck for an incredibly long time. Long enough that his mother had thrown away his clothes because they smelled like the cheese he had been hiding behind.

At that moment, Samuel would have preferred being back behind that wheel of cheese than standing there in front of an incredibly naked Penelope. Her hair had come undone, falling in alluring red swaths along her pale, freckled shoulders. He wanted to sweep a chunk of it into his hand, bury his face in it, memorize the smell of rain on it.

Instead he stood there like a child being scolded by the schoolmaster.

His shirt was half untucked, and his cravat had become wedged in his waistcoat. Mercifully, his trousers were still buttoned up and his boots were on. Hell, even his coat was on. It wasn't as if they had gotten very far.

But it was plenty far for him, which was farther than he had ever let himself slip before.

It was Penelope's fault. Not that he was blaming her. He

flexed his hands into tight fists at the thought. It came too close to what men like his real father were like. Men who took advantage of vulnerable women.

No, it was Penelope's fault because he found her too damn attractive. Appealing. He had never been tempted before the way he was around her. She had broken through his carefully laid restraints as if they didn't exist at all. He shuddered now and swiped a hand through his hair. He glanced at the door, his body yearning for retreat.

But at the opposite end of the room sat Penelope. Rumpled, naked Penelope. He could go through the door. Continue to deny the thing that ate him from the inside out. Or he could turn around. Answer Penelope's question. Take that one step forward until he could no longer turn back. Just tell her, and then she would know.

He turned. She still sat there with the woolen blanket pressed to her chest. The fire was burning strong enough now to cast streaks of orange across her pale face. God, she must be so tired. She hadn't complained once that day. Not when the carriage had become stuck. Not when she'd jumped out into the rain. Not when he'd had to share the saddle with her. Nothing through all of that. Just quiet acceptance and a steely determination to see their journey go on.

"Yes."

The word was softer than he had meant it, and he worried he would need to repeat it. But Penelope heard him. She unfroze at the sound in the small room. Her hands dropped from the blanket, and he thought she would stand, but instead she pushed herself further back on the cot and patted the space next to her.

He hesitated, feeling the freedom of the door behind him, pressing on his back as if to urge him the other way. He walked to the cot and sat at the very edge of it, leaving a solid foot of space between them.

"I would offer you a piece of my blanket, but you seem to be in possession of a great deal more clothing than me," Penelope said.

He stood immediately, ready to pounce on the pile of her discarded clothing only to be stopped when she called his name.

"I only kid you, Samuel," she said.

He settled back on the cot, but he didn't look at her.

"Most gentlemen of your age and circumstance do not find themselves in such a position as you seem to be in."

Penelope's toes peeked out from underneath the blanket. At least, he hadn't removed her stockings. They were wool stockings, very serviceable in nature and yet they were a warm cream color and not glaring white. Very Penelope.

"I realize that," he said.

"Would you care to tell me how you came to be afflicted so?"

He looked at her now. "Would you call it an affliction?"

"Some men would think so."

"I don't think so." He watched her face in the flicker of the fire, but her features remained calm and composed. He swallowed, unsure if he were so uncomfortable because of the conversation itself or because she appeared so relaxed while having it. It was likely the latter.

"I assume your affliction is by choice," she said.

He nodded. "Yes, it is my choice, but why do you say that?"

A smile slipped to her lips. "Because a man as handsome and powerful as you has likely not gone unnoticed by the female variety."

Heat spread over his cheeks that had nothing to do with the fire. "I'm not sure I can agree with you on that mark."

"Oh, you needn't agree or disagree," she said, adjusting the blanket around her legs. "It's an assumed fact of nature." She tapped him once on the leg. "I believe you will recall I did a lot of study on the matter on nature in helping my father. You'd be amazed at what natural order occurs in this world."

The thing inside of him stilled, not quite in fear but not quite in hope. Somewhere in between. "Natural order?"

She settled back against the wall of the quarters and flexed her toes toward the fire.

"Natural order," she repeated. "There's a way to things, you know. How natural history predetermines a lot of it. Like bees spreading the pollen for flowers to thrive. Or birds migrating as the weather changes." She turned to him, smiled. "Nature."

The thing in his belly tipped into fear, gnawing at him.

"So would it stand to reason that a creature born of another creature could exhibits the same attributes and tendencies as its creator?"

She stopped flexing her toes. "Why do I sense you are asking a much more complicated question than you let on?"

Samuel pushed to his feet, unable to sit still any longer. He tugged his cravat from where it dangled on his waistcoat and tossed it onto the pile of Penelope's clothes.

"It is the ultimate debate, is it not?" he questioned, striding to one end of the room. "Whether a creature acts as its predetermined qualities would suggest or if the influence of nature were so great as to overcome such obstacles."

"Are you suggesting that a creature's behavior should be influenced not by the environment but by its natural make up?" Penelope asked.

"Or the reverse," he said, stopping to regard her.

Her arms were long and white against the dark blanket, but her fingers did not twitch.

"Well, there is some debate in the scholarly circles my father used to frequent that would suggest organisms all developed from the same core components, and it's only through their exposure to differing environments that the creatures did, in fact, develop dissimilarities."

"So the creatures were more greatly affected by their environments and not their essential beings?"

She nodded. "Yes, but how does this cause you to be a virgin?"

She said the word with such casualness, his stomach tightened. He studied the fire if only to press through what he had to say. If he watched her face, her beautiful, open, inquisitive, understanding face, he'd never finish.

"I told you my sisters and I have different fathers."

"Yes."

"My mother became pregnant with me when she was very young. She was employed as a maid at the time, and her employers were having a house party. There were several guests of varying degrees of peerage staying at the estate." He paused, allowing the crackling of the fire to fill the space. Penelope did not speak, but he could feel her, sitting on the cot behind him. Waiting without prodding him to continue. "My mother is a very small woman. She was unable to defend herself."

There was a noise behind him, like a mouse scurrying through cotton, and Penelope suddenly had hold of his arm. She wrenched him about to face her. Her nostrils flared as her riotous hair settled along her shoulders. One hand clutched at the blanket while the other stopped the blood in his arm.

"Your mother was raped."

It wasn't a question. It didn't need to be.

"Yes."

Again, the single word spoken so softly.

"Who was it?" Penelope practically spit the words, each enunciated with cutting clarity.

The thing inside Samuel began to unwind. Just the

smallest of bits. Almost as if it no longer held its breath.

"It doesn't matter," he said. "My mother shot him."

Penelope released his arm so quickly, he stumbled backwards. Her almond eyes grew wide in her face, and her lips parted on an unspoken gasp.

He smiled, which surprised him. "He was a traitor. My father—the man who married my mother, that is—caught him smuggling noblemen to Napoleon for ransom. He tried to kidnap my mother, and she shot him." He shrugged. It had all happened so long ago, the story was more stuff of legend now.

Penelope took a step away from him. "Is this what you were saying? About your family working for the War Office?"

He thought back to that day at the coffee house when he'd been so young and naive. What else had he let slip that day?

"Yes, the Blacks regularly completed assignments for the War Office. That is how Nathan Black came to be married to my mother."

Penelope's eyes were still wide, but she'd at least shut her mouth.

"Does it bother you? The history of the Black family?" he asked.

Her eyes narrowed now, and she pierced him with a frown. "You just did it again." She pointed with the hand not holding the blanket to her chest. "You referred to them in the third person. As if they weren't your family." She rested her hand on his arm again. "Is that why you do it? Because your natural father is who he is?" She grimaced. "Or was, I should say."

He nodded and pushed away from her, striding over to the fire to poke at it unnecessarily. "They're not my family. It was only a matter of happenstance that they became entangled in my life." He poked at a log and added another. "And now I can't even protect them."

He had thought he had spoken softly enough, but then Penelope appeared at his side.

"One issue at a time, if you please." Her hair had begun to dry and fanned about her face as she squatted beside him. "The first is your father. The natural one. You have not had intimate relations with a woman for fear that you're like him. That's it, isn't it?"

"I am like him." He didn't look at her as he said it.

"Then you're an idiot as well," she said.

Now he looked at her. "I beg your pardon."

"You're an idiot. One's natural make up does not dictate one's eventualities. That's why God gave you a mind of your own. It would be a pity if you wasted it." She held up a hand before he could interject. "And what is this business about protecting your family?"

He straightened, but she kept a hand on him and rose with him.

"Samuel." She had a precise way of saying his name that brooked no argument.

"Someone tried to abduct two of my family members in the previous weeks."

"Abduct?" The hand on his arm twitched.

"Yes, abduct. I was unable to discover more because I was diverted by Wickshire on this mad scheme to retrieve the professor."

"It's not a mad scheme, and do members of your family often find themselves in danger?"

He nodded. "Yes, indeed, they do."

"You just agreed they were your family." She grinned at her trickery, but he only waved her away. "But tell me, Samuel, once upon a time you confessed a desire to marry me. How is it you plan to overcome your reluctance to have intimate relations with a woman on our wedding night?"

CHAPTER 12

*I*t should always be anticipated that while one is searching for clues, someone is searching for you.

From The Adventures of Miss Melanie Merkett, Private Inquisitor

HE WAS GOING to throttle her.

How he had not succeeded in doing so already surprised her. But Samuel was a man of powerful restraint, and nothing exhibited that more clearly than in his handling of her. He opened his mouth, and she raised an eyebrow in anticipation.

But she never got to hear what he would say as a knock came at the door. She jumped, nearly losing the wool blanket that covered her. Samuel turned swiftly, parting the door just enough to see who was on the other side.

"I'm so very sorry," came the voice of their hostess, of whom they still had not learned her name. "Someone's come looking for you."

Penelope felt a new cold then that had nothing to do with their sodden ride. Samuel's grip on the door stiffened.

"I sent them away," she hurried on. "I don't want any trouble here, and I said no one had passed by here on the road. I said no one would be traveling in this weather. But I must ask you to leave. You can't stay. I'm so very sorry."

Even before her words finished, Samuel shook his head. Penelope was beginning to have an entirely different under-standing of Samuel Black and his drive for justice, even in small matters.

"We will leave at once," he said. "I'm sorry to have put you in this position."

"You said you are with the Metropolitan Police," the woman said now, and the door thrust open a little wider. Penelope leaned around the edge of it as a wrapped bundle appeared. "My husband served as the constable in these parts. He was killed when he interrupted some highwaymen about to set upon a carriage." The woman's hands shook slightly on the bundle. "There's some food in here. It's not much, but it's what we can spare." Samuel took the bundle, cradled it against his chest. "I hope you find whatever it is you're after."

The door began to shut, but Samuel stopped it with a hand. "Wait, one moment." He handed the bundle of food to Penelope, and she awkwardly held it as she tried to maintain her grip on the blanket. Samuel went to their bags on the floor, pulling out a small pouch from a hidden pocket inside his leather satchel. He handed it to the woman at the door.

"It's not much, but your kindness is appreciated more than you can know." There was a stillness then, but Penelope knew from Samuel's face that the woman was grateful. "What is your name, miss?"

Again a stillness in hesitation. "Norton. Mrs. Walter Norton."

Samuel nodded and gave the woman an encouraging smile. "Mrs. Norton, if things here become too grave, you will find shelter at Lofton House in London. Tell them Samuel Black sent you."

Penelope could stand it no longer. She pulled herself around the corner of the door, heedless of her undressed state.

"Wickshire Place, as well," she said. "Tell them Penelope Paiget sent you."

There was a moment of recognition on the woman's face, in her wide eyes and parted lips, as she absorbed their secrets. She recovered and nodded. "Thank you. Thank you both. There may come a day when I will need to accept your kindness."

Penelope smiled as the woman backed out of the door, retreating into the darkness of the barn beyond. Already regretting putting on her still wet clothing, she turned back to the small room, setting aside the bundle of food even as she reached for her things. At least her stockings had dried.

"Are you not donning dry clothes?"

Penelope looked over at Samuel with her wet chemise hanging from her fingertips and then looked behind him at the still falling rain outside the only window in the room. "What would be the point exactly?"

He grimaced and found his cravat, tucking it into his pocket instead of retying it. He left the room still shrugging into his coat, and she dressed quickly. She retraced her steps to the main part of the barn only minutes later and found Samuel speaking in hushed tones with Mrs. Norton. He looked up at her approach.

"There's a road on the other side of this wood. It will take us around Oxford and hopefully miss the man who is following us."

Penelope turned to Mrs. Norton. "It is a single rider?"

Mrs. Norton nodded. "One gentleman. Finely dressed and riding good horseflesh. I cannot see a man such as he continuing on in this rain though."

"You think he'll stop at Oxford for the night?" Penelope asked.

Mrs. Norton nodded again. "I would suspect. You can take the road and go around if you're willing to travel in this."

"We must," Samuel said, taking Penelope's bag and going for their horse.

Penelope felt a stab of regret at rousing the horse from his dry bed. But after a few stomps of her feet and huffs from her nose, the animal pranced out into the barn, happy to accept the saddle and bags once more.

"If you're able, there's an inn at the crossroads, about five miles from here. It's a stopping point for the mail coaches. You should be able to find shelter and transport for your journey onwards."

Penelope looked at Samuel, but they needn't speak. What would be the possibility of meeting the mail coach Professor Mesmer was on?

With another expression of thanks, they made their way out into the barnyard and onto their horse. Penelope looked back long enough to raise a hand in gratitude to Mrs. Norton. The worn woman raised a hand in return, and Penelope thought she may have even smiled. But it might have just been a trick of the rain.

* * *

He was once more plagued with the proximity of Penelope Paiget.

At least the rain hadn't been as bad amongst the trees.

They didn't speak for the mile or so as they threaded through the woods, the horse finding its way through brush and branch. The ground was spongy, and Samuel worried for the horse, but the animal marched on confidently.

They had broken through onto the road Mrs. Norton had told them about in good time but found the way no better than the road that had swallowed their carriage. He kept the horse to the sides of the route where carriage wheels had not left deep scars, but even then, the mud sucked at the horse's hooves. The rain fell steadily about them, like a menacing, icy cloak.

"It could be worse."

The sound of Penelope's voice was startling in the constant hum of the rain.

"That's usually what someone says right before it gets alarmingly worse," he replied.

He felt more than heard Penelope's chuckle.

"It could be windy."

He supposed that was an accurate observation. He was wet and cold but not buffeted by unceasing blasts of cold air. He regarded the bit of Penelope's face he could see around the sodden brim of her bonnet. Her straight nose came to a gentle point, and her mouth was relaxed although not frowning. Of course, she would seek the brightest spot in a day that provided nothing but darkness even in the most literal interpretation of the word.

They only had to make it to the crossroads. It couldn't be more than a couple of miles further. He wasn't sure where the sun was at this point. He felt as though it were late afternoon or perhaps early evening, but the unrelenting gray sky provided no clues. They would make it to the crossroads. Find shelter. A hot meal. Maybe even a warm bath.

And if they were lucky, they would find the mail coach carrying Professor Mesmer. Their journey might be at an end. He didn't like the pang that pierced him at the thought, and he tightened his grip around Penelope. She patted his arm in response, but her gaze remained focused on the road.

They traveled like that for nearly an hour more before Penelope spotted it first.

"Light." It was the same word she had used when she'd seen Mrs. Norton's home, and he found it revealing that she would choose such a word. He urged the horse on, and the light grew until he could make out the details of a lamp post. He followed the line of the post until he could discern the outline of a crossroads.

"It's there," he said, and Penelope nodded, her bonnet brushing his cheek.

As if sensing a warm stall and fresh hay, the horse picked up speed, her ears going back as she plunged forward. They had almost reached the crossroads when an inn materialized by the side of the road, tucked into a copse of trees to one side of the junction. The horse trotted into the inn yard without guidance and stopped without suggestion as if indicating her finality of traveling for the day.

Samuel dismounted and reached up for Penelope, carefully setting her on the ground. Her boots sank into the mud of the yard as much as his did. There was an overhang above the door of the inn, and he drew her under it, handing her the lead for the horse.

"I'll inquire about a room," he said.

She nodded, but he noticed her eyes never met his. They were too occupied with scanning the make up of the inn yard, the wood of the overhang, and even the lighted windows. He watched for several seconds, marveling at how quickly her attention seemed to snap everything into her mind.

He pried himself away and entered the inn. The door let into the main tavern it seemed as he encountered several sets of tables and chairs, all empty except one in the far corner.

The bar keep looked up from where he scrubbed a glass with a rag. It was an older man, bushy white hair and sleeves that may have once been white rolled up his beefy arms.

Samuel nodded in greeting and removed his hat before stepping further into the room.

"Good evening," Samuel said. "Our carriage got stuck along the road to Oxford. We were hoping to find aid to send back to our coachman."

The bar keep set down the glass and leaned against the bar. "You won't be finding any help in this rain. It's got near everyone stuck indoors for miles around."

Samuel looked behind him at the one occupant in the tavern. It was a youngish man, but he looked solid about the shoulders.

"There isn't anyone about who could help?" he pressed the bar keep.

The man shook his head. "You probably didn't come up from Oxford along the main road, did ye? The rain's got the bridge washed out. Hasn't been any traffic through here in days."

Samuel stilled. "Days?"

The bar keep nodded and picked up another glass, resumed his scrubbing. "Don't know how long it will be until they get it fixed either. Not with this rain."

"Not even the post is getting through then?" He kept his tone light, his stance relaxed to avoid any suspicion.

The bar keep continued to scrub at the glass. "Nah, nothing of the like."

Samuel tossed his hat from one hand to another, deciding to take care of what he could at the moment. "Well, then I suppose a room will have to do. My wife and I are headed north. We'll need a tray of food and a bath, if you can accommodate it. We also have a horse that will require stabling and feed."

The bar keep perked up at the possibility of a coin, snapping his fingers at the lone man in the tavern.

"Tommy, see to the man's horse."

Samuel stepped into the yard just as the man called Tommy handed Penelope her bag, a hot blush staining his cheeks. Penelope was smiling as he asked, "What did you say to him?"

She shrugged. "I asked him his name."

Samuel doubted that was all. He took her bag and helped her inside. Their room was nearly an identical copy of the one they had shared that first night, but he supposed he would need to get used to such confines.

Penelope set down her bag and spun around, her lips already parting to speak as he set the bolt on the door. A flash of their unfinished conversation from earlier spiked through his mind and knowing he did not have the strength to continue such a conversation he cut her off.

"There hasn't been traffic through here in days," he said. "I fear we may have passed the professor."

* * *

SHE SAT down on the only chair in the room. A rickety wooden thing with a wicker bottom. Water began to pool in a halo on the floor as the hem of her dress settled around her ankles.

"Passed him?" she asked, her fingers twitching in her lap.

Samuel moved to the stove in the room and poked at the glowing logs until flames shot up. Was it only that afternoon that he'd done the same in the groom's quarters? It seemed so long ago.

"It's the only conclusion I can find," Samuel said as he straightened. "If the rain was bad enough to stop us on the road from Slough, then it was likely bad enough to stop the post."

"But surely at this point the professor is traveling an entirely different route from us," she pressed.

Samuel reached for the door. "We cannot assume that. We can't assume anything really." He gestured at her with a quick nod of his head. "I'm having a bath sent up. You must change out of those wet things immediately."

He left.

The door shut with a resounding snap behind him, and Penelope could only glare at the flecking paint on the back of the portal. Damn the man and his insisting ways. Of course, a bath sounded divine, and she would be happy to acquiesce immediately as per his instructions. But the part of her that had created Melanie Merkett wanted to defy him on principle.

Instead, she stripped. She had bundled herself into one of the blankets from the bed when the maids arrived with steaming buckets and a generous hip bath. She cast them a smile of gratitude as they curtsied and left.

Penelope discarded the blanket back to the bed and slipped decadently into the tub. The warm water scalded her chilled skin, and she recoiled, moving even more slowly until her body adjusted to the temperature. She took a good minute to just enjoy the heat seeping through her bones, but aware of Samuel, still wet and cold somewhere in the inn, she hurried through her toilette. The soap was plain but it did the job and soon she was feeling resplendently clean.

Stepping from the tub, she picked up one of the towels the maid had left. It had seen its fair share of backsides judging by its thinness, but again, it fulfilled its task nicely and soon she was dry and in her nightdress. She padded to the door, slipping it open just enough to see what she had expected.

Samuel, leaning against the wall opposite.

"Playing guard now, are you?"

He didn't smile at her prodding. "It's a part of the training one receives on entering the force."

It took her a moment to realize he kidded her. She laughed belatedly, and the corners of his mouth twitched.

"Come. You must hurry before the water cools all the way." She backed up enough to allow him to enter.

"You needn't worry. I shan't be bathing." He stepped into the room and gave a wide berth to the tub as he approached his bag where he'd dropped it on the floor.

"Of course, you're bathing," she said, shutting the door with a snap of the bolt. "You're soaked. And you're probably cold. You're just as susceptible to chill as I am."

He turned, dry clothes from his bag in his hands. "I think it would be inappropriate if I were to—"

"Have you forgotten that only hours before this you saw me naked?"

This stopped him.

"Precisely," she went on. "Now, in." She pointed to the tub.

He looked at her and then about the room. "Shut your eyes," he finally said.

Her jaw wanted to flop open at his ridiculous command, but she remembered their unfinished conversation and kept it shut. Samuel was serious. There was an unflinching part of him that demanded she retain as much propriety as possible. She walked to the stove, crossed her arms over her chest as she put her back to him, and closed her eyes.

"Will this do?" she asked.

There was some shuffling behind her before she heard, "Well enough."

"Good, now we were discussing the likelihood that we've passed the professor," she said as if he were not undressing behind her, because blast it all, she desperately wanted to peek.

She had seen a male cadaver once, but she knew that would be no mark for comparison to a warm, thriving man. Well, if not warm now, then soon. She heard splashing, and she screwed her eyes shut tighter. She would respect Samuel's sensibilities until she learned more of what caused him such distress. She owed him such kindness.

"The bar keep indicated as such. He said the mail coaches come through with surprising regularity, but he hasn't seen one in days. If the professor left Slough yesterday morning by mail coach, it would reason that it should have come through this junction by now," he said.

"How many possible routes are there from Slough to Edinburgh? Are we sure he wouldn't have just missed this crossroads?"

More splashing. She bit the inside of her cheek.

"I inquired as such. The bar keep remains steadfast in his determination. Something about the mail coach needing to go through Oxford and from there, the best route north would take them through this junction. We can only safely estimate that we've passed him."

"What if he took another route?" Surely there must be some other explanation. Some other possibility.

"What if he still hasn't left Oxford? What if we remain here at the inn and he shows up tomorrow?"

She hadn't considered this. "So it may be a boon that we've passed him?"

The sound of splashing grew louder, complex, and she thought he'd likely stood from the bath. There was a shuffling noise, and the distinct sound of water hitting wooden floorboards. She counted to ten in her head. In Greek.

"It depends," he said. "If we have truly passed him, we may

have the blessing of him catching up to us. But if we haven't passed him…"

"Then he'll reach Edinburgh and depart with John Herschel."

"Precisely."

"We'll never find out who killed Bobby Egemont or who is after Mesmer's telescope technology."

"Precisely again." She heard the tinkle of the metal clasps of his leather bag.

"So what do we do? Do we wait to see if Mesmer appears in the next day or two or take our chances for Edinburgh?"

"Edinburgh."

He said it with such assuredness Penelope turned around before she realized she was doing it.

"How can you be so certain?" The last word came out rather strangled as his hand remained affixed to the buttons of his trousers. "Sorry," she stammered and spun back around but not before she completely and utterly memorized every muscle, every valley, every curve of Samuel Black's bare chest.

Good Lord. She grabbed one hand with the other to keep her fingers from twitching madly.

"Edinburgh. You're certain?" She forced her mind to focus on the topic at hand and not at the dusting of dark hair across his chest. The way it tapered and disappeared—

"Yes, I think it's our only option. We know Mesmer is going to Edinburgh. At some point he must reach his destination. His path to that point is largely uncertain. We can only hypothesize his route, which is not a gamble I'm willing to take." She didn't realize he had stopped talking until he said rather more quietly, "Penelope."

She half-turned, propping a single eyelid open. "Yes?"

"You may turn around now."

She did so, popping both eyes open with glee only to be

met with disappointment. The blasted man had not only put on a shirt, he'd donned socks as well. Did he fear she would ogle his bare toes?

"So we continue to Edinburgh then?"

He sat on the chair she had used earlier and picked up one of his boots. "Yes. It's our safest option." He took one of the towels and wiped at the insides of the boot.

She took a moment to savor his words, his intent to continue on this journey of theirs. He had been all too clear in his desire not to find himself in such a position, and she found his assuredness in continuing a balm to her wounds. Not that she took his refusal to go on this endeavor with her personally. Now that she understood him better, she saw it more as a challenge.

She crossed to the bed and sat. "And what of our shadow?"

He set aside the boot and picked up its mate. "Hopefully, he'll catch us." She stared, not expecting that answer in the least. Samuel went on, "If he's able to catch us, then we'll at least know who it is that the professor is running away from."

Penelope toyed with the cuff of her sleeve, her fingers beating out a tattoo on her wrist. "So the prey wishes to be caught by the hunter?"

Samuel looked up. "Are you suggesting we're the prey?"

"Are you not?"

Samuel smiled, a smile that gave her quite a shiver. "I'm never the prey."

Oh, but he was. For a moment, Penelope could see it. Them. Married. Happily ever after and all that nonsense. But with the flash of insight came the rushing regret of the differences the past ten years had made, and she squashed the image, her fingers stilling against her wrist.

She looked down at her bag, sitting now in a pool of

water as it dried from the heat of the stove. She bent and retrieved her mother's writing box, unscathed thanks to the canvas of the bag. Opening it, she retrieved the sheet of paper she had begun to scratch on while still in the coach. She fingered its tattered edges, tears from having been thrust into the box so hastily. She looked at the words she had written there.

His kisses are better than trifle.

She shoved the note away and drew out a clean sheet of paper.

"I must write to Wickshire. Inform him of the developments." She paused, her hand on her quill. "Do you think perhaps someone will intercept this and try to learn of our endeavor?"

Samuel regarded her with a raised eyebrow. "Are you suggesting the need to communicate in code?"

She fingered the quill. "Is that necessary?"

He shook his head. "Even when my parents were engaged more thoroughly in War Office affairs, I doubt they ever communicated in code." He stood and headed to the door. "I'm going to see about our dinner."

She looked at him. His hair was still wet and dripped carelessly down his forehead, leaving splotches on the lawn of his shirt. He wore no collar, and his sleeves were rolled to his elbows.

That.

That was how she would write him. So undone. So free. One couldn't see his scars from here.

She swallowed and dipped her quill in the ink. "I'll have this written momentarily, and we can ask the bar keep about a special messenger." Her words faltered a bit, but she didn't think Samuel noticed as he closed the door behind him.

CHAPTER 13

*O*ne must always be keen on the opportunity to improve
one's skills.

*From The Adventures of Miss Melanie Merkett, Private
Inquisitor*

THE NEXT DAY they were back in a carriage.

Samuel wanted to feel a measure of relief at this, thankful
to not be crossing unknown country side on an unfamiliar
horse, jostling, intimately no less, against the thing he most
wanted to avoid. But other thoughts clamored for attention
in his mind.

The possibility that they had passed the professor.

The possibility that they had not and he would reach
Edinburgh first.

The identity of their shadow.

His thoughts bounced from one to the other only to
travel back to the first, scouring it for a detail he had missed.
Carrying on with their journey was the only prudent thing
to do. As a detective inspector, he relied on his training to

help him see the obvious answer. In this case, there simply wasn't one. However, he had faith he had chosen the best option.

It wasn't as if Penelope helped in making him feel assured of his decision. Although, to be fair, that wasn't her duty. She sat across from him. Happily scribbling on a scrap of paper atop her writing box as the carriage bounced its way across England.

He had sent off her missive to the Earl of Wickshire. He hadn't bothered to read it before she'd sealed it. He was certain her text would be adequate in updating the man on their voyage. Samuel had his own missive to send off before they went anymore off track.

They were due to pass Manchester that day. The rain had taken them wildly off course, and they were much further west than they ought to have been. It was this that had his thoughts bouncing between whether or not they had truly passed the professor. The coachman Samuel had hired had sworn to have driven this route several times over and promised Samuel he'd be sleeping in an inn in Lancashire that night.

Samuel doubted exactly how much sleeping would happen. He'd spent the previous night in a chair by the stove, refusing to share the bed with Penelope. The image of her standing in the grooms' quarters, bared to the waist ricocheted in his mind like a nightmare. A sensual, enticing nightmare. He didn't trust himself to be in the same room with her, and he damn sure didn't trust himself in the same bed as her. No matter that she wore a nightdress that looked as if it could cover the whole of Parliament in its folds. He knew what lie underneath it, and the billowing fabric only taunted him to pull it off.

And she would let him. Damn the woman.

He adjusted himself on the bench, crossing one foot to the opposite knee to relieve his agitation.

"Feeling cramped?"

He moved his eyes over to Penelope. She sat with the writing box in her lap still, her pencil poised above the paper.

"I'm fine. Thank you."

"You do not look it. For all I can tell, you've sat on a bee." She shuffled the papers she had been scribbling on and set them inside the box along with the pencil. She closed the entire contraption and slipped it back into her bag.

She had removed her bonnet when they'd entered the coach that morning, and the midday sun slanted through the windows, catching the vibrant tones of her hair in its playful grip. He imagined her portrait then. Shades of watercolors and pots of warmth. So visceral. So alive.

And then she stood up and plopped down on the bench next to him.

"I've a mind for a nap." She stretched and reached her arms toward the ceiling of the carriage. "Would you mind serving as pillow?"

She didn't give him time to answer. Instead, she dipped her head, putting her ear to his shoulder. It couldn't have been comfortable. He certainly wasn't comfortable, but then, he had more than a desire for slumber plaguing him.

"This truly makes you uncomfortable, doesn't it?"

Her voice was not at all sleepy.

"Uncomfortable is not the word I would use," he replied.

She straightened and looked at him. "Uneasy at the very least." She pushed away from him, settling in the corner opposite. "You will have to stand my presence for the after-noon I'm afraid. The sun is coming in much too strongly on that side."

She nodded at the bench she had occupied for the

morning as she slid down in her seat, propping her feet on the bench opposite. Bits of her stockings peeked out from where the hem of her skirts hitched up. He looked out the window.

"You never answered my question, you know," she said. He swung his gaze back, but her eyes were closed. "I do expect an answer at some point." She didn't open her eyes as she said this, and then she said nothing more.

Samuel gave up, slipping down in the seat as she had done and propped his feet on the opposite bench.

He awoke with a start when his body seemed to understand the carriage had stopped moving. He scrubbed a hand over his face, wrenching the sleep from his body. He didn't think he could sleep, and he hadn't expected to sleep for as long as he had. He glanced out the window, but the sun had dipped too low in the sky. Most of what he saw were shadows and darkness.

He threw the door open and leaped out of the carriage, ready to call up to the driver in protest. But the driver was not on the box and neither was the tiger. In fact, the horses were gone as well. The carriage sat unhitched in the middle of an inn yard very much like the one they had left this morning. He spun about taking in the surroundings. Unlike the inn this morning, this stop was clearly part of a hamlet as buildings sprang up along the road on either side. People milled about. Ladies in bonnets with baskets of wares. Men tipping their hats as they shuffled about their business. It wasn't a lively metropolis, but it was certainly no lonely inn on a crossroads.

But worse, Penelope was nowhere in sight.

He went back to the carriage and peeked inside, just to assure himself he hadn't missed her. He thundered around the carriage toward the inn, stopping abruptly on the other side. The sounds of metal striking metal pierced the air here, and he looked to the left. The sign of a blacksmith hung over the door of a wooden edifice. He inched toward it, his gut already churning with dread.

He recalled with far too great clarity the song the tavern goers had been singing with the help of a red-headed temptress. Passing under the blacksmith's sign, he could only imagine what devilish work she had attempted while he slept in the carriage.

The shade of the building swallowed him seconds before the heat of the furnaces hit him. He stepped back, feeling the instant sweat spring across his back. There were racks of iron implements spread out to one side. Farm implements from hoes to spades to rakes. Plows sat along the dirt floor ready for their owners to retrieve them. Horse shoes lined the walls in all shapes and sizes. A long wooden table stretched from one end of the room to the other, scarred with burns and dents.

Beyond all of this glowed the furnace, orange and beckoning.

That was where he found Penelope, of course.

She stood next to a man that looked far too much like the grizzly bears he heard could be found in the Western states of America. His beard grew down to his chest, gnarled and twisted like the metal he worked in his hands. He wore a leather apron over tattered trousers and rolled sleeves. The same gnarly hair grew long about his face. Some of it was caught back in a queue, but most fell around a face weathered and sagging, smudged black from the work at the furnace.

Penelope cast her glowing smile upon him, her almond eyes huge and round as she absorbed every word he uttered.

The dread in Samuel's stomach turned to ice. The blasted woman was determined to have him fail. How could he keep her safe if she continued to wander off like this? The tavern men had been bad enough, but to engage a blacksmith?

He stopped, turning about quickly. The shop was empty except for the worn blacksmith and Penelope. She consorted with the tradesman alone? Completely unchaperoned? His gut twisted, sucking the air from his lungs. Good God, what could have happened to her if he hadn't arrived?

Clenching his fists against the fire roiling inside him, he strode toward her, pulling a tongue lashing together in his mind.

It was then that the blacksmith handed Penelope the iron he'd been firing in the forge. Samuel was so arrested by the sight he tripped over his own feet, catching himself against the scarred work table. Penelope slipped her hands over the end of the iron, holding the rod back into the greedy flames of the forge. She turned and twisted it until the metal glowed red. She pulled it from the flames and held it aloft. The blacksmith said something, but the roar of the furnace was too great. He could only see the man nod, and then Penelope was moving, putting the iron back into the forge.

Samuel moved, too, freed from his momentary spell. He surged forward.

"Penelope!"

He really hadn't meant for his voice to be so loud, but the fire inside him thrust it out, erupting over the grumble of furnace and striking of metal. Penelope jumped, and he realized his mistake too late. The hand holding the metal rod skittered, and the horse shoe that had been dangling on the end of it, the one he hadn't seen, tottered. He watched it as if the entire world slowed to that one horse shoe, dangling, wobbling, and then...falling.

She did not wear a leather apron like the blacksmith. That was the thought that raced through his mind as the horse shoe fell, struck the skirts of her dress, and ignited upon impact. The blacksmith moved, reaching for something, but

Samuel no longer saw him. He only saw Penelope. On fire. On fire because of him.

He was on her in moments, swept her into his arms, and spun about. He raced back the way he had come, sprinting into the dying light as the flames smoldered through her skirt. The white of petticoat appeared, and Samuel stopped breathing. He cleared the carriage, and there. There was what he sought. Four more steps. No, he made it in three.

And then he let her go with a not gentle toss.

She landed with a resounding splash in the horse trough outside the inn. Water rushed up on either side of her, engulfing her as it drowned the flames. A wall of water hit him as he'd not stopped plunging forward as he released her. He leaned over on his knees, sucking in gulps of air until he could stand, pulled at Penelope's shoulders until she was looking at him.

"Are you out of your mind, woman?" He spit the words more than said them.

Penelope frowned. "I am not, but I'm beginning to wonder if you are."

* * *

SHE WAS GOING to have to do something about him.

He clearly did not understand that a woman such as herself could be trusted to adventure into unfamiliar circumstances and emerge unscathed. The water was cold, and the bottom of the trough was slimy from things Penelope did not care to imagine. She gripped the metal sides of the tub and wrenched herself free, standing only to have her feet slip on the slimy bottom. She pitched herself to the side and tumbled over the lip of the tub, rolling onto the ground.

She lay there, knowing full well that her skirts were singed, likely beyond repair, and that she was not only soaked from the grimy water of the horse trough, she was now also likely covered in dirt from the inn yard. She closed her eyes, trying to recall the thrill she had first felt at the possibility of this journey. She knew it was there somewhere.

Adventure.

The unknown.

Samuel.

The thought of Samuel had her cringing, and she slipped an eye open. He leaned over her, hands on his knees, face grim. The muscle jumped in his jaw, and for a moment, she wanted to reach up and stroke it, ease it back into relaxation. His eyes were so dark, darker than she'd ever seen them, and in them, she saw the bank of fear.

She was going to have to do something about Samuel Black, but she would need to take a very delicate tact.

"I take it you had a nice nap," she said, forcing a smile into her words if only to push away the taut lines bracketing his mouth.

"I don't recall."

Her smile fled. "Well, I certainly did, and I was quite rested and alert when Mr. Portridge offered to show me how to repair a horse shoe."

"Is that so?" Samuel looked back the way they had come.

Penelope turned her head, her hair grinding into the gravel and dirt of the yard. Mr. Portridge stood under the sign of his shop, his hands still holding the tongs he had had earlier. Worry had burrowed into his brow, squashing his bushy eyebrows together like caterpillars over his eyes. She raised a hand.

"I'm quite all right, Mr. Portridge."

The caterpillars disappeared from his forehead, and she thought she could even make out his smile through the brush of his beard. The man raised the hand with the tongs and turned back into his shop.

"One of the horses threw a shoe. We stopped to have it repaired." When she returned her gaze to Samuel, she found him in much the same state, her words clearly doing nothing to reassure him.

"Where is the coachman?"

Penelope pointed in the opposite direction as the blacksmith's shop. "Getting a pint in the tavern, I believe."

If she had thought Samuel was upset previously, he plunged directly into being irate the moment the words left her lips. He straightened, and not bothering to walk around her, he simply stepped directly over her, his hands curling into fists as his booted stomps struck up the dirt of the inn yard.

"Samuel!"

She hadn't thought him capable of actual violence, but now, she quite doubted herself. She rolled and got to her hands and knees before her burned skirts caught around her legs, their new holes finding ways to catch her knees. She stumbled. Fell. Her knees hit the hard gravel, and the sting of cutting flesh tore through her. She shoved it away and stuck her toes into the gravel to gain purchase when the idea struck her.

She looked up. Samuel was nearly to the tavern door. Releasing her elbows, she collapsed, striking the ground as she rolled and pulled her knees as close to her chest as her petticoats would allow.

And then she whimpered.

Or simpered.

Or some other such silly nonsense.

Samuel froze, his head going back at the new sound.

"Samuel!" She added tears to her call.

He spun about, saw her. He was back at her side within a breath, crouched in the dirt beside her as he reached for her, drew her into his arms and cradled her.

"What's wrong? Where are you hurt? I'll find a doctor." The words all rushed together, and she took advantage of his momentary panic to grab the lapels of his coat and pull him against her.

"Get a hold of yourself, Samuel." The words were low and stern, so unlike her, he stopped in an instant. "I am fine." She released one hand and reached up, sliding her fingers along his jaw and that ticking muscle. Just as she had suspected, it calmed at her touch. "Everything is fine. It's not inevitable that something terrible will happen to me the moment I am out of your sight."

He held her cradled in his arm, his body bent over hers, shielding her from the late afternoon sun but also from the rest of the world. It was an unsettling feeling. Being cocooned like that. Like Samuel really could protect her from everything.

"You need to trust me."

The darkness in his eyes fled at her words, but in their place, came something else. Something she couldn't quite name, but something she didn't like either. It wasn't fear, but it wasn't understanding. It was almost as though he were wary. Wary of her? Wary of them? She had touched something with those words, but if he wouldn't talk to her, she'd never know what it was.

"You need a doctor." He moved bringing his other arm under her legs and made to lift her.

She grabbed at the lapels of his coat again. "Samuel Black, I have no need of a doctor. Put me down at once."

"I haven't picked you up yet."

"That's of little consequence. Release me."

"No."

She opened her mouth, ready to fire her next volley, when the words crashed in her throat, and she choked.

"What?" she finally managed.

"No, I will not release you. I'm taking you to a doctor."

He looked away, adjusted his arms, and just as she felt the pressure increase against her back as he made to lift her, she moved. She plunged both arms around his neck and pulled his head down, crushing his lips to hers. He froze, but she continued, slipping her tongue out to run it across the seam of his lips.

He made a sound, almost a growl, and his grip tightened on her but not to lift her. It was as if he gathered her against him, closer even than she had been. She forgot what she was doing when he did that. Forgot that she was trying to prevent him from lifting her. Taking control.

She wanted the control.

She gentled her grip on his neck and opened her hands to push her fingers into his hair. Her other hand dipped, outlining the contours of the muscles of his neck. Feeling each corded muscle as he leaned further into her, changed the angle, and deepened the kiss.

She growled now, the sound low and throaty, and completely unexpected.

She didn't know kissing could be like this. In all the times she had written it, she had only thought of the mechanics of it. The pieces of anatomy. Lips and teeth and tongue. Hands and bodies.

But never the feelings.

The feeling of forgetfulness as the world fell away and all that remained was the point where lips met lips. It was the space between that mattered, the space that was conquered when two bodies came together in such a powerful act. She hadn't known that. She hadn't known how important that was. How addicting it was.

To wrap herself around him. To pull his body to hers and obliterate the thing that kept them apart.

"Oh, it's young love!"

The shrill voice made her jump, severing the kiss and allowing the stern expression to slip back over Samuel's face. Penelope frowned and looked up to find the owner of the voice. Mr. Portridge stood over them and next to him a near replica but in skirts and without the beard.

"Ned said someone was hurt, but he didn't tell me it was a lady such as yourself." She made a beckoning motion with her hands. "Come, my dear, let's have a look at you." The woman let out a tinny shriek. "Oh, child, it's burned clear through to your petticoats."

Penelope glanced down at her skirts for the first time and saw the hole that had made her stumble earlier. The heated iron had, indeed, burned clear through to her petticoats.

"I'm afraid the dress is a loss, but I may be able to save the petticoats. I'm rather deft with the needle, dear. Oh, my!" She fluttered her hands in front of her face. "Here I am carrying on, and you're sitting on the ground. Up you go!"

Before Penelope could protest, the woman had hold of Penelope's arm and launched her from the ground in one swift motion. Her head swam to be suddenly standing, and Samuel grabbed her arm without a word. She leaned into him, grateful for the contact.

"I'm Sally, dear. Married to this old curmudgeon for nearly thirty years, I have." Here she elbowed Mr. Portridge. "I'll take you to our little home and get ye fixed up. It's just beyond the shop." She gathered her skirts and twisted to move away when she stopped, turned back. "Ned here says you're traveling north. It's so late in the day. You should just stay with Ned and me for the night while you rest."

"That won't be necessary."

Penelope glared at Samuel, hoping her scold translated. "That's very kind of you, Mrs. Portridge, but we must really be getting on. There's likely another hour or so of daylight, and we could make several miles in that time."

Mrs. Portridge's face fell. "Oh, you must call me Sally, dear. And really, it's no trouble. You should rest after what you've been through."

Penelope was beginning to get very tired of everyone thinking she was made of fluff. "That's really kind of you, Mrs. Portridge, but we really must—"

The door to the tavern flew open at that moment, dispelling their driver and tiger. This hired driver was a thin man, long and lean like a fence post. He walked bow-legged with his arms swinging wide at the sides. He made directly for Samuel, pulling something from his pocket that he stuck in Samuel's hand when he reached him. She saw the flash of coin just before the driver straightened himself up with a great sniff of his nose.

"The barman says a gentleman's been through," he said, sticking one thumb over his shoulder as if to indicate the tavern. "Says he's looking for a young couple headed north to Scotland." Another great sniff. "I don't want any trouble, so you just take your coin back and me and my man will be on our way. Don't have time for a couple of crazy young things going off and making the greatest mistake of their lives." He nodded at Penelope. "And you, especially. I don't need your da coming after me with a gun because I delivered you there. No, sir, I don't."

The driver ambled away, tugging on the arm of his tiger to move faster. When they reached the carriage, the driver elbowed the tiger again, and the tiger reached inside, pulled out their bags, and dropped them on the ground. Penelope slid her gaze to Samuel.

So their shadow had followed them this far. The possibility was so outrageous as to be astounding. They hadn't told anyone where they were going. They were following no obvious route. There was no predicting the damage the rain had caused.

The man was good, whoever he was.

"Oh," cooed Mrs. Portridge, and Penelope reluctantly moved her gaze back to the woman. "You're running away to Gretna Green, aren't ye?"

Penelope didn't need even a moment to think. She slipped her arm through Samuel's, tugging him to her side, and plastered a bright smile on her face.

"Yes, we are," she said.

"Well, then you must stay. There isn't another coach for hire in town, and the post coach won't be through until tomorrow. You'll just need to wait it out. Come let's get you cleaned up."

Penelope did look at Samuel then, and when there gazes locked, she knew exactly what he was thinking.

The post coach.

Perhaps their journey would be over as soon as the morrow. If only they could get through the night.

CHAPTER 14

here comes a point in every investigation when one must speak the truth.
From The Adventures of Miss Melanie Merkett, Private Inquisitor

THE PORTRIDGES LIVED in a small house behind the blacksmith's shop. There was a wooden overhang above the front door that sagged on one side but had been shored up by a twist of iron that looked as if it may have once held a wooden barrel. The main floor of the house consisted of the parlor and dining room, kitchen, and a large bedroom at the back. Two small areas in the loft served as additional bedrooms.

This is where Mrs. Portridge took Penelope to change. Samuel watched them climb the stairs and noticed Penelope ducked her head as they neared the top. She turned when she reached the last step, her neck bent awkwardly to fit the space. She screwed up one side of her mouth and rolled her eyes up. A smile came to his lips involuntarily. She smiled, the gesture soft, and standing at the top of the stairs, enveloped in warm, fading afternoon light from a window behind her, he forgot momentarily why it was he'd thrown her into a horse trough.

"Come dear, I have some of my Sissy's old things in here. Let's get you changed." Mrs. Portridge's hand appeared from the room on the left and snagged Penelope inside.

Samuel turned into the parlor. The room was inviting, cluttered here and there by porcelain and needlepoints. A tabby cat lay in front of a fire, its head nestled on a pillow. The words *The secret to life is to learn to make your own luck* was embroidered on it, just above a stitched horse shoe. Samuel frowned at the saying, not finding comfort in it at the moment.

A grunting noise had him turning away. Mr. Portridge stood at the other end of the room, a glass extended in his direction. Behind him sat a small table with a decanter and several glasses. Samuel accepted the one extended to him, watching as the light struck the amber liquid inside. He took a seat on the settee under the window, thinking it the best place to sit as the other furniture in the room included a matching set of worn chairs by the fire. That was obviously where Mr. and Mrs. Portridge took their evenings.

He studied the chairs and their suggestion of domesticity. For a moment, the yearning for such a quiet life surged in him, and he wondered if he and Penelope would ever see the day. Mr. Portridge made another grunting sound as he set about clinking glassware. Before Samuel took a sip, Mr. Portridge crossed the room and left through the front door.

Samuel paused with the glass at lips, his eyes fixed to the shut door. Footsteps on the stairs drew his eyes back to the entrance of the parlor. Mrs. Portridge stepped into view, peered around the corner, and frowned.

"He left, didn't he?"

Samuel set down his untouched glass. "He did."

The woman shook her head, her upper lip encasing her top teeth in a scowl. "He doesn't like people much. You must excuse him." She held up a finger. "I'll just be a moment. Please make yourself comfortable. The cat is very friendly, but I wouldn't pet him. He's had a mysterious smell as of late."

Samuel looked at the cat with his head on the horseshoe pillow. "I'll remember that."

Mrs. Portridge smiled. Her front teeth protruded from the bottoms enough to remind him of a rabbit. "Would you like to freshen up? I'm getting some water for the lady. I wouldn't mind bringing you a bowl as well."

Samuel smiled and politely shook his head. "I'm quite unscathed from our journey today."

With a flip of her hand, Mrs. Portridge sauntered off. He heard her rather than saw her climb the stairs once more, and footsteps played across the ceiling overhead. There was rustling and muttered voices, and then more footsteps. Mrs. Portridge's head appeared.

"The lady will be right down." She smiled her rabbit-toothed smile.

Samuel nodded that he'd heard her. His drink sat untouched on a table beside him as he worked his fingers back and forth against the palms of his hands. His mind turned the possibilities of their shadow over and over in his head.

Only Wickshire knew of their intentions. How could it be that someone had followed their trail so succinctly? He thought back to each step of their journey. Each hired coachman and tiger had thought them husband and wife traveling north to visit family in Scotland. The only other persons they'd met along the way were Mrs. Norton and Mrs. Herschel. He doubted either of them had let anything slip. And the shadow had been at Mrs. Norton's farm when they had been there, and she had indicated she had revealed nothing.

Had Penelope's missives to Wickshire been intercepted? But then they would not have only been intercepted but deciphered. Penelope had not, in fact, written in code, but she had not been obvious in her correspondence. The shadow would have had to have had a certain degree of knowledge as to their endeavor in order to read anything into them.

There were Samuel's own missives. Two of them. But, no. Again, he had not been blatant in his writings. The shadow would still need a certain amount of background information to ascertain their meaning.

So who was it? Who had followed them from London? For surely, the shadow would have started there. It was the only way he would have been able to follow the trail.

Footsteps at the door had him looking up. Penelope stood there, her face freshly scrubbed and her hair neatly coiled at the nape of her neck. She wore a dress that was much too small for her frame. The cuffs of the sleeves ended in the middle of her forearms, and the tops of her boots showed from beneath the too-short hem. The dress was a faded blue with small flowers along the bodice.

"At least this one hasn't been set on fire," she said, as if interpreting his perusal of her.

"Not yet," he said and was rewarded with a smile.

She entered the parlor and took a seat next to him on the settee, glancing about them.

"Mr. Portridge apparently doesn't care for people," Samuel said at her gesture.

She looked at him. "He seemed to like me just fine. Until you arrived that is."

Her gaze penetrated him, and for a moment, he thought

she blamed him. But then he saw the corner of her mouth kick up in a smirk, and he knew she teased.

A clattering drew their attention to the door, and Mrs. Portridge bustled in, a tray clutched in her arms. Samuel stood and took the tray from her, setting it on the low table in front of the settee.

"I wasn't expecting guests, or I would have made a proper supper. With just Mr. Portridge and myself now, we don't take much for our evening meal. We usually share a plate by the fire in the evenings. I hope this will do."

The tray contained platters of cold ham, cheese, and loaves of dark, crusty bread next to a tea pot and two cups. The tea pot had once been adorned with little, yellow daffodils that had now faded along the sides.

"You have children then?" Penelope asked, reaching for the tea pot.

Mrs. Portridge pulled over one of the chairs from the fireplace and squeezed her large bottom into it. "Oh, yes, we do. All grown and gone now," she said with a little flight of her hands as if indicating the departure of her children.

"How many?" Samuel put ham and cheese on a plate for Penelope before tearing off a piece of bread for her.

"Six."

His hands stilled on the bread, and Penelope stopped pouring the tea.

"Six?" Penelope repeated.

Mrs. Portridge nodded. "Oh yes, four boys and two girls. Would have liked more girls, but it seems I was meant to make strapping boys." She shook a fisted hand in the air as if lamenting her fate, but a smile revealed her rabbit teeth. "But I already know all about me. I want to hear about you two."

Samuel handed Penelope the plate as she handed him the saucer and cup. Their eyes met briefly, and an unspoken message passed between them.

"We're eloping," she said, her voice bright and firm.

Samuel's gut tightened, and he stopped filling a plate for himself, leaving a solitary piece of ham on the china.

"Oh, how splendid," Mrs. Portridge cooed. "Do tell me. What is your love story?"

Samuel looked from Mrs. Portridge to Penelope, his eyes lingering on her. This woman who was pretending to be his intended. She was his intended, or at least, she would be once they returned to London. He planned to court her properly, as a real gentleman would. He only needed to get her back there without her reputation falling to tatters.

Tomorrow. Tomorrow with the appearance of the mail coach this could all be over. The thought sent an odd twinge of regret through him.

Penelope set down her plate and leaned forward, drawing as close to Mrs. Portridge as their positions would allow. She smiled, the kind that set her eyes alight as if she were passing on the world's most dangerous secret.

She whispered, "He took me to a coffee house in London." A pause. "Unchaperoned."

Mrs. Portridge pressed a hand to her open mouth. Her eyes darted back and forth between them. "He didn't?" she hissed when she removed her hand.

Penelope laughed, the sound light and fluttery. "He did, Mrs. Portridge. I had never experienced such a thing before." She turned, cast the warm gaze on him, and his chest tightened. "It was the most magical moment of my life."

"Oh, you precious thing," Mrs. Portridge whispered now. "How did he propose?" she asked on the next breath.

Penelope looked at the woman, her mouth slightly open. "It was a midnight rendezvous."

The color drained from Mrs. Portridge's face as her eyes grew as large as the saucers under their tea cups. "No!"

"Yes," Penelope said, her hands going to her knees. "Picture it, Mrs. Portridge. An inky black sky filled with pockets of twinkling light. A warm breeze filtering through the trees. And Samuel." She turned to him, one side of her mouth lifted in a coaxing smile as if she were drawing him into the story as well. "He got down on one knee."

"No!" Another exclamation from Mrs. Portridge.

"And he told me he wanted to be the witness to the rest of my life."

Mrs. Portridge made no sound then as Penelope watched him, her eyes wide, her lips relaxed. She appeared as though she meant it. As though it had really happened.

He thought about all he had put through already. The damage already done to her reputation. The things he hadn't been able to stop or prevent. Like the bawdy singing in the tavern. The debacle of that very afternoon. How many people in this hamlet had seen Penelope Paiget's petticoats? That had been his fault. His. And he was supposed to protect her.

His stomach churned.

But then Penelope smiled and reached for his hand. She turned to Mrs. Portridge. "What greater thing is there in this life than to have someone watch over you?"

Mrs. Portridge's eyes had filled with unshed tears. Samuel set aside his plate, his food untouched.

IT WAS SOMETIME LATER that they finally ascended to the rooms above. Samuel felt the weight of the past four days hang on him like manacles. He pulled himself up the stairs one step at a time, cognizant of Penelope's backside nearly at eye level.

The upper floor was even more cramped for him, and he crouched as he made the upper landing, bending almost to put his hands on his knees. Mrs. Portridge had made up only the one room, giving them a wink and a smile as she'd conveyed this information after their dinner of cheese, ham, and bread. Samuel wondered what illusions of romance Mrs. Portridge harbored to aide in such blatant impropriety. He was obviously ruining Penelope's reputation, and Mrs. Portridge was only too happy to help him along.

He made his way to a chair under the window at the back of the room, collapsing in it as Penelope made her way to the bed. She sat, her hands on her knees, and regarded him.

"Do you think he'll be on the post coach tomorrow?"

The question had plagued him all evening, and he knew as soon as they were alone Penelope would give voice to his torment.

"It would certainly be advantageous if he were."

A line appeared between her brows. "But you don't think he will be?"

Samuel shook his head. "I don't want to give the possibility hope. Nothing about this journey has gone according to plan."

She nodded, accepting his perspective. "Poor Bobby Egemont," she whispered.

Yes, poor Bobby Egemont, indeed. The man had died in the service of a friend. A mentor. And they were no closer to finding the murderer. If only the professor were on the coach tomorrow.

His eyes had drifted as he thought about Bobby Egemont, and it was several moments before he realized Penelope was undressing. He stood, immediately, ramming his head into the ceiling of the room. He shrank back, putting a hand to his throbbing head.

"I should give you privacy." He slouched toward the door.

"Samuel."

He stopped. The only other person to ever use such a

stern tone with him had been his mother, but he didn't turn around.

"Samuel, you must stop acting as though I will break at the slightest prick to my reputation."

He did turn now. "Your reputation—"

"Is my concern. Not yours. And I think it's precisely how I wish it to be." She slipped the bodice from her shoulders, tugging at the tight sleeves until her arms pulled free. She stood, and the gown fell to the floor. She stood in her stockings, chemise, and boots. It was a ridiculous picture, but one that sent a heat firing in his belly.

And then she stretched, lifting her pale arms as high as the slanted ceiling would allow. Her throat emitted a mewling sound that stoked the fire inside him, and her eyes closed at the ecstasy of a good stretch.

"I will be most elated when this journey is over." She brought her arms back down and opened her eyes. "Carriages can be so very cramping."

She stepped out of the pool of the gown at her feet and picked it up to set it across the chair he just occupied. He didn't move through all of this, and so when she turned, she nearly collided with him. She cast him a small smile, her eyes going up to his in the awkward space as she slide around him, her hands going to his chest as she did so.

"Excuse me," she said, a smirk at the corners of her lips.

He stopped her, his hands going to her bared arms. The moment he touched her, felt her bared skin beneath his fingertips, his mind went blank. He forgot he was supposed to protect her. He forgot he was supposed to keep her reputation safe. He forgot anything.

He cupped both of her upper arms in his hands, and he skimmed his palms up and down, her silky skin passing through them like a whisper. She was so soft, so smooth...so delicate. The way his head bent against the slanted ceiling

181

brought his lips almost to angle of her neck, and he could smell her. Lavender and sage. He could just dip his head a little. Taste her.

He should let her go. He should give her the privacy he thought she deserved. But he couldn't stop touching her. Just his hands at her arms, sliding up and down.

"Samuel." Her voice had gone quiet, but in her tone, he could hear the smallest suggestion of pleading. Desire. Want.

He dipped his head, and his lips brushed the line of her neck as it met her shoulder. The mewling sound came from her throat again, but this time it held an edge. An edge of pure lust. It spiked through him, cutting him where the fire burned in his stomach, and he parted his lips, allowing his tongue to stroke a line across her skin. Her fingers tightened against his chest, digging into him with a surge of instinct.

He let go of her arms to pick her up, propel her backwards until they fell across the bed. Her arms were around him, pulling him against her as his lips found hers. Drank. Nibbled. Cherished.

"Penelope." He didn't know why he said her name, but in it, he poured all of the doubt that warred with the heat raging inside him.

"Samuel." She answered his doubt with her own assurance. Her tone sure but more, wanting. Urging.

Her fingers were at his waistcoat. Buttons slipped free. His collar loosened, and his cravat fell away. His hands were under her chemise, riding up the smooth curves of hip and stomach. Finally, they touched breast. The delicate underside. He skimmed his hands just out of reach of them, and she arched, bucking into his hand.

"Samuel." Her tone was no longer sure and steady. It throbbed with desire, pleading him to touch her without saying the words.

He wrenched his hand free and sat up, pushing himself

away until he came up against the headboard, as far as he could get away from her in the cramped room. She lay sprawled across the bed, her chemise twisted at her waist, her chest heaving for air. Her hair had come undone and splayed across the bed in a riotous tangle of red. She still had her boots on.

Her eyes had opened as he'd retreated, but now they slid shut, her face falling into resignation.

"Samuel." Her stern tone had returned.

"Penelope, I cannot do this to you. I can't let myself be like —" He stopped. Unable to utter the words.

She rolled, coming up on her knees, and crawled across the bed to him. She pulled apart his knees to settle between his legs, pressing her small hands to his chest. Her hair fell in curtains around her face, and her eyes were wide and coaxing.

"Samuel, you're not like him. This—" She gestured behind her at the bed. "This is not like what happened to your mother. This...this is— " She seemed to struggle for the word, and then finally— "Love."

He got caught between her words, and the look of uncertainty on her face. He chose the words first.

He snatched up her hands, pressed them between his. "You don't know that. You don't know—"

"You're right. I don't. Because you won't tell me."

Silence.

She knelt between his knees, their hands tangled together as if caught in some strange prayer, and the beast inside of him was rendered captive.

Until he spoke. "I'm afraid I'm just like him."

He had never spoken the words aloud before. Had never told anyone of the thing that had wrestled inside of him for so long. The thing he was afraid to release because of what it might become. Perhaps what it already was.

"Tell me why you think that."

His mind cast backward, almost inexorably pulled to that night. When he had first taken up a watch with the Metropolitan Police. Felt the anger course through him at the sight of a prostitute being beaten by her john. The anger had been so real, so intense. Uncontrollable. It was this that had scared him the most. It took all he had to reign it in. But it had only gotten worse from there. At the next confrontation and the next.

But so afraid of the thing lurking inside him, he'd squelched it at that, holding a picture of Penelope in his mind. Centering himself on it until the pulsing subsided. He'd held onto that for ten years. The idea of marrying Penelope. Of making it right. Of making it proper and good.

He hadn't thought about this part. The part where he would need to let go of the thing inside of him. But just enough. Not too much. Now he worried he couldn't control it.

Penelope's eyes dimmed, and her hands slipped from his. He realized he had taken too long. She thought he wouldn't answer. He tugged her back, sitting up to grab at her shoulders and hold her in place before him.

"I get angry," he said, and the words rang with inadequacy. He tried again. "It's not like getting angry because someone is bothering you or has done something to displease you. It's a vile thing, this anger that I feel. It's strong, and it wraps itself around my mind, and I forget what I'm doing." He searched her eyes for understanding. She remained still but showed no sign of her reaction. "I'm afraid that if I let go it will take over, and I won't be able to control what happens."

Penelope regarded him with her wide eyes. "You think your natural father's anger lives inside of you."

"Yes." A single word had never been so painful for him to utter.

"You think the power of the environment in which you were raised was not enough to overcome that anger?"

He thought back to that first watch. "I beat a man," he said. "My first night on watch with the force. He was a john. He was beating one of his streetwalkers. I stopped him. Only…"

"You went too far." Her voice held no recrimination. No judgement.

"Yes."

"How old were you?"

"Seven and twenty."

Her face softened, her lips tipping into a sympathetic grin. "Oh, Samuel. You were so young. So inexperienced. How could you let something in a tender part of your life affect the rest of it?"

He shook his head. "I can't let it get out of control. I can't—"

She grabbed him now, tugging at the loosened front of his waistcoat. "Samuel. You are in control. I have never seen a person so in control. It's suffocating." She said this last word with a laugh and a smile that had his grip on her shoulders relaxing. "You've had all these years to change. To grow. To gain wisdom. What if you tried again? What if you found out you are better than you think you are?"

He had started to shake his head and stopped. He planned to marry this woman. He planned to spend the rest of his life with her. What would that life be like if she were right? What if she were wrong?

"Penelope," he said, allowing his head to shake now. "When we're married, things will be different. Things—" He halted, and the words he had been about to say collided in this throat. He choked on them.

Her face had changed. Slipped into something murky and

185

dark. Something like hesitancy. Something like fear. His gut twisted.

"You want to marry me, don't you?"

She didn't answer, but her shoulders slipped out of his grasp. Slowly. Imperceptibly. But he felt it. The loss of her heat. The loss of smoothness of skin. He scrambled, his hands finding her, pulling her back.

"You do want to marry me, don't you, Penelope?"

CHAPTER 15

he most dangerous thing a lady can possess is a profession.

From The Adventures of Miss Melanie Merkett, Private Inquisitor

YES.

That was her first response. Then. Now. Always. Yes. Yes, she wanted to marry Samuel Black.

Only...

She sat back, her shoulders tugging against his hands, and realized she still had her boots on. She opened her mouth, ready to tell him everything. To tell him that she was Melanie Merkett. That she was a...novelist. The worst crime in a potential wife that didn't involve promiscuity but it may as well have.

For one heartbreaking moment, she believed she could tell him. That it wouldn't be so bad. But staring at him then, as she sat between his legs, having only moments before tasted his kiss, felt the planes of his body under her palms, she couldn't do it. A detective inspector for the Metropolitan Police could not take a novelist for a wife. It would be socially unseemly and professionally fatal.

And yet...

She couldn't give up her writing any more than she could give up Samuel.

"I do want to marry you," she whispered, but she knew he didn't believe her.

His eyes slid away from hers before she finished speaking, and suddenly it was too late. In that precious second, she'd lost him. She felt it like a physical loss. As if something were wrenched from her. She gasped silently, sucking at air that wouldn't come in, and she pressed a hand to her chest.

Samuel stood, and the bed bounced with the absence of his weight. He went to the only window in the room and put one hand against the slanted ceiling to bend and look through it. Night had fallen, and the yard below had taken on a silvery glow. But she didn't care about that.

She watched him breathe. Watched the pull of his coat against his back. Her fingers wanted to touch him, and she even raised a hand to do just that. But then he spoke.

"You say it doesn't matter. It doesn't matter who my real father is, and yet—" She could hear his swallow in the following silence, but in its place, she heard what he didn't say.

She stood and went to him. She placed both hands on the muscles of his back as she wanted to do, absorbing their pull as he straightened away from her, recoiling from her touch. She snatched her hands against her chest as if she'd been burned.

"It doesn't matter," she said. "It matters no more than that I have my mother's red hair. It's only a matter of nature. This —" She stepped forward, ignoring his attempts at retreat and pressed her hands to his chest. His heart thundered against her hand. "This isn't dictated by nature. This comes from those who have loved you in this life."

She stared up at him, bent as he was against the low ceiling, his face came close to hers. She wanted to kiss him again. Forget they ever started this conversation. For just a moment, she wanted nothing more than to be two bodies in a close space. Two bodies that yearned for one another. Cherished one another. Desired one another.

But there was no desire in his eyes. Only questions. And doubt.

The hand against his chest curled, pulling the fabric of his waistcoat into her grip once more.

"Samuel, there's something about me that you don't know." The words were out before she could stop them. She had to clear his gaze of the hurt that haunted it, and the only way she could do that was to make him understand. To give a part of herself that would condemn her forever. "There's something that I've done, something that I am that makes it so I don't deserve you for a husband."

The doubt vanished. She sucked in a breath, not believing her luck, not believing that so little held so much power. But her relief was fleeting as wariness replaced the doubt. Wariness and the unmistakable glint of a male determined to fix whatever it was that had gone wrong.

He seized her, his hands going to her shoulders once more, but his touch no longer held the heat it had only moments before. Now it held resolve.

"What are you talking about, Penelope?" She usually loved the way he said her name, pronouncing each syllable as if it deserved special attention. But not now. Now he said it in a rush as if to get it out of the way and to the heart of the thing that needed fixing.

Because that was the horrible truth of it.

She needed fixing.

Penelope.

Puh-nel-uh-pee.

The thing she had dreaded for so long suddenly became real. Absolute.

Bad.

She had always known what she did, what she was, was not acceptable. Was frowned upon. That was the polite phrase used by society matrons. But it had never become real until that moment. That moment when she saw the look on his face.

It was then that she realized a part of her, a very small part, had believed he would accept her as she was. That he would be all right with a novelist wife. That he would keep her secret and if the day should come that it would be revealed, he would support her. She hadn't known she had been harboring such hope until right that very moment when it was stripped from her before she could enjoy it.

She stepped back and shook her head.

"It doesn't matter, Samuel." She said his name with each syllable carefully enunciated. "It can't be changed. Not by you. Not by anyone."

He followed her even as she retreated. "Anything can be fixed." A self-deprecating smile came to his lips. "My own family is evidence of that. The bastard son of a duke marries a former housekeeper? And now they're received in drawing rooms of society's most prestigious peers."

She wanted to believe him. She wanted to soak in his smile and his story. But this was different. She was different. No one ever approved of a woman taking pen to paper.

She stepped back until the backs of her legs hit the bed. She sat.

"I think it would be best if we discussed this tomorrow," she said, forcing a smile to her lips. "We'll need our strength if the professor really does appear on the mail coach."

He hesitated. His hands still reached for her even though he hadn't moved. But she had known exactly what to say, what point would divert him from this dangerous course.

The mission.

He dropped his hands only to pick one back up and scrub at his face as was his habit. "You're right. It's been a long day, and tomorrow may be even longer." His eyes found hers again, and she knew they had not settled this thing between them. She had merely diverted it.

She shed her boots and slid back in bed, taking up the far side to leave room for Samuel. She closed her eyes, not wanting to see him strip off his coat and waistcoat. Not wanting to see the way his linen shirt outlined the muscles of his chest. Muscles she had only begun to explore.

The bed dipped, and she let her eyes open, expecting to see Samuel's feet by her head as he had slept that first night at the inn outside of London. She flinched when she found his eyes on hers, his mouth inches from her own.

He smiled and tucked an arm underneath his head. The angle let the moonlight through the window strike him full in the face, and she could only stare at this beautiful man who shared her bed. Who wanted to marry her. Who wanted to fix her.

She closed her eyes against the sight of him, but sleep did not come.

* * *

"ARE YOU WITH CHILD?"

The question was whispered to her by none other than Sally Portridge herself the next morning as she raised a forkful of eggs to her lips. She slid her gaze sideways at the woman as she hovered by her elbow, teapot in her hands as she pretended to pour Penelope another cup.

They were alone in the Portridges' dining room. Penelope had heard Mr. Portridge leave the house as dawn lightened the window in their cramped room. His footsteps were heavy, plodding, and he made blustery noises through his beard that had traveled up the stairs as he'd let himself out. Penelope had feigned sleep until Samuel had risen and left and had only ventured downstairs when she knew him to have gone out.

She set her fork down. "I am not with child."

Mrs. Portridge frowned and finished filling Penelope's cup that did not need filling. "Oh, bother," she muttered. "I had only wished. Well, seeing as how you look this morning."

"How do I look this morning?"

She stopped in her bustle around the table. "Well, it's only that I meant—" She stopped. Shook her head. "It's only that you look a little careworn this morning, darling."

Careworn.

What a harmless word to describe the horrible way she felt.

She had not slept, but more, she had spent the night attempting at all costs to avoid touching Samuel. Which had not worked. In fact, it had failed spectacularly when somewhere in the middle of the night he had rolled over, slinging an arm and then a leg over her, pulling her tightly to his chest.

Samuel was strong. Very strong even in sleep, and she had spent the better part of an hour by the estimate in her head cataloging all of the words she would use to describe how she felt in that situation if only to accurately describe such a scenario should it ever occur in the adventures of Miss Melanie Merkett.

The word *loved* came up at an alarming rate.

"I'm just weary from all the travel." She picked up her fork again.

Mrs. Portridge took a seat opposite even though she had no plate. The older woman leaned an elbow on the table and rested her head against her fist as if settling in for a conspiratorial chat.

"I can wager how you'd be feeling. I was afeared you were carrying a child, and that would only make the matter worse, wouldn't it, darling?" She sat back and patted her rounded stomach. "I know a thing or two about such things myself, you understand."

Penelope smiled around a bite of toast.

"Ah, well," Mrs. Portridge muttered and stood, pushing heavily against the table to gain her feet. "I'll leave you to your breakfast. You'll want to be well nourished for the journey today. But you'll be resting for a day or two once it's done, won't you? That will be a nice spell, I suppose."

"I beg your pardon?" She set down her toast.

Mrs. Portridge turned back. "You'll take a day or two to rest before beginning the journey back, won't you? There won't be the urgency, you know, once you're good and married. Why, it should be all over by tomorrow. Even tonight if you can rouse a blacksmith to do the job."

"Tonight?"

Mrs. Portridge's brow folded in concern. "Why yes, child. We're not far from Gretna Green. I'm supposing that's where you're headed to have the deed done."

She picked up her tea cup and took a satisfying gulp before replying. "Yes, of course."

In the chaos of their journey over the past several days, she hadn't understood how much distance they'd traveled. If Gretna Green was only a day's journey away, how far was Edinburgh? If the professor was not on the mail coach, how much longer did they have to travel? Perhaps she wouldn't be pressed into company with Samuel Black for much longer.

The thought drove a spike through her, and she set aside

her napkin and rose from the table. She smiled carefully at Mrs. Portridge, hoping to hide her inner tumult.

"Thank you for your kindness, Mrs. Portridge," she said. "My—" Her throat closed on the word *husband*. She swallowed. Tried again. "My husband and I can never thank you enough."

Mrs. Portridge waved at hand at her. "Nonsense, child," she said. "I'm only too happy to hear a good love story."

Penelope fled the room before Mrs. Portridge could see the tears in her eyes.

CHAPTER 16

he most obvious clues are often the most difficult to find.
From The Adventures of Miss Melanie Merkett, Private Inquisitor

PENELOPE EMERGED FROM THE PORTRIDGES' home about the same time he'd lost feeling in his legs from where he'd perched against the blacksmith's shop, watching the road from the south in anticipation of the mail coach.

At the sight of her, their conversation from the previous night came rushing back to him. The thing that he had kept so tightly wound inside of him for so long was not there this morning. He didn't think it was gone. It was just...hibernating. For the first time, he truly considered the impact of those who had raised him. First his mother. Instilling in him the ethics of hard work. Then Nathan. Teaching him what it meant to be a gentleman. His uncle Alec teaching him the value of a good wardrobe. His grandfather.

A pain sliced through him at the thought of Richard

Black. The grandfather he had had for too short a time. The man who had left them so recently.

But even as the pain ebbed, a smile came to his lips. Surely a man as revered as Richard Black, the previous Duke of Lofton, would not have taken in a child who possessed a tainted potential. Richard Black must have seen something in young Samuel. Something Penelope saw.

She shielded her eyes from the early morning sun as she crossed the yard towards him. She wore a gown that fit her properly, and he thought Mrs. Portridge must have repaired her petticoats.

"Good morning," she said as she stopped beside him.

There were dark circles under her eyes, and her hair was not as tightly wound into a chignon as it normally was. He straightened from his perch on the pretense of stretching his legs.

"Did you sleep well?" he asked.

She didn't look at him as she answered. "Splendidly."

He followed her gaze to the road, and he knew she looked for the mail coach just as he did.

"Mr. Portridge says it usually arrives before nine in the morning. It's half eight," he added when she looked at him.

There were definitely dark circles under her eyes. Had he kept her awake? Had he done something in his sleep that he'd been unaware of? He had felt emboldened by her confession of something in her past preventing her from marrying him. For one terrible moment, he felt like a chivalrous knight from the stories Lady Jane used to tell them as children. He thought he could protect her. He thought marriage to him might save her from whatever it was that plagued her.

So consumed by his own demons, he had never considered that she may have demons of her own, and now perhaps, he could vanquish them.

She didn't say anything more, and he touched her elbow. She jumped although she tried to hide it.

"Are you certain you slept well?" he asked.

She peered up at him, her smile broader and obviously more forced. "Of course."

He didn't believe her but just then the sound of a coach drew his attention back to the road.

The mail coach was a haphazard thing with bags strapped to the top and trunks belted to the back. A solitary driver slouched on the seat and called out the name of the hamlet as he stopped. People tumbled out, rumpled and weary, stretching arms and legs as they plodded away from the coach. It had likely left the place where it had stayed the night at the first light of dawn, which would mean it was traveling for a good three hours or more by the time it arrived in Oxenholme. The travelers had been packed in, one after the other like the pages of a book.

He moved his gaze to Penelope and found her fingers tapping against her leg. He peered at her, his mind working the problem of her devastating secret over in his mind. He realized then he didn't know much about Penelope Paiget. He knew where she had come from. That she was employed. That she was well respected by both her peers and her employer. She was quick with a smile and had a way of putting people at ease.

But if he didn't know better, he would have said she would make an excellent spy. For in her, he saw a variation of every female member of his family. And as he thought it, he realized he had no reason to believe she wasn't a spy.

His chest tightened, and he crossed his arms over it to ease the pain.

Could Penelope be a spy? Could she be the one after the professor and his technology? Ready to intercept it and pass it off to the highest bidder?

It sounded ridiculous but the inspector in him paused, mulling over the possibilities. She had opportunity. As Wickshire's secretary, she would have been privileged to his diary, known his schedule in advance. She would have seen he was attending the lecture of the astronomical society. Might have even found a way to attend herself.

She had motive. She was the secretary of an earl. The daughter of a respectable member of the gentry. But that didn't amount to much in a society where titles carried more weight than deserved. A king's fortune would go a long way to alleviate that.

He stared at her as she watched the travelers meandering about the yard. She appeared utterly relaxed and yet...

The dark circles under her eyes.

Her tendency to wander away from him.

Her mad scribbling of notes purportedly to send back to Wickshire.

The nervous habit of her fingers. Twitch, twitch, twitching.

Passengers began to re-board the coach as the driver called out their next destination. A few remained, however, picking up their bags from where the driver had tossed them into the yard.

Penelope turned to him. "Do you suppose one of them is the professor?"

She didn't ask the question with any discernible interest above what would be expected in her capacity on this endeavor. But he had never analyzed her speech, her movements as the guise of a spy before.

He observed the remaining passengers. There were five of them in total. Three lone gentlemen and a couple. The professor could have been any one of those men, even the man traveling with the female companion. As evidenced by his own situation, appearances could be used to mislead those who were watching.

"Possibly," he said, taking her elbow to follow the newcomers into the tavern of the inn. "There's only one way to find out."

* * *

THE FLOOR of the tavern was sticky under her feet, and she pulled at each foot as if the next step was sure to find her boot permanently affixed to the floor. She was quickly becoming acquainted with the accommodations of inn taverns, and her eyes swept the room, completing an inventory of sorts.

This tavern had round tables. It was becoming clear that round tables offered more room for patrons, and thus increased the likelihood of gatherings, which turned into profits for the tavern owners. There were three bar maids in the requisite uniform of smudged skirts and artfully draped, billowing bodices. The women were all overly thin, which accentuated their extraordinary bosoms. The bar ran along the back of this tavern, which remained relatively quiet at this early hour.

The passengers from the mail coach had taken spots at the tables, and the three bar maids scurried about to fill orders. Pots of tea were gathered as well as trays of food, eggs and sausages and kidneys. Samuel slipped into a table and pulled her down next to him.

He hadn't shaved that morning. When she'd risen, she'd found Mrs. Portridge had left water for her morning toilette, but perhaps Samuel had risen too early, eager to get out to the courtyard to wait for the mail coach. The fine dark hairs covered his cheeks and jaw, and she wanted to reach up, feel how it scraped the soft skin of her hands.

"Do you know what this professor may look like?"

Penelope's gaze drifted away from his beard to find his steady gaze on her. She shook her head. "Of course not. Why would I know what he looked like?" She shifted so she could more easily take in the room without appearing to twist her head around backward. "I wasn't at that meeting of the astronomical society."

"But you've been to previous meetings?"

Samuel's tone had taken on a curious edge, and she turned back to him, regarding his expression instead of allowing his dark good looks to distract her. Something was different about him this morning. She shouldn't have been surprised as their conversation the previous night had not gone according to anyone's plan, she was certain.

But he seemed to study her with greater care now. With more nuance and less acceptance. Of course, he did. She had told him she had a secret. A secret he couldn't fix. If there was ever a way to attract a man's attention it was to present him with a dilemma that could not be solved.

"Yes," she said but faltered on the next word when she realized she was picking her words carefully. Something she had never done around Samuel. She should never have even hinted that anything were wrong. Let alone that she held a secret that would prevent her from marrying him. It was so much easier handling people who only existed in one's imagination. "Sometimes Wickshire asks me to accompany him to take notes. Usually when it's a lecture of particular interest to him. He finds he often gets carried away with the speaker and fails to ascertain all aspects of the lecture. He relies on me and my thorough notes to put the entire picture together for him after the talk."

"So you've learned a great deal about astronomy then?"

The fold along his brow suggested this was more than a casual curiosity.

"I've learned a great deal about many subjects through the course of my work." Samuel's expression did not clear. "Is there something you're not asking me, Mr. Black?"

He straightened, his brow unfurling faster than Wickshire shed his clothes in a state of mental rapture.

"No, not at all." He scanned the room only to peek sidelong glances at her. "It's only you're a rather unconventional sort of woman, Miss Paiget."

"Unconventional?" Her hands twisted into her skirts, smashing the petticoats Mrs. Portridge had just mended.

"Do you have many friends, Penelope?" The fold appeared along his brow once more.

"That's a rather odd question."

He shook his head. "It's only I can imagine a woman of your intelligence would find it difficult to make acquittances of any worth."

"I beg your pardon." Her hands went flat in her lap only to allow her fingers to twitch wildly.

"With so unusual an intelligence as yours, I can only presume people would constantly barrage you with their ideas of what you should do with it."

Her fingers froze.

He shrugged. "I would find it tiresome if people deigned it acceptable to tell me what to do with my life at every turn." He gestured toward her. "You're quite accomplished in my eyes. I don't see that there's any room for improvement." He said this last bit with a beguiling twitch to his lips, and something in her chest softened.

"There is a strong desire for people to tell me what I should do," she said. "I've grown rather used to it, I'm afraid."

He didn't say anything more. Simply nodded and turned his gaze back to the room. "So if we don't know what this man looks like, we'll have to go on speech."

"Speech?"

He grinned, and for a moment, he looked not unlike a hound at the ready, listening for his master to give the tally ho.

"We're looking for an American, aren't we?"

She twisted around, her eyes traveling the length of the tavern room and back. "I suppose we are." What fun. She hadn't considered this aspect of their mission as fully as she ought. She'd never encountered an American with such potential for intimate exchange. There had been the many colleagues of Wickshire's she'd been introduced to at various meetings or other but never had she the chance to study an American. Listen to his patterns of speech. Study his mannerisms. Her fingers twitched madly, and she reached up, signaling one of the barmaids to occupy her wayward hands.

"Tea, please," she said to the young woman. "Have you eaten?" This was directed at Samuel.

As he was studying the patrons around him, it took him a moment to realize she spoke to him. He gave her a confused shake of his head before saying, "No, I haven't."

She smiled at the barmaid. "And breakfast."

The barmaid grinned and leaned precariously over the table toward Samuel. The position tipped her ample bosom into his line of sight, and nearly immediately, his attention was arrested back to the table. Penelope frowned.

"You like kidneys, sir?" She was missing a tooth, and her tongue poked through the gap as she spoke. "We's got some lovely…kidneys 'ere."

Did the woman shift her bosom or had Penelope only imagined it?

Penelope regarded her own bosom. Gave her shoulders an experimental twitch, but nothing happened. She looked up to find the barmaid gone, and Samuel staring at her.

"What is it?" Color was noticeably absent from his face,

and if his jaw became any tighter, he was going to break a tooth.

"What are you doing?"

She nodded in the direction of the barmaids. "Did she just do something with her bosom?" She couldn't find the barmaid in question, so she returned her gaze to Samuel to find his jaw was no longer in danger of murdering his teeth. His mouth had fallen open instead. "Oh surely you saw what I did. Do all barmaids do that?"

Samuel swallowed and licked his lips a time or two before saying, "I think it is safe to assume that young woman augments her earnings here at the tavern with some salacious work after hours."

She leaned in and lowered her voice so the other patrons wouldn't hear. "You believe she's a streetwalker."

Samuel regarded her with a narrowed expression. "I would think it's safe to assume that." His eyes narrowed even further. "Have you reason to be acquainted with street-walkers?"

She shook her head and straightened as the barmaid returned with a tea tray and breakfast. She placed them on the table with a little wave of her fingers at Samuel. Although Penelope knew the woman only did it in the hopes of some coin, it still proved to have the oddest effect on Penelope. And not a desirous effect at that.

"Have you?" Penelope asked the question just as Samuel took a bite of toast, and the poor man choked so hard, a spray of crumbs cascaded over the table. "I suppose not then," she said and brushed the crumbs from her bodice.

Samuel eyed her, his toast forgotten. It was most definitely time to return to the case at hand. She smiled, hoping to coax him from his dark mood, and turned her eyes to the patrons.

Two of the gentlemen had taken a table together while a

third gentleman sat alone. The couple sat nearest the door, both of them turning their heads periodically towards the windows as if waiting for someone.

"Do you think it's the lone gent?" she whispered and reached for the teapot.

Samuel shook his head. "I wouldn't want to make such a presumption."

She studied the other two men then, but they were deep in conversation, and there wasn't much to discover. They looked like working men judging by their soiled boots and trousers. They carried sacks with them that had been repaired several times over with different patterns of cloth. The third gentleman carried no such luggage.

She elbowed Samuel. "Are you sure it's not the lone man? He doesn't have a bag with him."

He swallowed his eggs and leaned closer to her. "You're assuming the professor didn't have time to pack one."

She scowled at him. "Well, of course not. Isn't he running for his life?"

He raised an eyebrow. "That's rather dramatic. I don't think whoever killed Bobby Egemont would kill the professor immediately. They would need to get his technology from him first."

She hadn't considered that. It was just at that moment that one of the barmaids placed a tea tray on the table of the lone gentleman. The man looked up and gave a polite smile before reaching into his coat pocket. She expected him to withdraw a coin to pay for his food, but instead he slipped a book from his pocket. It was rather worn. The cover showed the signs of having lived in his pocket for quite some time. But the gold letters along the cover were unmistakable to her.

Uncovering the Cabot Caper
From the Adventures of Miss Melanie Merkett

She must have made a noise because Samuel touched her elbow.

"What is it?"

She shook her head, her mind already moving her body before she'd realized what she was going to do. Samuel tried to reach for her, take her arm in his grip, but she slipped free, stood, walked over to the lone gentleman.

"That's one of my favorites," she said, leaning against one of the empty chairs at the table as she beamed at the lone gentleman.

The man looked up, and she caught his look of surprise before it slipped into something resembling pleasure. Nothing untoward. More of a weary traveler finding a kindred spirit on a long journey. Perhaps the man *had* been on a long journey.

Or being chased by scoundrels who wanted his creation.

"Ah, that Miss Merkett. What a wee cheeky lass, eh?"

It took all of her power to keep her smile in place at the man's Scottish accent.

"She certainly is." She tacked on a laugh when her words came out overly bright. She pointed at the book in his hand as if it needed to be indicated. "It looks like you've had that one for a while. Been carrying it in your pocket long?"

The man smiled, and she realized he was quite younger than she had originally thought. Not much older than she and Samuel really. Startling blue eyes rimmed by thick lashes hid behind round spectacles. Lines fanned out from those eyes when he smiled, and the man did have a rather fine smile. A lot of nice straight teeth. Everything about him cried normal chap passing through.

It was harder to hold her smile now as she remembered Mrs. Portridge's words from earlier that morning. Scotland wasn't that far away. Perhaps he was just on his way home.

"I've had it longer than you ken. The words, ye see. It takes my mind off the matters what plague me, lass."

Penelope's heart pinched at the words, and she wanted nothing more than to throw her arms around the man. This. This right here was why she defied convention. This moment, this man. With his warm smile and crinkly eyes. She'd given this man a spot of joy, and for that, she would give up all the conventions a woman like her should expect.

Her eyes skittered involuntarily to where Samuel sat, and she recognized the lie for what it was. She forced her smile wider.

"I couldn't agree more," she said. She wished the man a pleasant journey and made her way back to Samuel.

He stared at her as she sat but didn't question her. He would have been close enough to hear that the man was not American.

"I don't think the professor was on that coach," she said after some time had passed.

Samuel stood and tossed a coin to the barmaid to pay for their meal. "No, I don't think so either. And now we'll get a late start for Edinburgh."

CHAPTER 17

*O*ne's destination may not be where one is meant to go.
     *From The Adventures of Miss Melanie Merkett,
Private Inquisitor*

IT WAS after luncheon before another coach arrived that would carry them into Kendal, a much larger village where they would have a better chance at hiring a coach to take them to Edinburgh.

For once, luck seemed to be on their side as several coaches were available for hire once they reached the larger village. He selected the best outfitted carriage as he held out hope that this would be the last leg of their journey. He wanted Penelope to be comfortable for such a distance as remained.

They were well underway as the sun moved past the midpoint, and he had hopes of reaching the Scottish border before nightfall. If he had known that their journey would have taken them this far north and through this many challenges, he would have defied Wickshire at the mere suggestion of Penelope undertaking such a journey.

But now as he sat across from her, he wasn't thinking about his objections. He was attempting to puzzle her out.

She had removed her boots some miles ago and rested her feet on the bench beside him, her toes flexing back and forth in time to the scratching of her pencil. The writing box had emerged far earlier than her stocking clad toes, and the scratching of pencil against paper had become nearly as constant as the rumble of carriage wheels along the road. Mrs. Portridge had packed them a bundle of food as well, and she chewed at some cheese in one hand as the pencil scurried in the other. He wondered briefly if she realized what a striking tableau she made.

No other woman of his acquaintance would have been found in such a state. Bare feet. Legs spread to hold the writing box. Intently munching on a morsel. It was terribly domestic. Intimate. A far greater transgression than Samuel had committed on their journey thus far, and yet, he couldn't honestly accept the blame for it.

It was largely her fault. She was the one to point out the absurdity of his worries. One night so early in his career. When he had been so green. Exposed to such horror. He should have seen it. He should have believed it. But it had taken her, Penelope, to point out the extremeness in his reaction. While his gut still simmered at the possibility of ruining Penelope Paiget, it no longer haunted him at every turn. Now, it merely ate at him.

"That's a very long note to Wickshire."

The pencil stopped as if it struck a hole in the paper. She raised only her eyes to him, her lips molded carefully around the piece of cheese between her teeth. He tightened at the sight of her lips, of her delicate fingers, and he felt the thing inside of him perk up. He squashed it back down.

"Are you giving away all our secrets for someone to possibly intercept?" He had meant the words in jest but as they emerged, he recalled his earlier misgivings about her. He had all but dismissed them, but something still lurked in his mind.

What secret could Penelope Paiget have that would keep her from marriage? Was it marriage in general or marriage to him in particular?

It wasn't as if one would be easier to solve than the other, but one would most definitely be easier to approach. The one that didn't see her marrying anyone but him.

"It would seem so," she said, but she didn't finish the morsel of cheese, instead placing it alongside the piece of bread she had ripped off of the loaf Mrs. Portridge had packed.

She dropped her feet and straightened, setting the writing box beside her on the bench. He felt a sudden regret at disturbing her so and wondered if he could coax her back into such a reclined position. For he enjoyed watching Penelope so relaxed. So at home. So comfortable around him.

It was a startling notion. That she may be comfortable around him. For the past ten years, he had been so focused on ensuring he was a man deserving of Penelope for a wife, he had never stopped to consider what it would feel like to actually have her for a wife.

The intricacies of it. The exchanges they would have. The secrets they would share.

Ah, but she wasn't sharing her secrets, was she?

He leaned forward and put his elbows on his knees to look out the window.

"We'll reach the border tonight as long as we keep up this pace."

"Bah!"

He shot a glance at her to find her frowning at him.

"Don't speak out loud the thing you wish to happen for it is certain not to."

He raised an eyebrow. "What fairy tale is that?"

"It's not a fairy tale. It's common sense." She placed her notes inside the writing box and snapped the lid shut with a resounding thud. She tucked it back into her bag and in the same motion, picked up her boots.

"I didn't mean disturb you so." The words came out softer than he had meant them to, and he wondered if she'd even heard him.

She had for she cast him a small smile. "Oh, it's not that." She tied off a single boot and reached for the other. "I have a tendency to get caught up in my—" Her eyes never left his, but he could tell she searched for a word. An elusive word or a damaging word, he couldn't tell. "Writings that I sometimes forget I am in the company of others." She finished tying her boot and set her feet back to the floor. "I shouldn't be so rude."

"You weren't being rude. I would daresay you would be sick of my company by this point."

She laughed, her eyes lighting with expression. "Hardly. You're rather easy to be with."

He stilled. "Is that so?"

She nodded and reached up to tuck a piece of her hair back in her chignon as she sometimes did. "It's likely the result of having a large family. One needs to be tolerant to survive in such situations."

His mind cast over the large family she referenced so casually. The one he never took for granted. Not since that day when he'd realized how different he was from them.

"I suppose you are correct."

She smiled at him and looked out the window. "Will we travel much further today? It's getting dark out there."

Samuel followed her gaze and noted the sun was dipping precariously low.

"It shouldn't be much further."

"What shouldn't be?" She looked at him sharply.

"Gretna Green."

She wrinkled her nose. "Are we truly stopping there? It seems rather overdone."

He shrugged his shoulders and leaned back. "It's part of the ruse, isn't it?"

She seemed to consider this. "I suppose it is, but couldn't we be a little more original about it?"

They traveled in silence for quite some time, and he thought she may have fallen asleep when she said, "I think I see lights."

It was becoming a common expression with her, and he smiled before he realized it. He leaned forward again and noted the lights she likely saw. They were dropping down along the road into another hamlet like the many they had traveled through already. This one was fairly more robust. The road well maintained. He wondered just how many people traveled this road. Running away from someone. Or perhaps running toward someone.

Their driver pulled the coach to a stop at the Hen and Hound just as the last of the light slipped over the horizon.

"This looks lovely," Penelope said as she sat up and gathered her things. "How much further is it to Edinburgh?"

He grimaced and raised an eyebrow at her.

"You're right," she said. "I suppose I shouldn't ask such a question with the luck we've been having."

He stepped down into the yard and held a hand out to help her down. The driver was already speaking to a stable boy that had run out at their approach, so Samuel let his gaze scan the space, searching.

This inn was like the others they had stayed in. Bricked

along the bottom half with a wooden upper floor. A weathered wooden sign hung over the door depicting a hen riding a hound. The noises of laughter and singing drifted out into the night, and warm yellow light spilled from the windows of the first floor.

A shadow detached itself from the wall of the tavern and stepped forward into the light.

Penelope stiffened beside him. "Samuel." Her voice was low and ominous. "Samuel, is that the man who has been following us? He's headed right toward us." She gripped his arm, her fingers digging into him. "Samuel, he looks...he looks like he could be a spy."

Samuel smiled. "That's because he used to be one. Penelope Paiget, I'd like you to meet my father. Nathan Black."

* * *

PENELOPE STARED.

"I've never been to Gretna Green," the man said as he came to stand before them. "I'd always thought I would need to chase Alec here one day, but I didn't expect it would be you I was following."

Her gaze traveled between the two men, her mind racing. Samuel's father? When had this happened? Why was he here? Her gaze settled on Samuel as he laughed at his father's quip. And really, who was Alec?

"I'm sorry to have put you through the trouble. Our mission became a great deal more complicated than we had anticipated."

Complicated, indeed.

"The only trouble you caused was in me having to convince Elizabeth she could not come."

Samuel laughed harder. Elizabeth. That was his younger sister. Mr. Black reached out then and drew his son into a

212

strong embrace. She could see the way the man's fingers flexed along his son's back in the dim light from the tavern windows.

She nearly swallowed her tongue.

What was wrong with Samuel? Clearly his father loved him. Clearly he had been raised in a nurturing environment. Why was he so plagued with the possibility of something other? Why had he let one night consume the rest of his life?

"Miss Paiget," Mr. Black turned to her as he released his son. "I apologize for your current situation. It must be rather unpleasant."

Penelope stilled, her thoughts colliding with one another as her hackles rose. She prepared herself for the inevitable. The speech that always followed such a proclamation that she should be employing herself elsewhere. But that's not what happened.

Mr. Black's mouth twisted into a mocking grin. "You're not only stuck with this bloke for interminable hours on the road, but now you're irrevocably tied to the Black family. I believe that may be far worse."

She choked on a laugh, so unexpected were his words that she hadn't fit the right emotion with the correct response before it came blithering out.

"Oh, he's not that terrible." She leaned in as if she were conferring a secret to Mr. Black. "As long as you keep him well fed and rested."

Samuel frowned at her while Mr. Black laughed. When the sound died away, she realized what it was that truly bothered her.

"I'm sorry to be so forward, Mr. Black, but what are you doing here?"

He looked at Samuel, his lips parting in confusion. "Samuel sent me a note that I should meet you here. He said your endeavor had not gone according to plan."

She recalled instantly the letter that Samuel had posted along with her own the morning they left Mrs. Herschel. She peered at Samuel now and knew that if there had been enough light, she'd be able to make out the flush on Samuel's face. She also knew that it was not out of concern for their objective that he had written his father. It was out of concern over a manufactured sense of his own failings.

She smiled although she felt anything but jovial just then. "Ah, yes, of course. Then I appreciate you accommodating us."

Mr. Black regarded Samuel with a keen eye, and she knew he did not believe her for a moment.

Samuel gestured to the tavern. "We should go in and see about rooms."

Mr. Black stopped him with a hand. "There's a gentleman in there asking after you."

Samuel glanced at her. "A single gentleman?"

Mr. Black nodded. "Well dressed, too. Good hygiene. I ascertained he's been here for several days. Asking after a pair of young lovers eloping here. One is a young woman with red hair."

They both looked at her, and she wanted to reach up and pull her bonnet more snugly against her incriminating hair.

"He's been shadowing us since nearly the beginning. I had thought we lost him in the confusion of our journey, but it appears we did not." Samuel's brow wrinkled. "Although, why he would stop in Gretna Green, I cannot say."

"He likely heard word of the ruse somewhere along the way. I think it speaks to our effectiveness in planting the story." She looked between both men.

Mr. Black frowned. "I'd say you did a fine job of it then. He's quite convinced he'll find you here eventually. What is your plan from here?"

"I'm going to confront him. If he's traveling alone, he's outnumbered, two to one."

"Three." She didn't miss the grin on Mr. Black's face at her interjection.

"Three to one," Samuel amended. "We need to find out who he's working for. We don't want to keep mitigating the symptoms. We need to find the root of this."

"Do you think to confront him head on then?"

He peered at her through the darkness. "If he's looking for a woman with red hair, he might not know what I look like. I'm going to go in and try to befriend him. What does he look like?"

"He's wearing a black coat and fawn trousers cut into Hessians. Navy waistcoat. Cranberry cravat. He has an excessively large chin."

Something tickled at the back of Penelope's mind, but she gave it a mental shake. He'd just described half of the male population of the ton. Surely, it couldn't be who she thought it was.

"Stay here. I'll come back when I've made progress."

Samuel strode off in the direction of the inn, leaving Penelope to stand in the dark with the man who held all the secrets to what made Samuel Black so sure he wasn't good enough.

CHAPTER 18

It's quite possible to be too good at one's profession.
From The Adventures of Miss Melanie Merkett,
Private Inquisitor

THE YEASTY SMELL hit him first as he entered the low-ceilinged room. Here the tables were rectangular and long, each flanked by a bench, crowded at this hour with all matters of men and women. There were men in simple clothes, farmers and stewards from neighboring estates. The women with them wore plain dresses that showed careful mending in different colored-patches affixed to elbows and skirts.

The travelers were somewhat better dressed, but their clothes carried the rumpled and dusted appearance of the road. Children scampered about between the tables. Their faces smudged with filth and food as they found entertainment while their parents idled on in their boring chatter.

He made his way up to the bar, slipping between a farmer

and another man, possibly a blacksmith from the soot staining his trousers.

The bar keep saw him and signaled to him with a nod of his head.

"A pint, good man," Samuel called over the din. "And two rooms if you have them."

The man pulled the pint and sloshed it across the bar to him. "'Ere's the pint. And I'll have the lass set up the rooms for ye." He turned away and called, "Meghan, two rooms for the gent." His voice boomed over the open space, but none of the patrons seemed to mind. It was likely a common occurrence anytime someone came in requesting a room for the night.

At the far end of the bar, a head appeared, covered in a white mop gone brown with age and grime. But the face beneath it was young and pounced on the bar keep's word.

"Aye, all right then," she hollered back with just as much strength and slipped out from behind the bar toward a dark stairwell in the back of the tavern.

"It'll just be a minute or two, gent," the bar keep said and moved down the bar to other thirsty patrons.

Samuel picked up his pint and used the excuse of taking a sip to survey the men at the bar. None of them appeared to be their well-dressed shadow. These were all hard working men, their uniforms of grime and weariness plain to see. He scanned the tables next, noting the two groups of obvious travelers. The tables of men so enthralled in conversation, he thought they might be regular patrons of the Hen and Hound.

Then there were the other odd tables here and there. Smaller groups. Some deep in discussion. Some sitting quietly as they consumed a meal of pies and pints.

Their man was sitting by the door. That was why he hadn't seen him when he'd come in. He sat alone with this back to the wall, his eyes on the doorway. A half-finished pint sat in front of him along with a plate riddled with only crumbs. An empty chair sat across from him.

Samuel pushed off from the bar and made his way back through the room to the man, noting each detail of his appearance as he approached. He did have a rather large chin and a broad, thick forehead. His hair was cut short and pushed back from his head in a flamboyant sweep. He cut a stunning figure in perfectly tailored waistcoat and trousers. His Hessians gleamed even from where Samuel stood. A finer dandy Samuel had not seen in quite some time, but there was something about the man that didn't seem to fit. As if the man merely played at the role of dandy. Not that he came to it naturally.

"Good evening," he said when he reached the table. The man's eyes shifted, but his body didn't move. Samuel raised his pint in greeting. "I apologize for my forwardness, but it seems to be a packed room tonight. Would you mind sharing the table until my room is readied?" He pushed the pint towards the ceiling as if to indicate his room being readied above.

The moments ticked past, and Samuel waited, his mind skittering between the fate of recognition, what the man might do, and the opportunity of invisibility. If the man did not know who it was that approached him, then Samuel could get close, question him. If not...well, he hoped his father reached him in time.

The man smiled, the expression slow and easy, reaching his eyes last. He pushed at his empty plate to clear a spot in front of the empty chair.

"Sure," he said. "You've had a long day, I assume."

The words did not reassure him but neither did they raise alarm. Samuel was dressed like many of the other travelers in the room even though Mrs. Portridge had tried her best to brush some of the dust from his coat.

He returned the smile and sat, raising his glass to the stranger. "Thank you, sir. Your kindness is appreciated. It's been a long journey from London."

He watched the man carefully for a reaction, but he needn't have bothered. The stranger's face lit up, his eyes going wide and his smile relaxing. "London, you say? Why, that's where I've just traveled from. It's always nice to encounter someone from your home city when you're traveling, isn't it?"

A keen sense of trepidation stole over Samuel but not for reasons he had expected. This man was exceedingly polite. Encouraging, almost. If he were a spy or a worse, a mercenary, would he be so accepting of a stranger he met in a tavern?

Unless perhaps he knew who Samuel was.

Samuel did not carry a weapon unless on duty. The presence of a weapon always increased the likelihood that one would be tempted to use it. Sitting there in the tavern, he began to rethink his policy on the matter.

"It is at that. Have you been traveling long? The roads the past few days have been deplorable."

The stranger scoffed and shook his head. "You cannot imagine the downpour I had to ride through just to reach Manchester. It really shouldn't have taken as long as it did, and the journey was miserable. I assume you found no better luck on your way."

Samuel shook his head. "I'm afraid not. I'm headed further north but the rain washed out the road, and I was painfully diverted. I had hopes to meet my colleague much earlier than this, and I only hope he is still in residence by the time I make my way into Scotland."

He hoped he had peppered his speech with enough clues

to bait the man, but the stranger's expression never changed. He only shook his head.

"I can only hope we can instill our trust in these new railroads they've been building. Surely innovations such as these will improve travel in the years to come." The man took a drink from his half-finished pint.

Samuel regarded him carefully. A man interested in innovations. Curious.

"You enjoy technological pursuits?"

The man set down his glass, his eyes coming back to Samuel with a noticeable spark. "Oh yes, very much. I like to think of myself as a man of study." He said this with a smile that betrayed a certain level of pride. "There is nothing grander than the undiscovered coming to light. Wouldn't you agree?"

What an interesting choice of words. Samuel sat forward in his seat. "I do at that. Is there any particular field of study that interests you more than others?"

The man sat back with a huff of air, his hand moving between them as if cataloging his interests. "There are the usual fields, of course. The chemical arts are always of interest to me, but I must say the strides they are making in astronomical endeavors are simply extraordinary."

Samuel clutched his pint glass. "Is that so?"

The man nodded and leaned an elbow against the table, drawing nearer to Samuel as if to confide in him. "I'll let you know, man, I have exclusive knowledge of some of the latest developments in astronomy." He raised an eyebrow over his self-assured grin.

While his words gave cause for concern, the cocky manner in which they were delivered did not quite match, and Samuel's suspicions faltered.

"What sort of exclusive knowledge?"

The stranger laughed, the sound genuine and throaty.

"Oh, I can't tell you that, good man. Academics never reveal their secrets to the public too soon."

"You're an academic then?" Samuel caught at the revelation.

The man smiled, showing a thick row of brilliant white teeth. "Oh, of course." The smile faltered. "I thought perhaps you recognized me. No?" The smile slipped some more.

Samuel shook his head. "No, I'm sorry. I'm not really a man of letters."

The stranger brushed him off with another sweep of his hand, and his smile relaxed into a friendly grin. "The name's Sir Devlin Cross."

* * *

"Are you aware your son summoned you to act as chaperone?"

Mr. Black didn't look at her when he answered. "His mother thought as much."

"His mother?"

"She's aware that something is troubling him just like the rest of us. Only she is not keen to allow him to wallow in it until he comes to peace with it." He did look at her now. "Only I have a suspicion you know what it is."

She didn't speak. She only stared at that this man who had become Samuel's father. It wasn't her secret to tell, but more than that, this man was the very thing that proved Samuel's misgivings were unfounded. This man who had traveled the length of a country at the request of a son that did not come from his issue proved such. This man who now stood in an inn yard in the middle of Gretna Green as dark lay all about them and mildly conversed about what it was that troubled his son. Who knew that she knew and yet did not press her. That was a man worthy of having Samuel Black for a son.

She nodded and neither of them spoke for several minutes. She watched the lit windows of the tavern as if she could see Samuel through them. See the man that had followed them all the way from London. She could see nothing, of course. The windows were marred with a layer of dust from the yard and the road beyond, and she doubted they ever came fully clean. The tavern beyond was only noise, drifting like forgotten whispers through the night air with corresponding smudges of light and dark through the windows.

"Did you really wait all this time for my son?"

The question came out of the darkness at her, and she flinched as if it carried a sting. "I beg your pardon?"

"Samuel introduced you as Miss Paiget, and I recall your face." He studied her through the dark. "Even now in the dark, your face is unmistakable. Samuel took you for coffee a very long time ago, didn't he?"

Her mind flew back to that day in the coffee house. When Samuel asked her to wait. What had prompted his rash request.

"You were there."

Mr. Black nodded. "Only briefly. I was attempting to keep his mother from interrupting your interlude."

"Thank you for that." She paused. Thought about it. "His mother is sounding more and more like a quite fearsome creature."

One side of Mr. Black's mouth propped up in a familiar grin. "You can only imagine."

Her fingers twitched against her skirts, and she didn't miss Mr. Black's gaze diverting, noticing the gesture. She forced her hand to stop.

"You didn't answer my question, Miss Paige."

She had quite honestly forgotten what he'd asked and now searched for what it was he wanted to know.

Had she waited for Samuel?

She regarded the windows of the tavern as she sought her answer. Yes, she had waited for him. For a time. But then... But then her work had become more important than waiting. Than anything else really.

"Does he know you're Melanie Merkett?"

Her gut wrenched at the softly spoken words, and a gasp caught her throat, spilling out like a strangled choke.

"You know?" The words hardly registered in the din about them.

Mr. Black passed her that lopsided grin. "Of course. Samuel came to see me before he left London, and given the nature of the situation, I investigated your background. Your publisher is only too keen to offer information regarding your person to the right bidder. You should consider taking your stories to another publication."

She unclenched her jaw. "Did he?"

Mr. Black nodded. "I would think with the level of recognition your work has achieved, you could take your stories to a more reputable publisher."

"I think you're quite right, Mr. Black." She crossed her arms over her stomach to dull the pain there. "You won't tell him, will you?"

His expression hardened so much, she could see it through the dark. "That means you have not told him."

She shook her head. "I haven't—" She had been about to say she hadn't found the right time to tell him, but they'd been traveling for five days already. Most of that time spent locked together in carriages. It would seem most unusual if she declared not finding the right moment as the reason for keeping her secret.

"You're afraid that if you tell him, he'll make you stop writing when you're wed."

She shut her mouth. Opened it again. Turned with her fisted hands to her hips. "How do you know that?"

"Because you're a lot like that fearsome mother of his." Mr. Black returned her steely gaze with one of his own. "I think your position on this matter relates to commonly held viewpoints on the subject of female authors and not those held by my son on the subject."

"Your son is a detective inspector for the Metropolitan Police. He cannot marry a novelist." She had become so irritated by the line of conversation the last word came out as if it were a blast from a cannon. She clapped a hand to her mouth and peered around as if someone had heard her utter the word.

Mr. Black frowned. "You should speak to Samuel."

She shook her head, her lips grating against her glove. She dropped her hand. "I can't. He already thinks—" Again, she faltered.

"You think you're protecting him by not telling him."

"You are very irritating, Mr. Black."

He smiled. "My wife often says the same thing. I think the two of you would get along quite well."

She had nothing to say to that, and so she let the conversation drop off, returning her attention to the tavern and the occupants within. Several more minutes passed, and worry for Samuel eclipsed her irritation at their previous conversation.

"Do you suppose he's all right in there?" she asked when she could bear no more. They didn't know who this shadow was, and they were operating on the very unsound conclusion that the man wouldn't recognize Samuel and immediately render him incapacitated.

Mr. Black shrugged. "I think Samuel can hold his own against any bloke who carries a walking stick."

Her pulse skipped. "What did you say?"

Mr. Black's brow creased at her concern. "Walking stick. The gentleman looking for the red-haired woman carried a walking stick."

She swallowed. "Did the walking stick have an unusual ornament at the top?"

His eyes narrowed. "It was a rendering of Poseidon. Why?"

She didn't answer. She picked up her skirts and ran for the tavern.

But now, to hear him say the words, something shifted inside of Samuel.

They were words he spoke so often himself, only slightly different. He was an agent of the Metropolitan Police. He fought for domestic safety while his father had fought for international security. The uneasiness spread inside him. Perhaps he had been thinking about this entirely wrong.

Sir Cross had wedged himself against a bench now, and his lips quivered as he reached up with a placating hand.

"I don't know what it is that you think I've done, but I promise you it wasn't me." He licked those trembling lips. "My name is Sir Devlin Cross. She can vouch for me." Here he pointed a shaky finger behind Samuel.

He turned and for the first time perhaps, realized Penelope stood behind him.

And she was furious.

"If you are quite done protecting my honor, Samuel Black, I would be happy to explain who this gentleman is." She paused, and he knew he was supposed to say something but everything had become jumbled in his brain. "Perhaps you'd like to wait until after you beat him into oblivion. Would that be more convenient for you?"

She was mad at him. This didn't make any sense. This man, Sir Devlin Cross, had followed them from London. Was certainly a part of the scheme that had ended poor Bobby Egemont's life. Was now driving Professor Mesmer to run for his life. And yet, this was his fault?

"Sir Cross is Wickshire's colleague and an esteemed member of the academic community in London." He thought she was going to say more but she halted, her eyes moving unsteadily to Sir Cross. Back to Samuel. Back to Sir Cross. She seemed to make a decision because she stepped forward, putting her shoulder to his as she put her back to Sir Cross. The position allowed her to press her lips to his ear, which felt altogether too good and did not help to unmuddle his brain. "He's mistakenly infatuated with me and was quite upset when I declared I was running away to Gretna Green to marry you."

She stepped back. Regarded him with eyes that said he should have understood what she'd just said.

Sir Cross was infatuated with her? Penelope? His Penelope?

Well, that was simply a great deal worse than treason.

"You're here for her?" Samuel gestured to Penelope with a clenched hand.

Sir Cross's eyes wavered for a moment, his mouth opening and shutting with no sound.

"Sir Cross, I promise not to commit further harm to your person if you will simply answer the question."

The man stared at him but would not hold his gaze. His eyes kept straying to Penelope until finally he seemed to make up his mind.

"Penelope," Sir Cross said and flipped over to crawl on his hands and knees over to her. "Penelope, my love, you are making a terrible mistake. You cannot marry this man." He reached her and came up on his knees, grasped her hands in his. "Penelope, it is I you should be marrying. I can make you happy. I can make you a woman of the peerage. I can make you everything you deserve to be."

Penelope's lips folded tightly against a speech Samuel knew she was dying to emit. But as he also knew of Penelope, she wouldn't utter a single word to deflate Sir Cross's horribly bold proclamation.

"Sir Cross, I must apologize, but you have completely misunderstood. I do not return your feelings and for that, I am sorry if I misled you in anyway."

"But—" he stammered, his eyes flicking to Samuel and back. "But he's...he's just a policeman."

Penelope looked at him over the top of Sir Cross's head, and he wondered what she saw. He was rumpled from days of travel. He hadn't shaved. He hadn't bathed for that matter. And Sir Cross was right. He was only a policeman when it came down to it. He couldn't offer Penelope the things Sir Cross could.

But then Penelope's eyes shifted, her gaze going beyond him to something else.

Someone else.

His father.

His father stood behind him. Standing between Samuel and the disgruntled and confused bar keep. Nathan Black was tall and solid, gray appearing at his temples and lines marking his face. Lines from smiling at his wife. Lines from laughing at the antics of his children. Lines from worrying for his family. Nathan Black was a good man who had led a good life and now he stood behind Samuel.

Samuel Black.

The by-blow of a man who thought nothing of raping a woman to get what he wanted.

Samuel's gut clenched.

"Oh no." She watched Samuel as she said it, something bright lighting her eyes. "Oh no, he's much more than that."

"So you're really going to marry him?" Sir Cross remained on his knees peering up at Penelope.

Penelope's gaze met his, and through it, she cast a thousand questions.

Yes, Samuel was going to marry Penelope. But not like this. Not now.

He felt his father standing behind him. The whole reason he had sent for him crashing into him until he thought he might break under it. His father was supposed to stop this from happening. He was supposed to arrive in Gretna Green in time to stop them. Save Penelope's reputation despite it all being a ruse. No one in London would be the wiser of what really happened here.

But kneeling there on the floor was the very reason Samuel was going to marry her now. Like this.

Sir Devlin Cross was a witness Samuel had not accounted for in his plan. Sir Cross could return to London. Could relay his account of the events. Penelope arriving in the taproom. Unchaperoned. Her appearance giving every indication of having traveled for days with Samuel. Sir Cross could ruin Penelope with a simple slip of those quivering lips.

No matter that he planned to marry her. The damage was done. She would be ruined.

And it would be his fault.

The very thing he dreaded most had happened. Nothing he had done had stopped it. Even forcing his father to travel the length of England hadn't prevented it. He had failed.

"Yes," Samuel said then, loud enough for the entire taproom to hear. "Yes, we plan to wed. Tonight." The last word had been an afterthought but as it had emerged he felt the inevitability of it. Why not tonight? There was no sense in waiting now that the deed had to be done.

But that second, that moment between speaking and drawing his next breath. Before the room erupted into chaos. Before their audience came to congratulate the happy couple one by one, giving their blessing and hope for a bright future. Before he could locate the blacksmith to perform the ceremony. Before any of that, he heard a noise.

A small noise.

So small anyone else would have missed it. Anyone including Sir Devlin Cross.

But Samuel heard it because it was Penelope's voice. And Penelope's voice was a sound he could hear fathoms away.

He watched her face when it happened. Watched her lips

part on that small sound, watched her eyes go wide with disbelief and worse, fear.

Heard the words as they slipped free.

"Oh, no."

He died inside then.

The thing he had fought for so long had won, but it wasn't a victory he had expected. It was much crueler than anything he could have anticipated. In the dark nights, in all the dank alleyways where he had fought the madness, he never considered this.

Penelope did not want to marry him because of what he was.

She did not want to marry him because she didn't want him.

* * *

Sir Cross acted as witness to their marriage.

The thought struck her as ridiculously absurd that this was how it would end. The blacksmith's shop in Gretna Green was not as quaint and homey as Mr. Portridge's shop had been, but then, Penelope considered the amount of traffic this blacksmith's shop likely saw. How many others had stood where Penelope had stood? Waiting for her fate to be sealed?

For that's how she had felt.

As she stood next to Samuel, repeated the words that would make her his wife, his property, she had felt a door closing on all the things she had worked so hard to obtain. She sat on the chair in their room at the inn, regarding the hands that lay in her lap. Her fingers never twitched as the minutes ticked by.

Samuel had deposited her in their room some time ago

and gone off with his father. She hadn't looked at him since he had spoken the words that would be the end of it all.

Yes, we plan to wed. Tonight.

She hadn't had enough time. Time to speak with Samuel. Tell him her secret. Explain to him why she couldn't marry him. And now it was too late.

His wife was a novelist.

She closed her eyes against the ramifications. What would happen if her secret ever got out? What would people say? Would Samuel's reputation be tarnished? Worse, would his career be ended because of her?

A sob stuck in her throat, and she choked on it, coughing and pounding her chest until she could breathe again.

God, this couldn't be happening.

She couldn't have done this to the man she—

Loved.

The tears came now, hard and mercilessly, streaming down her face as she released the torment that had built inside of her for so long. She bent over with the force of it, her arms wrapping around her middle as if she could stop it. She remembered crying when her mother had died, but those were the tears of a child. While she had loved her father, theirs had been more of a professional relationship rather than father and daughter. She had been saddened at his death, had cried appropriately, but then again, it wasn't the ripping emotion of what swept through her now.

This was Samuel. The man she loved. The man she was so proud to see accomplish those things he had set out to do with his life. And accomplish so much in so little time. Her mind skated over his career, his achievements, the things she had gathered in their short time together. Samuel could be proud of the things he'd done, and she should be proud as his wife.

Another sob ripped through her, and she pressed a fist to her mouth to stop from crying out.

She had ruined everything for him, and he didn't even know it yet. She would stop immediately, of course. There would be no more Melanie Merkett stories. There couldn't be. What if someone found out? What if someone tied her back to Samuel?

His father already knew.

Anger, sharp and vicious, tore through her sadness. She would be finding a new publisher. With her success, she didn't doubt she would find someone to take her next work.

But even as the thought entered her mind, she dismissed it. There could be no further stories. Now she was a wife.

A wife.

For nearly ten years, she had thought of it. After she'd blown out her lamp for the night, tucked under the covers and staring at the ceiling of a room that was only hers as long as she was employed. She had thought of what it would mean. To share her life with Samuel. What it would be like. How she would feel.

She hadn't expected to feel like this.

For a moment, she regretted ever setting pen to paper, but she scolded herself for such a feeling. Her Melanie Merkett stories had brought so many joy. She knew it. Just like that morning in the tavern in Oxenholme and the traveler who carried her book in his pocket. There was proof that her words had done good. She would never retract that.

But now it must remain a secret.

She stood and went to her bag, dragging her writing box from it. She unlatched it, rummaged inside until she found the notes she had been taking, the ones she planned to use in her next novel. She tore them from their cubby inside the box and was surprised when tears stained them. She swiped at her face, only to make it worse, and her eyes flooded. She faltered, swiping again to no avail.

She set down her notes, tugged a handkerchief from her bag, and properly wiped her face clean. When she could see again, she looked down at her scribbles.

His kisses are better than trifle.

The ache bloomed anew in her chest, and she sat without thinking, perched on the edge of the bed. She traced the letters with a solitary finger, not believing that she had written them not more than a week previous. How could so much change in so short a time?

As she pondered her words, a silly flash of hope burst through her torment. Samuel would be a good husband. He would make her happy, of that she was certain. She already knew he suited her when it came to her baser needs. Needs she hadn't known she had until that first time he'd touch her.

Another sob caught her throat, more of a choke than anything. She recalled all too clearly the kiss on the pavement in front of Wickshire Place. So swept away with the power of his kiss, she'd forgotten to think of the damage it would do.

Samuel was right to protect her as he had done. She was a lot more trouble than she was worth.

She stood and went to the stove in the corner of the room. Coals flamed through the grate, and she bent, opened the door with a twist of the handle. She stared at her writing for a moment more before lifting the first paper to the fire.

She wasn't sure if the door had opened earlier and she had not heard it with all of her sobbing, or if she was so absorbed in what had happened in the past hour, that she had missed it opening entirely.

But suddenly Samuel was there. He wrenched her to her feet with two strong hands at her shoulders and tore the papers from her grasp.

"No!" The word was out before she could stop it, her hands going for her notes. Notes she never let anyone read.

It was as she stretched for the papers that she noticed Samuel's face. It was hard. Tense.

Angry.

She had never seen him angry. Not like that. Not as if she'd done something despicable.

"You don't understand," she said quickly, and it sounded just as guilty as her hasty no.

And then Samuel's face changed. It was the smallest of contortions, but then softly, his anger fell away. He switched to another paper and then another. Until his expression had gone from hard to bewildered.

He looked up at her, his mouth open with no words coming out. But his eyes. His beautiful, brown eyes. They held hurt and disbelief. Worry and regret.

She closed her eyes against his stare, unable to bear it. But even as her lids closed, the words slipped from her lips.

"I'm a novelist, Samuel."

* * *

IT WAS ODD, what happened then.

He laughed.

The sound so rich and deep, it startled him. He blinked at her and then down at the papers in his hands.

When he had walked in to find her kneeling before the stove, papers at the ready to be burned, he had only thought one thing. She was destroying evidence of her betrayal as a spy.

But instead, he had found...

Well, he honestly didn't know what he'd found.

His kisses were better than trifle?

That was something he was going to remember. It would be excellent blackmail in their marriage.

Their marriage.

Not more than an hour ago, he had wed this woman despite her revelation of not wanting to marry him. But now, staring down at the writings in his hands and hearing her confession, he knew exactly what had prompted her desire to not wed.

He laughed again. "You're a novelist? That's your secret?"

She blinked at him, and he finally took in her face. Realized she had been crying.

He sobered immediately, stepping forward to pull her into his arms, but she resisted. Pushed against him.

"Do you think this is funny?" Her words were sharp against her thinned lips.

He knew he was smiling when he answered, but he couldn't help it. "It's a relief, is what it is. Pen, darling, I thought you were a spy."

He watched her mouth contort as if to admonish him when her lips froze on the first word. She visibly changed direction.

"Spy?"

"Yes, can't you see?" He waved the papers at her. "You said you had a secret. Something that would keep us apart. And then I found you trying to burn these papers. What was I supposed to think?"

Her face cleared, only the tracks down her cheeks evidence that she'd been crying. "You truly thought I was a spy?"

He nodded and this time, she let him take her into his arms. He rested his chin against the crown of her head, inhaled the scent of her. "Oh, God, Pen, you had me terribly frightened."

She squirmed out of his arms. "But this changes nothing. And since when did I give you leave to call me Pen?"

He smiled, again unable to help himself. He shook the papers at her. "I find it terribly fitting."

She scowled. "I'm a novelist, Samuel. I can't marry you."

"We've already proven that you can actually. Perhaps you remember the little thing we did at the blacksmith's shop not more than a—" He stopped, the events of the past day colliding in on themselves like a runaway horse cart thrown into a market. He sat down on the bed, his legs collapsing beneath him.

And again—

He laughed. The sound so unexpected, he pressed at his chest as if something were physically wrong with him.

"It all makes sense," he said, his eyes still taking in the room but seeing everything else as well. Their entire journey. Her twitching fingers. Her delight in asking questions of things she didn't know. Her propensity to wander off.

She was exploring. Learning. Discovering.

So that she could one day write it all down into a book.

His laughter ceased. "Oh, God," he said, his face falling as the ramifications of this hit him with greater accuracy than his sister's thrust. "Oh, God, I married a novelist." He sat forward, putting his head into his hands. The papers he held scraped at his face, and he pulled back to look at them again. It was then that he saw she had started crying again.

He lurched to his feet. "That's not what it sounded like, love. I promise you. I only meant—"

She shoved him away again. "Don't call me that. You can't possibly—"

"I can't possibly what? Love you?" He eased his expression, not wanting to frighten or upset her more. "I've loved you since the moment I first saw you."

The words struck something within her because she

collapsed on the bed, the tears drying on her cheeks. He sat next to her and picked up the hand closest to him, held it in his.

"Ten years is a long time to love a person, Penelope. We've both changed in that time." His mind skittered to that dark night, and he pushed it away. "If you can love me, knowing what you know now, then who is to say I can't love you? Even if you're a novelist?"

She glanced at him but wouldn't hold his gaze. "It's not that simple."

"It is actually that simple." He thought of his own parents. The bastard son of a duke and a former housekeeper. Theirs was a relationship plagued from the start and yet here they were more than twenty years later. Happy. Old. And still in love. "It really can be that simple." He stroked a thumb over the back of her hand, noting each and every freckle that dotted it.

"A detective inspector for the Metropolitan Police cannot be married to a novelist."

His thumb froze. "Is that what this is about?"

She turned watery eyes on him. "Of course, it is."

Again, the laugh came without him realizing it would. "Good God, woman, you know nothing of my family, do you?" His words only made her lips tremble. He turned, cupped her cheek with his hand. "Penelope, darling, I promise you. In a few days, this will all make a lot more sense. But right now, you'll need to trust me. It's going to be all right. I love you, and that's all that matters." He didn't ask if she loved him. She was so fragile sitting there next to him. If he prodded her for an answer, she may just flee. "We need to find the professor and return him safely to Wickshire. And then—" He smiled softly, encouragingly. "I'll explain why having a novelist for a wife is nothing extraordinary to a member of the Black family."

She didn't believe him. Her eyes continued to search his, and he kept his smile in place in the hopes to finally convince her of his honesty. When resolve appeared in her eyes, he knew she had decided something, but he wasn't certain of what.

"All right, Samuel," she said, her voice weaker than he'd ever heard it. "I'll wait."

"Thank you," he said, and then looked behind them at the bed where they sat. He cast a sidelong glance at his wife. His wife. He would never get tired of that. "You know, Mrs. Black, I've heard novelists are quite creative types. Would you care to demonstrate?"

Her face went red in a flash, and it was almost as if her freckles had all connected. "I write adventure stories, Mr. Black, not love stories."

"Well, I think adventure will have something to do with it."

CHAPTER 20

It is best to change one's course than to wallow over a misunderstood clue.

From The Adventures of Miss Melanie Merkett, Private Inquisitor

SHE AWOKE to a stream of sunlight in her eyes and an odd pressure against her left arm. She blinked at the light and glanced down to find Samuel's head on her shoulder, his arm over her waist, and his leg tucked through hers. She blinked again, coming fully awake as she recalled the events of the previous night.

Her husband.

She lay entwined with her husband. Her husband who had been right about the lack of definition between love and adventure stories. There had been quite a lot of adventure last night.

Their wedding night.

She hadn't honestly given it much thought as she had always imagined her chosen profession would preclude her from engaging in such an event. But as circumstances had demanded such, her profession had proved little barrier to the inevitable.

She was Samuel's wife now. Even more so having consummated the act. Three times.

It was all a great deal more splendorous than she had given it credit for, and she began to ponder the merit of writing romantic stories instead. This avenue of research had never been open to her before, and she suddenly found it vastly appealing. Perhaps if she—

"You're thinking."

Samuel's voice was muffled against her neck, and she flinched at the heat it sent spiraling through her.

"I'm sorry?"

She felt him shift, the pressure easing even as his hold on her tightened, drawing her more fully against him. His lips found her neck again, nuzzling this time, tempting with distracting kisses.

"You're thinking." His lips pressed to her flushed skin, and his words sent a tingle into her torso. "Don't try to deny it."

"I was doing no such thing. It's only—" She swallowed, attempting to find the words his attention scattered. "It's only you're being very inconsiderate of my attempt to speak."

He laughed and sat up. He leaned on one elbow to look her in the face. His hair was mussed, sticking up at odd angles, and he hadn't shaved for a couple of days. He looked loved and rumpled and delicious, and she wondered if they had enough time to make it four times. Four was a good number. She thrilled at the prospect.

"Do you always wake up with your mind spinning?" He brushed a single finger along her brow and down her cheek, leaving a trail of heat in its wake.

"Only when you give it something to spin about."

His finger stopped, and his gaze sharpened. "What do you mean?"

"I was thinking about what you said. About love stories and adventure stories and how the two might mix. I think I suddenly have an opportunity to explore the possibility of a romantic writing endeavor."

He removed his finger entirely, his jaw clenching. "You mean you'd put this in a book?"

She smiled, but it was a devious smile even for her. "Oh, Mr. Black, did you not realize the true danger of marrying a novelist?" She reached up, pushed the hair off his forehead as she stroked the line of his tight jaw. "Whatever happens from now on may end up in a book. It's just the nature of it."

"Is that so?" His expression did not soften.

"It is, and instead of being angry about it, I would suggest another avenue of approach."

"And what would that be?"

"You should strive to provide only the best bits on which I could practice my talent."

He raised an eyebrow. "The best bits?"

She countered his raised eyebrow with a smirk. "If you can manage it."

He pulled the sheet from her quite naked body before she realized what he was about. A small shriek escaped her, muddled by the laugh she could not hold back as he pounced on her.

"I had thought I'd already demonstrated the best bits, Mrs. Black, but I would be happy to remind you."

The reminder nearly made them miss breakfast.

It was all she could do to keep the blush from her face as she met Samuel's father and Sir Cross in the taproom nearly an hour later. The occupants of the inn had risen long before and most had already resumed their journeys, wherever they may be going. The remaining patrons were few and far between, so their entrance was not missed.

Mr. Black looked up from where he'd been in conversation with Sir Cross. There was no plate before him, but he held a cup in one hand he used to gesture toward them. Samuel led her into the room with a hand at the small of her back that once upon a time she might have brushed off. But right then, there was something territorial about the gesture that she simply wanted to enjoy.

She took the chair Samuel pulled out for her and greeted her father-in-law and Sir Cross with the best smile she could manage while resolutely avoiding eye contact. As if he sensed her discomfort, Mr. Black offered a neutral gambit.

"The eggs are good, but I'd avoid the sausages if you want to have a pleasant journey." He smiled at her in a kind way, as Wickshire sometimes did when they shared stories of discovery in front of the hearth after a long day's work. Mr. Black was a natural at being a father, and she looked askance at Samuel, wondering why he would ever doubt the power of the influence this man had had on his upbringing.

"I shall take your advice to heart, Mr. Black," she said with a nod.

"Nathan, please." He gestured again with his cup of coffee.

Her smile came easier now, and she looked to Sir Cross to bid him good morning when he cut her off with a jovial, "I trust you slept well!"

Samuel stopped as he'd been about to offer a pot of something to her, tea or coffee, and looked at Sir Cross. The man only smiled, his chest out and chin up in the pompous way he had. Only now when she looked at him, she didn't see a braggart. She saw a man too keen in the unpopular field of academics, thrust into the spotlight, and trying to make a go of it. She realized this was likely Sir Cross's only moment to be cherished for his talents, as haphazard as they were, and he truly just didn't know how to conduct himself in polite society.

So she smiled harder, returning his jovial tone with, "I slept marvelously! They must launder the sheets regularly in this inn. Not a single louse!"

Sir Cross lifted his own mug to her with a hearty laugh. The tension was broken after that, and they discussed the impending travel for the day. Sir Cross had only come by horse as a single rider, but he thought he would hire a coach for the journey back to London. The dry weather would likely make the return journey more hospitable.

She thought of their own journey to Edinburgh and glanced at Samuel. Now that they were wed, how would they carry on with their plan to find the professor? Wasn't their secret elopement part of the ruse? And what of Mr. Black's arrival? Nathan, that was. Wouldn't his presence suggest their plans should come to an abrupt end? She would need to discuss this with Samuel once they were without Sir Cross's company once more.

When they had finished breakfast, Samuel and his father went into the yard to see to their own conveyance, but Sir Cross stopped her with a touch to her elbow.

"Penelope, may I have a moment, please?" For the first time, Sir Cross appeared almost sincere, his eyes filled with a hope she'd never before witnessed.

"Of course." She stopped just outside the taproom and gestured to a spot in the shade where they could speak with some semblance of privacy.

Sir Cross shuffled on his feet for a couple of moments, the gesture so unlike him, she grew nervous.

"I'd like to apologize," he said. "I never intended to cause you any harm or to prevent the occurrence of something with which you found great—"

"Devlin." At her use of his given name, he stumbled on his

words, stopping altogether as she took his hands in hers. "I want you to know I appreciate what you did. There would have been no one else who would have followed me across the entire country, through rain storms no less, to stop me from making a terrible mistake. I'd like to thank you for that and to hope I may count on you as a friend."

The look of sincerity and hope vanished from his eyes as she spoke, and for a moment, she thought she had hurt him. But then his eyes filled with an unusual happiness, and for a painful moment, she wondered if Sir Cross had any true friends. Not just the kind who reveled in his presence because of his notoriety. But real, true friends.

He gave her hands a squeeze. "I would think that an honor."

She smiled and released his hands. "I'm only sorry you'll have such a long journey back to London." She began walking toward Samuel and his father where they waited in the yard as a hired coachman and tiger readied their carriage. Samuel was speaking to the coachman as Nathan handed up their bags for the tiger to secure them on top of the vehicle.

"It's all right," Cross said. "It gives me time to mull over some hypotheses I am hoping to test when I return."

"What sort of hypotheses?" She hadn't been aware of anything new he was working on since his misinterpreted weather discovery, and she knew Wickshire would want to hear about it.

But Cross only smiled. "It's just ideas for now, dear Penelope. It will be quite some time before I am able to pass you anything you can share with that rascally Wickshire."

She laughed, unable to contain her mirth at the idea of Wickshire as a rascal. Perhaps Cross perceived more than he let on.

"I will keep that in mind."

They had reached the waiting men just as Samuel finished his conversation with the coachman.

"We've only heard good things on the road from here to Edinburgh. Should be a speedy, uneventful trip." The coachman wiped his nose with a handkerchief and turned about with a wave toward the seat.

"Edinburgh?" Cross asked, passing a look between her and Samuel.

Samuel paused, his eyes traveling beyond Penelope to Nathan behind her.

"Yes, Edinburgh. Wickshire, rascal that he is, asked me to stop in on John Herschel while I was this far north. You know how fond he is of the Herschels, and he's most interested in the younger Herschel's work."

Cross shook his head, a frown creasing his brow. "Well, then I'm just glad I overhead the coachman. John Herschel isn't in Edinburgh. He left more than a week ago for Portsmouth. Found himself a place on a research vessel headed around the cape of Africa." Cross looked up at the sun as if to find answers lurking in the sky. "He's probably on board the ship by now."

Penelope darted a look at Samuel. "Are you certain?"

Cross nodded. "Quite. Mr. Herschel wrote to me to ask for more specifics on my discovery so that he may test the theory in the African climate. He wrote in his letter when he planned to leave and by when he required a response. Of course, I responded immediately, so my answer would reach him in time."

Samuel turned away but not before she saw frustration crease his features.

"Well, it appears Wickshire will just not be getting what he wants this time."

* * *

JESSIE CLEVER

THE CLOSER THEY got to London, the more his gut decided to clench.

The fact that Sir Devlin Cross had become their unexpected traveling companion did not help matters.

Once it was determined that their journey to Edinburgh would be fruitless, it was obvious they should return to London as quickly as possible. They had received no word from Wickshire since they had left more than a week ago, although the earl would likely not have been able to guess at where their travels would take them. Even if he had sent a letter, it would likely not have reached them as the weather had driven them so far off the main road from London.

And to actually have married in Gretna Green.

He regarded his wife who sat beside him, scribbling at her writing box as they bounced along. She had been scribbling quite madly since they'd left Gretna Green, but he couldn't bring himself to move his eyes to her pencil, to see what it was that so consumed her.

But as he'd watched her the past couple of days on the road, he began to understand more and more what it was going to be like having a novelist for a wife. She continued to wander off, but where at first, he had pursued her, stricken with fear for her safety, he now followed behind her, hoping she didn't injure another person in her curious explorations. When she set to bouts of scribbling, he merely watched. It was only on the second day that he realized he wished she would share some of her scribblings with him.

He hadn't expected to take an interest in his wife's work beyond his natural inclination to support her. He had been honest when he'd said there was nothing disagreeable about her chosen profession, but he wasn't exactly sure how it was he was to support her further. The fact that she wrote furiously across a writing box in a bouncing carriage suggested there was a certain level of manic to her habit. As if she couldn't stop the words from flowing.

It was odd to him. Foreign. But he thought it not unlike his drive early in his career when he had done all he could to influence the passing of the police bills in Parliament.

But thinking of his early career days had him thinking about that night. He glanced at Penelope again, thought about what she'd said. He had been young, that was true. But still. Her words had done much to convince him he may be making too much of the incident, but another part of him held steadfast to his conviction.

He had married her though. Penelope. It still seemed strange that she was his wife. Surely if his true father's blood ruled in his veins, he wouldn't have done the right thing. But then, he'd wanted to marry Penelope. Always had.

It was all of this and more which twisted his gut so mercilessly the closer they got to London.

Sir Cross was not a terrible traveling companion, he had to admit, but he didn't like the surreptitious glances he threw in his wife's direction. Penelope had relayed in some detail who the man was and his connection to Wickshire, but it still didn't let him settle. He got on well with his father though, and the two chatted amiably on different scientific subjects they found they had in common. Particularly those relating to agricultural discoveries. There was apparently something fascinating about the use of water to irrigate rotating fields of crops and how it could be reused if a proper system were put in place.

Samuel was sure Jane would find it marvelously interesting, but the topic did not prevent his mind from skittering back to the fact that they had failed to rescue the professor. His mind was happy to race down all the possible paths of what may have happened to the professor, but all paths inevitably led to the professor being either kidnapped or killed, neither of which he cared for.

And the more mired in the situation he got, the more Penelope noticed.

As the confines of the carriage and the nearness of their traveling companions precluded intimate conversation while on the road, Penelope cornered him when they stopped for what was likely their last night before reaching London.

"Something has you twisted about a maypole."

He hadn't even managed to set their bags down before she'd slid the bolt on their door and pinned him with an unwavering stare.

"What is it?"

She hadn't even given him time to address her first statement. He set the bags down at the end of the bed and turned to her.

"I'm worried about the professor."

"No, you're not." She studied him with narrowed eyes and had even put her fisted hands to her hips.

He smiled at the sight of her. "Has my wife already turned into a shrew?"

Her eyes widened at this as her mouth fell open. "Samuel Black—"

He caught her in a kiss before she could finish the sentence. She resisted for all of a second before her arms snaked around his neck, and she yanked him closer. He laughed at her impatience and tumbled them both back on the bed.

"And here I was worried about your performance on our wedding night."

Her words had him stilling. But the stilling was smaller now, more like a trip against the carpet than a fall down the stairs.

"Oh, no," she said, reaching up to frame his face in her

hands. "We've already discussed this, and you're not allowed to go back there."

He sat up, pulling out of her grasp as if peeling off a layer of himself. He raked a hand through his hair and scrubbed at his face. "It's not as easy as that."

She sat up beside him, took one of his hands into her own. "Sometimes it is."

Her voice was so soft, he looked at her, recalling his own words from their wedding night. It was warm, and a fire had not been lit. Only the light from the fading sun from the window beyond illuminated her face. She looked wonderful. For a woman employed in a genteel fashion, she had worn their tiring journey well. He wasn't surprised at all by this. Penelope would likely do anything well.

Including being a wife.

"I'm worried about what I've done to your reputation."

She either scoffed or gave an aborted laugh. "I'm sorry?"

"Cross was not factored into this. Neither was Mrs. Norton. None of this was. I can't control what gossip reaches London, and I fear I may have done more damage to your reputation than I ever meant."

She squeezed his hand. "You're being ridiculous. You married me. There's no harm done. To my reputation at least. I'm still concerned about yours."

"Mine?"

"You really think being married to a novelist will not affect your professional reputation. What about your affiliation with the House of Lords? I know you're quite respected in that circle. What if you're looking to have more legislation passed? What happens when they find out your wife is—"

A niggling began at the back of his mind, urging its way forward. "My wife is who?"

She looked about the room and out the window. Finally,

she looked quickly back at him, uttered—"Melanie Merkett."— and looked away again.

The words were so quickly said and so perfectly mumbled, he could hardly guess at what he'd heard.

"It sounded like you said you're Miss Melanie Merkett."

Her eyes flashed back to him. "I did say that."

The thing that had tripped inside of him before fell off a cliff. "I'm sorry?"

"I'm Miss Melanie Merkett."

She said it with such conviction it was almost as if she thought it were true. He shook his head. "You can't be Miss Merkett."

"I am, I'm afraid. But I did warn you that marrying me was ill advised. You proceeded to do just that. Not that I'm surprised such behavior would come from someone such as yourself."

"What does that mean?"

She blinked at him. "You always get what you want. Haven't you realized that?"

He shook his head, pulled his hand loose, and stood to pace. "What are you speaking of?"

She gestured as if to encompass all of England outside of their small room. "The entire Metropolitan Police Force. No one fought harder for that than you."

"I think that's an exaggeration."

"It is not." She stood, stopping him in his path. "Samuel Black, stop being a pig headed, stubborn man and for once, look at the world as it truly is. You're an accomplished detective inspector of the Metropolitan Police Force. You are seen as the son of a well-respected and well connected family of the ton. You've achieved so much. How can you only focus on the things in which you find fault?"

"I don't find fault in you even if you are Melanie Merkett."

She tried to hide a smirk from him and failed.

"Are you certain you're Melanie Merkett?" He thought about all the mad scribbling since they'd left Gretna Green.

"Oh yes, quite." She nodded at the door. "You can ask your father. He found me out from my publisher." She held up a hand before he could speak. "I shall be finding a new publisher when we return to London. One who practices a great deal more discretion."

He leaned in, resting his forehead against hers. "This is not how I wanted to do this, Pen." He slipped his hands up, caressing her neck, sinking the tips of his fingers into her hair. "This is not how I wanted to marry you."

"But it's how we're married never the less."

She was right. He could wish for something different all he wanted, but in the end they were still wed.

"What do you think will happen when we return to London? Do you think I'll be blacklisted by every matron in society?"

He laughed. "I'm not sure you'd care."

"You would be right." She tilted her head in his hands and laid a gentle kiss to his lips. "You must stop worrying. It does no good to plague yourself now before anything has happened."

"But so much has happened."

She pulled out of his arms. "I think you need a hot meal, and a good night of rest in something that isn't moving." She smiled at him. "You'll feel better in the morning."

"In the morning, you'll finally be able to meet my mother. I don't think I'll feel better then." At the stricken look at Penelope's face, he laughed. "Who is worrying now?"

CHAPTER 21

One must be careful not to apply character assumptions based on class, wealth, and hearsay to one's suspects.
From The Adventures of Miss Melanie Merkett, Private Inquisitor

"WATCH OUT BELOW!"

The cry came just before Samuel snatched her out of the way, tucking them both against the wall in the foyer of Lofton House. The house was large, ornate, and beautifully appointed. Samuel had informed her all of the Blacks made this their home when in town. She wondered just how many persons that entailed when the shout rang out through the space.

She looked up towards the source of the call when her eyes met the person in question but could not quite register what it was she was seeing. It was a lad, perhaps a bit older, a young man then, but the baggy costume of trousers and lawn shirt billowed around a slight frame suggestive of youth. The boy held a rapier aloft as he put a thigh to the balustrade and proceeded to slide down the length of it.

Penelope jumped, but Samuel's arms were fast around her as the lad dropped to his feet directly in front of them. With a valiant swish of the sword, he sheathed the weapon and most curiously, bowed. The lawn shirt, which was indeed much too big for his person, rippled like a sail as he tucked his arm to his chest.

"The prodigal son returns," the lad said, and it was only then that Penelope realized her mistake.

"You're a girl," she said before she could stop the words from spilling out.

The girl straightened, a wide smile splitting her face. "I am at that!" She put fisted hands to her hips, hips Penelope now realized were much too wide for a lad's. "I'm the troubling sister, Elizabeth. I apologize in advance for the amount of times Mum must yell at me in a given day. I am trying to reform, you see, but being me is just so terribly fun."

Penelope watched the girl, a smile rising unbidden to her lips. The girl, young woman, really, had Samuel's eyes and mouth. She looked between the two of them and was struck by the strength of resemblance. Did Samuel even look like the father that plagued him so? Penelope doubted it.

"Elizabeth!"

At the scold, Penelope looked down the hall, expecting to see the mum of whom Elizabeth had warned. In that second, she steeled herself, drawing in a tightening breath to square her shoulders. She was an accomplished woman with professional accolades to her name. She loved Samuel, and although her chosen profession would be a detriment to her son's career, Penelope was sworn to being as good a wife as possible. She had only to prove this to the mum.

But it wasn't the mum that walked down the hall to them. It was another young woman with Samuel's eyes. Wide eyes of a deep brown set over a thin, straight nose and small mouth. Fringe dangled in those eyes and obscured her features, and it was something about the timid way the woman walked with her arms full of ledgers that Penelope knew who this was.

"Elizabeth, are you trying to scare the poor woman? She hasn't even met Mother yet. She's likely to turn tail now before she's even had the chance."

While the young woman's words were tight with reproach, her expression was encouraging, as if she were providing an aid to her sister before the dreaded mother had time to scold the girl properly. But it wasn't the words that had Penelope pausing. It was how Samuel relaxed against Penelope at the appearance of this sister.

"Jane," he said, a smile evident in his voice although from her position under his arm, Penelope could not quite see his face. "You are all right? Nothing has transpired since I left."

The blush came hot and fast to Jane's face, spreading from every inch between that little mouth and that copious fringe. Penelope's eyes widened, and her fingers twitched compulsively. There was most definitely a story there, one she certainly wanted to discover.

Elizabeth gave a snort. "Nothing in the matter that you mean."

"Elizabeth!" Jane scolded again, pressing the ledgers more tightly against her chest as if they were a shield.

The door opened then, and Penelope's stomach knotted instantly. But it was only Nathan, slapping the road dust from his trousers as he shrugged out of his coat. He stopped at the tableau in the foyer and turned a frown to Elizabeth.

"What did you do?" he asked, his tone excessively fatherly but quite resigned as well.

Elizabeth smiled her wide smile. "Nothing," she said with an innocent shake of her head.

Nathan turned to Samuel. "You warned Penelope about this one, right?"

Samuel laughed. "I thought a warning would not do the matter justice."

"You're probably right." Nathan handed his coat to the footman waiting by the door and moved into the foyer to take the stack of ledgers from Jane. "You checked the accounts again? I thought you settled the discrepancy with the mills."

Jane shook her head as she handed the ledgers to her father, the blush seeping away from her face as if it never existed. "I'm still not satisfied with the rate of return on the shares. I think we should consider alternative investment options."

Penelope stared. Was Jane giving unsolicited business advice to her father? It was most unheard of for a lady to do such, but Jane appeared confident in her statement. In fact, she appeared the most relaxed since they had entered the house. Penelope's fingers twitched again.

"You're probably starving," Elizabeth said and grabbed Penelope by the elbow. "How about let's get some grub?"

Penelope stared down at this eccentric young lady who was now her little sister and smiled involuntarily. "I would love something to eat, Miss Black."

Elizabeth waved a hand at her. "The name is Lizzie. None of this Miss Black nonsense. I'll leave that to Jane." She tugged on Penelope's arm. "Let's off with you." The girl stopped and looked back at Samuel. "I can borrow your wife for an afternoon, right?"

Samuel smiled and gave a nod. "I was hoping you'd do just that. I must speak with Uncle Alec about Stryden Place."

Nathan paused in his perusal of the ledgers and looked up. "You're going to accept his offer then?"

Penelope's gaze ricocheted between the two men as

Samuel shuffled his feet, looked at his hands. "It seems most appropriate."

"The two of you," Jane said, shaking her head and stepping forward to take Penelope's hands in her own. She gave them a reassuring squeeze. "Speaking in riddles in front of poor Penelope when she's just suffered the introduction of Lizzie." Jane smiled, an expression that was all Nathan. "Stryden Place is the home of the son of the Duke of Lofton but as the son of the current duke is only fourteen years of age, the house has been sitting unoccupied. Uncle Alec has been asking Samuel for ages to take up residence there, but my stubborn brother insists on being a man of his own bearing. Ridiculous not to accept help from his family."

Penelope's gaze darted to Samuel, and a look passed between them. She could understand only too well why Samuel had never accepted the offer, and now she felt another pang of guilt at forcing his hand when it came to their unexpected marriage.

Lizzie punched her in the shoulder. "Come on. Let's have some food, and you can tell us all about your adventure."

Nathan frowned at his youngest daughter. "Jane," he said, the single word containing a good deal of annoyance.

Jane held up a placating hand. "I will ensure she does not get any ideas."

The door swept open at that very moment, and a gaggle of women spilled in, all talking at once. Hats, reticules, and shawls were discarded in a mad flop, but all conversation ceased as one of the women stepped forward, worry wrinkling her brow.

"What adventure?" she asked, her eyes sweeping the entire room with a single blow. "Elizabeth Sarah Black, if you so much—"

"Mum."

The word was softly spoken, but it might as well have

been a blast of icy cold water as the woman who so sternly degraded the occupants of the space before her calmed. She turned, and her entire face opened, her mouth seeping into a smile at the same time her eyes crinkled against tears.

"Samuel." The word was spoken much as the single word before it had been.

Samuel opened his arms, and his mother stepped into them. Penelope wished harder than ever that she had her writing box and a piece of blank paper at that moment. Never before had she witnessed such joy in a single gesture.

But then the woman pulled away, the domineering countenance returning to her features.

"What did you do?"

Samuel blushed. Penelope nearly made a noise of surprise as the redness sprang to his face. A grown man slayed by his mother. Outstanding.

The woman spun about and strode directly for her. Penelope squared her shoulders.

"Whatever Lizzie has done, I must apologize. We are all not heathens in this house." A stark line of concern speared the space between Mrs. Black's eyes.

Penelope had no response, and it needn't matter because just at that moment another cry erupted from the top of the stairs.

"Tally ho!"

"Oh God!" the three women still standing at the door cried in unison.

And then a chorus of names being yelled erupted at the same time a herd of floppy-eared, short-legged dogs stampeded down the stairwell.

"Michael! Maddie!"

"Eloise! Edwin!"

Penelope had no time to react. As soon as she spotted the waterfall of hound, Mrs. Black tugged her away as Lizzie stepped in front of her to block the impact. Nathan swept Jane away from the stairwell and together with Samuel they all pressed against the wall.

It was then that Penelope realized Mrs. Black whispered in her ear. "I assure you, my dear, we are all not this uncivilized. We are truly a wonderful family, and I hope you will be happy here."

The words were not at all what she had expected, and a tiny flame of hope sprang to life inside of her. The words although soft and nearly drowned out by the cacophony of mothers yelling at a corresponding herd of children that had appeared after the dogs reminded Penelope too much of her own mother. Tears pressed against her eyes, and a smile wobbled to her lips. Samuel and Nathan corralled the hounds as the other women addressed the children, sending them not off to their rooms as Penelope had expected but down to the kitchens to peel potatoes. What an odd punishment and yet decidedly more vexing than sitting around one's room.

When the uproar had ceased and the dogs had been cleared, the eldest of the women approached Penelope, a soft hand extended.

"It used to be I who delivered the most eyebrow raising introduction, but it seems I have handed down that accolade to my yawning brood."

Lady Jane. This must be Lady Jane. Penelope dropped into a hasty curtsy, but Lady Jane snatched at her hand, drawing her back up.

"Oh please, child. I am too old to stand on ceremony. I'm hoping you're famished from your journey, so I may indulge as well." The older woman carried a walking stick, which she used to tap against the balustrade. "Ladies, shall we retire to the library to get to know our newest member?"

The other two women who had yet to be introduced

smiled, tired but happy from their run-in with their apparent children and dogs.

Mrs. Black moved out from behind Penelope, an equally weary expression on her face.

"I am so sorry. After everything, that is how you're welcomed home." She shook her head. "I cannot begin to apologize. Once we've had a chance to sit down and discuss things, we'll see that everything is rectified." Again, she shook her head. "You didn't even have the chance to write your family. Will they be overly upset at what's happened?"

None of what the woman said made any sense to Penelope, but then she realized the poor woman didn't know anything of Penelope.

"I have no family," Penelope decided to say, and the answering look of despair on Mrs. Black's face had that tiny flame of hope erupting into a fire inside of her.

"Oh, child," Mrs. Black said, that line of concern appearing again. "You do now."

CHAPTER 22

*T*he hardest part of any case is waiting.
     From The Adventures of Miss Melanie Merkett,
Private Inquisitor

"TELL me the bit again where Samuel set you on fire."

She frowned at the Earl of Wickshire who was taking far too much glee in her recounting of the events of their journey north.

"He didn't set me on fire," she said. "He startled me, which caused me to set myself on fire."

"How very interesting," Wickshire muttered. "Go on. What happened next?" He leaned his head on his fist as he rested an elbow on the arm of the chair.

They sat in front of the hearth, dormant today, in the drawing room where they had discovered poor Bobby Egemont. The previous fortnight was a bit blurry to her. What with being wed unexpectedly and moving out of Wickshire Place to Stryden Place. It was helpful only to have to replace the name and not the entire epitaph.

But the rest.

The rest had not been helpful. But had not been precisely unbearable either. Just different.

After that tumultuous introduction to Lofton House and all of its occupants, Penelope was starting to ascertain her expectations of marriage were not at all in accordance with fact. So consumed had she been with the potentially fatal effects of her profession as a novelist, she had never considered the other parts of married life.

Her in-laws for example.

Although, she was fairly certain she could never have predicted them. Jane and Lizzie, and Nora and Nathan. Mum. Nora had asked her to call her Mum. She bit her lip as she recalled it. The indomitable mother. She had been so worried by the picture everyone painted of the woman that the reality of her had quite swept Penelope away. She was not domineering and foreboding. She was resilient and strong. Marvelous. Inspiring.

Lady Jane.

What words to use for Lady Jane? She was...unreal. Simply unreal, and Penelope only feared having not enough time with her.

The afternoon of their introduction the women had just returned from an organized meeting on the subject of labor rights for domestics.

Penelope's fingers twitched at the thought. Labor rights. For domestics. And Nathan. Hardly the dominating husband disappointed in his wife's actions had asked her how the meeting had gone and if she were hopeful for the outcomes. He had even offered his assistance in speaking with some members of Parliament.

Penelope could not fathom it.

Samuel had disappeared almost immediately to seek out this Uncle Alec that she had yet to encounter. Stryden Place had been opened and staffed at once. Well, staffed after Penelope herself had given her recommendations on the character of the applicants for the positions. Samuel hadn't even bothered to question her methods. He had simply handed the matter over to her and gone off to the police commission.

They had fallen into a sort of routine in the past few days after all of her things had been moved to Stryden Place. She hadn't brought much with her, but the house was fully furnished. She'd spent more hours than she cared to admit just wandering the sumptuous townhouse. There were four drawing rooms, a sewing room, and a billiards room. There was a library which was different than the study which was different from the earl's office. There was a breakfast room and a dining room and a tea room. What was she going to do with the tea room? She still hadn't figured out this bit.

Did the wives of police inspectors host teas?

Such entertaining was going to require a serious consideration of her wardrobe. She would need to entail the help of Samuel's Aunt Sarah, for certain.

Aunt Sarah had been one of the women who had returned that afternoon with Nora. Mum, that is. Aunt Sarah and someone else known as Lady Maggie. The hounds, Penelope learned, were the fault of Lady Maggie. The entire web of the Black family was slowly unraveling for her, but it was still quite a complicated mess.

A wonderful, loving, happy mess.

"You've heard that part already," she said to Wickshire now.

He frowned and waved a hand at her. "I know, but I wish to hear it again. It's just so fascinating."

"It is not. I could have been seriously injured."

"But you weren't, and now you have great fodder for your books." Wickshire paused, concern darkening his face. "You will keep writing, won't you? Now that..."

He didn't finish the sentence. He didn't need to.

Penelope shook her head. "We haven't discussed it really. Not explicitly." She thought of the few minutes she and Samuel had had together since returning to London. Those encounters did not include a lot of talking by nature. There were a lot of other noises made, but not really distinguishable words. Her face heated at the thought.

But there had been other things that had taken up their time. Opening the house. Adjusting to their new staff courtesy of the Duke of Lofton.

And poor Bobby Egemont.

They had met with Wickshire the day after they'd returned to London only to discover Wickshire had netted about as much useful information as they had.

Whoever was after the professor and whoever had killed Bobby Egemont had run to ground. Wickshire had met with nothing but dead ends in his inquiries while they had failed to find the professor entirely. Samuel had attempted to confirm Herschel's presence in Portsmouth, but even those reports had proved unreliable. That left them with no professor and no suspect. Leaving the murder of Bobby Egemont unresolved irked Samuel. Penelope could tell in the way he avoided speaking of the matter. But there was something else that was bothering Samuel. Something that left a lingering taste of tension hiding among the domestic bliss of their newly settled married life.

"Samuel professes to be supportive of my career, but I'm not sure how much of that is speak and how much is true."

Wickshire pushed at the sleeves of his shirt, which he had already rolled to his elbows. His waistcoat and cravat had long been discarded. "If I know the Black family, and I think I do know them well enough, I would say young Samuel will be true to his word and support you in your endeavors." He gestured with a hand. "When is your next story due to your publisher?"

It was Penelope's turn to frown now. "That's another thing. It seems I have need of a new publisher. One who practices a great deal more discretion."

Wickshire's eyebrows rose up. "Is that so?"

Penelope nodded. "Mr. Black, Samuel's father, discovered my secret before I had a moment to tell Samuel."

"Had a moment to tell him or the courage to tell him?"

She did not honor that with a response. "As I am now his wife and if I should continue my writing, I will need a publisher who is appreciative of my need for secrecy."

"Or you could just come out with it. Secrets only hold power if we let them. If you just come out as Miss Melanie Merkett, you no longer have need to worry."

"But that would indubitably damage Samuel's reputation."

"Will it?" Wickshire leaned forward. "Tell me, have you met Miss Elizabeth Black? Commonly known as Lizzie?"

Penelope straightened. "Have you met her?"

Wickshire scoffed. "Met her. Darling, I've sparred with her. The girl has a good arm. I think with a sister like that, Samuel would have no worry over a novelist for a wife. It may even lend some credence to the Black family name."

She pondered that for a moment. "Still, a wife for a novelist seems just a bit too risqué."

"That's what the duke is for. As the nephew of the Duke of Lofton, Samuel need worry about very little. The Duke of Lofton title carries a mighty weight of prestige."

"But wouldn't my profession incur a toll on that title?"

"You give yourself too much credit."

They lapsed into silence then, each contemplating the remnants of the tea that sat between them.

Finally, Wickshire spoke. "Is there anything else that is

troubling you, dear? More than your husband's position in regards to your professional acumen?"

Penelope opened her mouth to reassure him that everything was fine, but she shut it almost immediately. Other than Wickshire, Lady Delia was Penelope's only other confidante. She thought that would likely change as her relationship with Samuel's sisters grew but as this pertained to Samuel, she thought it was likely not a good topic of conversation for those sisters.

So she said, "Samuel is ignoring the invitations we have received since we returned."

"Invitations?"

"To teas and balls and dinners. We've received more than half a dozen. It could be ascertained that our marriage has been accepted by the ton or that it's terribly curious of it and wishes to observe it for itself. Regardless, I have several invitations to which I have not responded because Samuel will not talk about them."

"How odd. Does he not care for the social aspects of the season? As a detective inspector, I would think he would understand the need for social integration."

She shook her head. "It's not that, I'm afraid. It's more—" She didn't know how to word this. "It's more that I think Samuel is afraid to witness the damage he may have wrought to my own reputation."

"Your reputation?" Wickshire laughed. "What could he have possibly done to your reputation?"

Although Penelope knew exactly the things Samuel could imagine he had done to her, it wasn't her secret to share with Wickshire. So instead, she said, "He believes by eloping to Gretna Green he has irrevocably ruined me for polite society. He thinks I shall be snubbed at every turn."

Wickshire leaned his elbows on his knees, a smirk coming to his lips. "Penelope, dear, I will tell you what to do with those invitations. You respond to each one in the affirmative, and you advise your husband of your social commitments as a wedded couple." He held up a finger before she could protest. "You of all people should know the ton enjoys a good story." His smirk dissolved into a daring smile. "Give them one."

Before Penelope could respond, Mrs. Watson appeared in the doorway.

"I beg your pardon, my lord. A young woman has turned up at the door. She says Miss Penelope Paiget sent her."

Penelope stood and turned to Mrs. Watson, her fingers twitching against her gown. "Does she have a young girl with her?"

Mrs. Watson pursed her lips. "It would appear so."

A smile came to Penelope's lips. "Please show her in."

"Is this another piece of your adventure?" Wickshire stood next to her now.

"A most important piece."

When Mrs. Norton and her daughter appeared in the drawing room, Penelope felt a rush of ease sweep over her. She stepped forward, taking the woman's hands into her own. "You've come," she said. "I'm sure the journey must not have been easy. Physically or emotionally. But you are welcome." She bent to the little girl. "And it just so happens I know several young ones who would love to have your company, Miss—" She waited, hoping Mrs. Norton would give the child's name.

Her voice was soft and hesitant, but finally Mrs. Norton said, "Emma. Her name is Emma."

Penelope smiled. "What a beautiful name."

The little girl hid in her mother's skirts but not before Penelope saw her small smile.

Penelope straightened. "Mrs. Norton, it seems I misinformed you. I shall have need of your assistance at Stryden

Place. I hope you don't mind being a housekeeper. I should like to employ someone with whom I hold a measure of trust."

The woman's care worn face opened at her words. "I shan't mind at all, miss."

Penelope's face heated. "It's missus, actually." And then hurried on to— "For real this time."

Mrs. Norton raised an eyebrow but said nothing, the tell-tale sign of a good housekeeper.

* * *

"I don't like it."

Samuel spiked his fingers through his hair before putting his palms to his desk, leaning in as he glared at the Marquess of Evanshire, who stood on the other side of his desk at the police commission.

"I don't like the silence."

Evanshire regarded him with a nonplussed look. "I'm sorry it's not something different. If the fiend had made a move while you were absent, it would have been my pleasure to apprehend him. You know that, Samuel. But as it is, all is well and quiet. I don't like it any more than you do."

After two near kidnappings before he left London, Samuel found the resulting inactivity glaringly upsetting. Someone was testing the barriers of the Black family now that Richard Black, the previous Duke of Lofton, and Samuel's grandfather had died. It had been more than a month since the funeral now, and while the two near kidnappings had happened almost on top of each other, nothing had happened since. It was almost as if their test had proved something, and the culprits had gone to ground to recoup their offensive.

Samuel sat in his desk chair and put his head back. He was missing something. He knew it.

"And you were with Lady Black the entire time she was in public?"

Evanshire nodded. "Unfortunately. Your cousin has a spectacular ability to make one uncomfortable."

Samuel thought about his cousin, the daughter of the now Duke of Lofton, his uncle Alec. Emily Black had a personality that only lent itself to certain tastes. Evanshire's was not one of them.

"Any ideas on how we proceed?"

Evanshire gave a deprecating laugh. "How do we trace a man who has only used hired thugs to do his bidding through a third-party administrator?" He laughed again, his lips twisting into a cold smile. "Whoever this is, he's experienced in avoiding detection. It's almost as if he's made a profession of it."

Samuel sat up. "Are you suggesting he's a professional?"

Evanshire shrugged, tossing his hat between his hands. "A professional what would be the question. Who makes a career out of avoiding detection?"

"Spies." The word hung between them as if it were a guillotine, set ready to chop their heads off.

Samuel's mind thought back to his grandfather, the famed spy for the War Office. He stood.

"We need to find out the names of every person in attendance at my grandfather's funeral."

Evanshire stopped tossing about his hat. "You think this is someone your grandfather routed out in his work?"

Samuel shook his head. "We don't know anything yet, but I think you're right. This is someone who has played a game of deceit before and has a questionable level of skill at it. We need to proceed carefully. Once we've determined who was in attendance, I want to do a cross check against any of my grandfather's known enemies."

"This sounds like something from a Melanie Merkett novel."

Although the words were spoken casually, they rendered Samuel motionless.

"Melanie Merkett?" he finally asked. "You read those novels."

Evanshire shrugged with a sideways smile. "Everyone reads those novels."

Samuel closed his eyes only to re-open them as his office door opened after a short rap.

One of the commission's lads popped in, a paper extended in his fingers. "Message for you, Inspector. It's from yer lady wife." The lad gave a cheeky grin before scampering back out.

Samuel picked up the letter from where the boy had tossed it on his desk. The note was short, brief, and cuttingly to the point.

"It appears my lady wife has accepted an invitation to Lady Southington's ball." He looked up at Evanshire. "It's this evening."

Evanshire pulled out his pocket watch and regarded the time. "Then you'd better get a move on, chap." He tucked his watch back into his waistcoat and gave Samuel an encouraging smile. "Come on, old boy. It's the season, as they say. You'll be obligated to attend such functions now. At least, I'll have someone to converse with of an appropriate intelligence."

Samuel eyed him. "You attend these things?"

"The curse of a marquess, I'm afraid."

Samuel shuddered. "No, thank you."

Evanshire shrugged and placed his hat on his head. "It's

your curse now as well, Inspector Black." He gave a mock bow. "I'll see you this evening, chap."

* * *

"PLEASE DON'T PRETEND to be enjoying this just for me."

Her sarcasm was met with a glare from her husband as he led her into Lady Southington's ballroom. Penelope had been quite surprised when her response to Lady Southington's invitation in the affirmative had received a response of its own. Lady Southington had written to express her keen joy that Mr. and Mrs. Black would be making their first society appearance at her ball that evening.

Wickshire was right. The ton did enjoy a good story.

Penelope had attended many balls as Lady Delia's companion and was not at all affected by the crush that greeted them in the ballroom, but it appeared Samuel was. He tensed under her hand, his gaze darting about the room.

"Are you all right?" she whispered.

"I'm noting all possible exits."

She frowned. "I'll leave you home from now on then."

"Don't threaten me with a good time, Pen."

She ignored this as he brought her to the edge of the ballroom where Jane stood. Penelope unlatched herself immediately from her husband at the stricken look on Jane's face.

"What is it?" Penelope asked, taking the other woman's hands into her own.

"Nothing." The word conveyed one meaning while its tremulous nature suggested another.

Jane was young, perhaps seven and ten. Penelope squeezed the girl's hands. "Is this your first season, Jane?"

Jane's eyes, which had been lingering somewhere over Penelope's shoulder, zeroed in on her. "How did you know?"

Penelope frowned. "It's rather obvious, my dear." She

272

patted Jane's hands, and then drew her arm through her own. "I assure you it's not as terrifying as it appears."

Jane shook her head. "My father had promised we'd skip this year. What with Grandfather's death and all." Jane's voice had tripped on the word grandfather.

Penelope peered over at her husband, but he only shook his head. She squeezed Jane's arm. "Well, consider the positives. You'll get the first year over and done with. That's always the best way to start an unpleasant task. Simply jump right into it."

Jane shook her head. "It's not that. I've already selected a husband, you see. A very practical match. The son of a—" The girl nearly swallowed her tongue.

Penelope stared in fascination as heat flooded Jane's face. Penelope turned her head about and encountered the most extraordinary man emerging from the crowd toward them.

"Black!" the man called, raising a hand in greeting.

Penelope looked at her husband. Back at the man. Back at poor Jane. The girl was going to burst into flame at any moment. Penelope snatched her arm out from under Jane's and prodded the girl in the back to stand up straight and accentuate her good features. While the girl was somewhat timid and rather thin, she had a quick mind and excellent judgement. She must put that first if her reaction to this man betrayed feelings she was obviously trying to squelch.

Practical match. Ha. Penelope knew a good story when she saw one.

She smiled as Samuel introduced her to the Marquess of Evanshire. She couldn't help an eyebrow from popping up.

A marquess. She regarded poor Jane, still simpering on the side of the ballroom. The girl could do a lot worse considering she was the daughter of the bastard son of a duke.

She turned back to the marquess to exchange the usual

pleasantries when their little tete a tete was shattered with a shrill— "Evanshire!"

Samuel turned, his jaw clenching as if he recognized the voice when a girl, surely she was not of age, pranced into their circle, her mop of blonde curls swinging about her face.

"It's been so long!" the girl cried, tripping into a curtsy that displayed an enormously developed bosom for such a young thing.

Before the girl had risen, a man stepped from the crowd behind her, grabbing her arm and pulling her to her feet. Penelope stilled. If she hadn't known better, she would say this man was Samuel's father, the resemblance to Nathan was so striking.

"Emily. You forget yourself." The man's voice was tight and his features tighter.

"Father," the girl whimpered, sticking out a fat lower lip.

Aunt Sarah emerged seconds later, blowing an escaped tendril of blonde hair out of her face. She grabbed this Emily's other arm.

"Evanshire," she said with a weak smile. "What a pleasure to see you again." Aunt Sarah took hold of Emily's arm with a great grip and gave a good yank, popping her out of the other man's grasp. Sarah's smile turned from weak to simply gritted teeth as she took command of her wayward daughter.

Uncle Alec.

The famed Uncle Alec of whom she had heard much but had not yet met. As if hearing her thoughts, he turned a smile on her.

"You must be the newest Mrs. Black." He frowned. "I'm very sorry for that. You could have done much better than this idiot." He gestured to Samuel.

"I can only assume she and Aunt Sarah will have a lot in common," Samuel replied.

Alec gave a great laugh and thumped Samuel on the back.

"That we can both be assured." He stepped forward and bowed in front of Penelope. "Pleased to make your acquaintance, Mrs. Black."

She curtsied. "Likewise. And I must thank you for your hospitality. The house is lovely and—"

Alec cut her off with a wave of his hand. "Think nothing of it. I had nearly forgotten about the place entirely. It is you who does me a favor in no longer having to worry over it."

"Would you please excuse us?" Aunt Sarah asked to no one in particular. "It seems Emily and I require the retiring room."

"Mother—eek!" Sarah yanked the girl away before she could say more.

Alec shook his head. "I'm sorry about that, Evanshire. We were most adamant about keeping Emily out of society for one more year, but then when Jane stepped up to take her season...." He looked at quiet, little Jane as if the fate of the world rested on her shoulders. He shrugged. "Well, we hoped her calm countenance would have an encouraging influence on Emily." Again, a shrug. "One can wish and one can hope, but in the end, things will be how they'll be." He crossed his arms over his chest. "Any developments in the, eh, kidnapping thing?"

Penelope stared at how casually he addressed the potentially perilous situation involving his daughter and niece, a situation she had only gleaned herself.

Evanshire shook his head. "I'm afraid we haven't. The trail's gone cold."

Alec looked at Samuel. "Same as that thing with the professor?"

Samuel nodded. "We're in odd times, it seems."

"Odd, indeed." Alec rubbed a hand against his chin. "God, how I miss the old days sometimes. Do you know what I did today? I contemplated the merits of labor rights for domestics." He shook a single finger in the air. "I have your mother to blame for this one." He thought a moment. "And my wife, I suppose. And Lady Maggie." He shook his head as he developed an ominous frown. "How did we get tangled up with such women? God save us from their intellects." His tone was so humorous Penelope could not stop the laugh that bubbled up inside her. Alec regarded her with a cutting glance. "Don't you start," he said and leaned in, lowering his voice so only she could hear. "Samuel has told us your dirty secret, Miss Merkett. Don't think we're going to like you any better because you apply your intellect to ink and pages."

Penelope stopped laughing, but then the blasted man winked at her. The laugh came again with a skittering ripple. And lud, Samuel smiled at her. For the first time since their unexpected wedding, he truly and deeply smiled at her as if he'd suspected what his uncle had whispered to her.

This could not be happening. This life. This happiness. Marriage was supposed to mean imminent doom. And here, her family, her new family, were making light of her profession. But really, a novelist was a far cry from women who advocated labor rights. Perhaps she was not the danger she had perceived herself to be.

"Crawley, my good man!" Alec had turned about as another man approached.

Penelope surveyed him. He was tall and rather plain. Sunken in the cheeks and eyes as though undernourished. She thought he'd fall over with a strong breeze or perhaps faint away in a dead sleep of boredom. His eyes were devoid of any light, and his expression was nothing in particular. Straight features and straight countenance. Terribly dull, really.

But Alec seemed to take an interest in him.

"Crawley, have you met the new Mrs. Black?"

Penelope dipped a crusty to Crawley's bow. "Penelope,

dear, Lord Crawley has the dubious honor of having worked with the Blacks in our more officious matters in years past." Alec slapped Crawley on the back much as he'd done to Samuel, but where Samuel had enjoyed the display of masculine approval, Crawley twitched an eyebrow at it.

"Mrs. Black," he said, and his voice was equally as sleepy as his appearance. "It's a pleasure. Your uncle is correct. I have spent a great deal of time in service with the Blacks. It is an honor to make your acquaintance."

"The feeling is mutual, Lord Crawley." Although she knew the Blacks had a legacy of spies, she didn't know how deep the legacy ran or what this Lord Crawley's involvement was. Her fingers twitched in anticipation only to be rewarded with Crawley's next statement.

"Would you do me the honor of a dance, Mrs. Black?"

While she firmly believed a dance may kill the man, it would also provide her with an opportunity for investigating. She cast a glance at Samuel and was surprised to find he watched Lord Crawley with a certain degree of intensity.

"Yes, of course," she replied, but her gaze didn't leave Samuel as Lord Crawley took her hand.

The dance was a waltz, and a part of her thrilled at the opportunity for conversation such a dance would allow. But as Lord Crawley turned her about for the first time, her gaze caught Samuel's again, and a thrill of wariness crept up her spine.

Her husband watched her. Not with jealousy. Not with annoyance. No. He watched her like an inspector would watch a suspect. He watched her with deliberate calculation, but she knew his mind saw something else. And whatever else it was, it was dangerous.

CHAPTER 23

*O*ne most always record one's findings. It is a sign of inexperience to rely on something so traitorous as one's memory.

From The Adventures of Miss Melanie Merkett, Private Inquisitor

"WHAT ARE YOU DOING?"

Penelope jumped as he caught her closing the door on the room she often frequented since they'd moved into Stryden Place. He couldn't remember if it was the library or the study. It faced the back of the house, overlooking the gardens and the mews beyond. It wasn't exactly an exotic location in the house, but he knew why Penelope would find it attractive. It was the perfect room if one were trying to hide something.

They had fallen into a pattern over the past several weeks. They rose early, breakfasted together, and then he went to the police commission while Pen did God only knew what. Their investigation into the missing professor had stalled, and he'd been forced to file a report on the murder of Bobby Egemont as an unsolved case. Lady Pemberly had notified the War Office of the matter as the case contained too many clues that pointed to treason or at the least, a mercenary venture, but Lord Crawley had deemed the evidence insufficient. Samuel couldn't fault the man that. It *was* insufficient. The matter plagued Samuel like no other case had in his years on the Metropolitan Police Force.

His inquiries into the attendants at his grandfather's funeral had proved a dead end as well. There was no one on the record who didn't have a past of which any pope would be envious. Evanshire persisted in the effort, though, maintaining his careful surveillance of Lady Emily, but Samuel had a suspicion is was really an excuse to see Jane. He would need to address that matter at some point. His sister was out, for certain, but she was still young, and the instinctive urge to protect her roared up at the sight of Evanshire within speaking distance of her.

But for now, he had his wife to contend with.

She straightened after realizing who it was, and she smiled, stepping forward as she coyly put her hands behind her back and tilted her head at him, a coquettish smile on her lips.

"Why, Mr. Black, you gave me a fright."

She stepped close enough for him to wrap his arms around her, but instead of pulling her close, he seized her wrists and pulled her arms in front of her for his examination. Ink stained her fingertips, palms, and even the cuffs of her gown. He met her gaze.

"Up to no good, Miss Merkett?"

She started at his accusation, and then likely saw the smirk he was desperately trying to hide because she yanked her hands free, fisting them at her hips.

"Samuel Black, you know very well—"

"That I married a novelist. I do indeed."

She studied him. "What are you doing home?"

He felt a flare of something at her use of the word home, and it was odd to think that he had come to think of Stryden Place as such. Until very recently, it had always just been another residence in the Lofton clutch, and as a child, it was his Uncle Alec and Aunt Sarah's home. He'd come here on holidays from school to play with his young cousins. Ashley more so than Emily if he were honest. But now it was his home.

Home.

And he found himself smiling at his wife.

"What is it?" she whispered when he'd clearly been smiling for too long.

He shook his head. "Nothing." And then he recalled her question. "I am home, lady wife, because I believe you mentioned an unsavory affair we must attend this evening."

She blinked at him. "Oh, lud, I'd forgotten. What time is it? Are we late?" She looked about her as if a clock were readily available.

"It's only half six. You've plenty of time to dress before we must be underway."

While Stryden Place had become home, the more social aspects of their marriage had not settled so easily with him. Penelope had taken it in stride with alarming alacrity to receive and respond to the invitations that had started flowing into the house upon their taking residence, and she had developed a keen ability to manage all of their social obligations. All obligations which he steadfastly wished they could ignore. But just as she'd been right about so much, she was right in her deductions of their social position.

In the span of several weeks, he'd made more connections than he'd ever hoped to make. Connections that would likely aid him in expanding the police force, strengthening its power, and protecting the citizens of London. It was as if Penelope knew exactly the people whom he should meet and where they would be.

It was likely a talent she had developed as the secretary to a man who thrived on connections to aid him in his academic endeavors. But while he appreciated it, he didn't like it. Ever since their return to London he had been waiting for the inevitable crash. The moment when society would realize what he'd done. Done to Penelope. Eloped with her. Married her. Ruined her. But with every ball, soiree, dinner, and tea, nothing happened. The matrons of society welcomed them with a smile and a wink. Yet the dread continued to pool in his stomach.

Tonight was no exception.

The situation was further exacerbated by the fact that tonight's ball was to be a masquerade. It was the annual Brownlow affair that marked the end of the season before all of God's people fled the heat and filth of London to pass a quiet, tranquil summer at their country estates. He could remember his grandmother and grandfather attending the ball years before, and then his aunt and uncle, and then surprisingly, his own mother and father. Everyone went to the Brownlow ball. Everyone. The illusion of the masquerade allowed those of a more questionable social standing to mix with those of impeccable breeding.

He hated the thing.

As a police inspector, all he saw was a field ripe for debauchery. Pickpocketing. Outright theft. Excessive alcohol consumption. Not to speak of the sexual escapades that left debutantes ruined and marriages in shambles. But as it was the landmark event to cap off a season where everyone sought to be seen, everyone attended for one last bit of frivolity before retiring to the country.

The Brownlows' massive estate sat on the other side of

Piccadilly. A sprawling affair, it was constructed in the Egyptian style so popular at the turn of the century, and its twisting and turning structure encouraged such misbehaviors as ran rampant at the ball.

And now Samuel was to escort his wife there.

His very impressionable, curious wife.

"You'd like to say something, wouldn't you?"

He started at the question. At his wife's ability to guess at his mood.

"I'd like to lay some ground rules for this evening, but I know you will only balk at them."

She laughed. "Ah, my husband, the police inspector." She stepped forward and slid into his arms. "Always looking to protect the lives of London citizens."

"I'd settle for just protecting yours."

She pulled back to look up at him. "And hasn't that always been the problem?"

He felt the thing inside of him twist guiltily at her words, and he set her aside. "I believe I am getting better at it."

"And I believe you are avoiding the situation by immersing yourself in work and avoiding social encounters that would draw attention to the utter lack of ruination I have suffered at your hands."

He began to reply when he stopped at the confident twist of her lips. "I was not the only one to enter this marriage with a certain misgiving. You seem to have lost yours somewhere."

She shook her head. "I haven't lost it," she said. "I simply acquired support in the matter."

He frowned. "Is it my sisters or my mother?"

"Your aunt actually," she said and stepped around him to proceed down the hall to their bedchamber. "Did you know she taught me how to fire a pistol?" She looked over her shoulder. "A real firearm. It was marvelous."

He groaned before he could stop himself, and she laughed.

"It's really not all that serious, is it?"

He closed the door behind him and snatched his wife into his arms eliciting a squeak of surprise from her. "It is very serious indeed. And I believe you should be reprimanded for it."

"Reprimanded?" She cocked an eyebrow. "And just what do you believe should be my punishment?"

He eyed the bed beside them, and she giggled. "I can think of one or two things that might be appropriate."

"I think you lied to me, Mr. Black."

"How so?"

She pulled out of his arms and backed up to the bed until she could sit, leaning back on her elbows in a seductive sprawl. "I think you came home early for entirely selfish reasons."

He smiled. "There's only one way for us to find out."

* * *

WHEN THEY ARRIVED at the ball, Penelope had but one question.

Would anyone notice if she took her notebook out of her reticule?

Of course, she had brought a reticule. She never left the house unprepared. The small leather-bound book always came with her. Along with two sharpened pencils in case one broke. One could never be too careful.

But could she find a quiet corner to take notes in all the bustle?

Sarah and Nora had warned her of the Brownlows' estate off Piccadilly. The house itself was massive and ornate bordering on the ostentatious. The Egyptian motif was strong in coloring and design, and the halls and rooms through which they filtered took on a catacomb-like feel. She clutched at Samuel's arm lest she get lost.

Finally they emerged into a grand ballroom, lit from above in a glittering cascade of chandeliers. Mirrors reflected the light and the scene of the dancers below. She stopped involuntarily to stare up at the scene. A kaleidoscope of color and movement. She adjusted her mask to see better. In the reflection, she could make out the orchestra at the very far end of the room. They were costumed as well. She gave a small laugh as she realized they were dressed as American dandies in red, white and blue.

A footman swept in front of her, drawing her attention back down to the crush around them. The servant was costumed as well, in a mock representation of knight's armor. She couldn't keep up with the varying themes, and that was likely the point. Dizzying distraction. She laughed and squeezed Samuel's arm.

He regarded her with less than enthusiasm.

"Oh, bother," she said. "You police types just do not know how to enjoy yourselves."

He leaned down and pressed his lips to her ear. "I'll enjoy myself when I get you back home."

A thrill shot through her at the words as she recalled why it was it had taken her so long to dress for the evening. Her husband was terribly distracting and left absolutely no time to transcribe her notes. She tightened her grip on her reticule. She really needed to find that quiet corner.

But there wasn't a single one to be found in the entire room. They were pressed to the side as the crowd shifted around them, and then almost miraculously a familiar face appeared.

"Jane!" Penelope called through the noise, and a look of utter relief appeared on Jane's face.

Jane's costume was a simple rendition of Athena, allowing her face to remain free except for the edges of her helmet which encroached at her cheek and brow.

"Jane, you look lovely."

Jane did not appear confident in Penelope's assessment as her eyes darted about her, and her hands pressed against her stomach. "I feel rather silly."

Penelope shook her head. "Nonsense. Everyone is allowed to be silly once in a while. I think that's the point of the evening."

Jane shook her head now. "Silly has a rather uncomfortable fit on me."

"Jane, are Mum and Father here?"

Jane looked up as if only then realizing that Samuel stood behind Penelope.

"Why aren't you wearing a mask?" she asked without hesitation.

Penelope regarded her husband with resignation. She had asked him the same question at least a dozen times before they had departed Stryden Place, but he had adamantly refused to wear one on principle.

"Police inspectors do not wear costumes," he said just as he had every time she'd asked.

"That's utter nonsense. If I must wear a costume, so must you."

Penelope stifled a laugh at the very thing she had said to her husband. She liked her new sister-in-law a great deal just then.

"I must not. Is Father here?"

Jane frowned. "He's somewhere with Mum. I think Peel wanted a word with him."

Samuel raised an eyebrow, but Penelope cut him to speech. "Peel, as in Sir Robert Peel?"

Jane nodded. "He'd like Father's support, I think. He's likely to be Prime Minister, you know."

"I do enjoy a woman who is keen of the world around her."

Jane squeaked, quite undoing the confidence she had displayed only moments before as the Marquess of Evanshire joined their group. He, too, was dressed in the Greek style with little covering his face except the wisps of a gray wig.

"Oh God," Jane muttered much too loudly, and the marquess had the decency to look away and engage Samuel while Jane recovered herself.

Penelope tucked her arm through Jane's and pulled her sister-in-law against her for support.

"He's dressed as Hephaestus, isn't he?" Penelope whispered in Jane's ear.

Jane mumbled something that sounded like agreement as she panted, obviously struggling to regain normal breathing.

"Isn't he said to be the soulmate of Athena?" Penelope couldn't help herself. The poor girl truly needed to gain her feet, and she would not do so if she ran at every challenge.

More mumbling that may have been agreement.

They were all saved by the appearance of Sarah and a far too effervescent Lady Emily. Lady Emily because that is how she'd asked Penelope to address her. She was the only one of the Black family that did not sit well with Penelope.

Stepping back imperceptibly, Penelope withdrew her notebook from her bag while the rest of their group exchanged pleasantries. She had just pulled a pencil free when someone jostled her from behind. The pencil slipped, and the lead point streaked across her white elbow-length glove. The black mark it left behind marred the surface, and she muttered an oath at the clumsy fool who had bumped her. To be fair though, the room was quite crowded, and how could anyone know that she'd been trying to take notes on the affair?

She touched Samuel's shoulder.

"It seems I have need of the retiring room. I'll be back in a moment," she said when he leaned down to her.

He seized her arm before she turned away. "I don't want you wandering around here by yourself."

She smiled, but she knew better than to undermine his concern. She knew Samuel honestly believed her to be in danger at every turn, and if she disregarded his concern, it would only be disrespectful. "I promise to be careful, and I will only go directly to the retiring room and back." She smiled harder when he didn't speak. "I promise."

Something flashed across his eyes, but then his grip loosened. "There and back directly?"

She squeezed his arm and nodded in reassurance. He let her go, and she moved to the corridor where she thought the retiring room likely was. She realized quite quickly enough that she had been overly confident in assuming there was a direct path to the retiring rooms. In the monstrosity of the Brownlow estate, she couldn't be really sure anything had a direct path.

She rounded a corner and then another until she was in a corridor lit only with interspersed torches. Torches being the appropriate word as they really were torches. The walls of the corridors were presented in the manner of tomb walls with jutting columns and geometric designs in turquoise and yellow. She stopped and stared at the architectural details, her fingers twitching madly.

She roused herself and pressed on, promising to return and take copious notes as soon as she attempted to clean the pencil mark from her glove. She had only gone a few feet when she heard the first footstep.

It was subtle, almost masked, as though the person did

not wish to be heard. She did not falter in her step but kept her stride keen and sure, her ears alert for any sound.

The swish of clothing came next. The tell-tale sign of trouser pants brushing one against the other. She slowed her step, decreasing her pace as her eyes darted from side to side, searching for an escape. Her heartbeat had increased its pace, but she resolutely kept her breathing normal. If she had to run, she would need the air in which to do it.

For a moment, she considered herself absurd. She didn't know if she were truly being followed or if it were only another lost guest. She was likely being silly. And this would also assume whoever it was had recognized her behind her own mask. Samuel had raised an eyebrow at her costume, but when she had returned his stare with one of her own, he'd backed down. She wore trousers under the split skirt of her dress, and a jaunty hat pinned to her head. The costume was quite like the one she'd imagined for her adventurer, Miss Melanie Merkett. For surely, a private inquisitor would have need of movement and ease. As she listened to the footsteps following her, she was glad of her costume decision.

She rounded another corner and found herself in a passageway bordered by a row of glass-paneled doors that looked out onto a garden of sorts. Moonlight spilled through the windows in a rush, and the sudden brightness had her faltering. She reached out a hand to right herself, and her fingers met cloth.

She retracted, but it was too late. Her pursuer gripped her wrist and tugged, swinging her about until she was pinned to the wall, his hand at her neck, thrusting her head back.

She smelled sweat and fear and alcohol. His grip on her throat restricted air, and she moved her mouth like a fish out of water, gasping for any oxygen she could draw in.

"Where is the professor?" He spit the words at her, dampness disgustingly striking her face. She balked at the invasion, but she couldn't move her head.

Her hands scrambled for purchase, but her gloves kept her from getting a good grip on his shoulders to haul herself up. To get herself air.

"Where is he?" he hissed now and slammed her head against the wall.

Black dots swam into her vision at the concussion, and she thumped at his back, trying to break his hold even though she knew it was no use. Her reticule thumped along her wrist, and inspiration struck.

There was one remaining sharp pencil in her reticule. If she could reach it…

"I don't know," she tried to say but the words came out blurry as she couldn't draw a full breath.

The hand at her throat squeezed dangerously.

"You are hiding him. Where is he?"

She shook her head, desperate to convince him that she didn't know the professor's whereabouts any more than he did, whoever this man was.

At the thought, her novelist brain kicked into action. When she survived this, because God blast it, she would, they would need to identify this man. She needed to catalog everything about him as if he were a character in a Melanie Merkett novel. Instead of peering at the gardens behind him through the glass, she moved her gaze to his face.

He wore an unadorned mask of white that covered most of his face except for his mouth and small holes at the eyes. It was too dark to take in their color. Her gaze moved on. He was tall, but his shoulders were unusually narrow. He was rather thin for his height. He wore gloves, judging by the scraping against her throat, and his clothes were of a dark color. She couldn't see more than that about the rest of his person.

The reticule slipped open under fingers, and she plunged her hand inside, searching for the pencil.

His hair was a darker color. Black or brown, maybe. It was too hard to discern color in the misleading moonlight.

Finally, her fingers seized wood, and she pulled her hand free. Swinging her arm wide, she thrust. The wretched scream tore through the quiet of the corridor as the pencil met its mark in the man's neck. He dropped her instantly, his hands going for the spot between his neck and shoulder where she'd hit him.

She pushed along the floor, her gloves and slippery heels preventing her from gaining her feet. But she needed to create distance between them if she were to have any hope of escape.

"You bitch!" he cried after her. He was still much too close, but she couldn't look back to make certain. She had to get away.

But he was on her before she had made it very far at all. He wrenched her to her feet, and she regretted dropping the pencil when she'd made contact.

"You little—"

He didn't finish the sentence because just then a gunshot split the air. He screamed again, tearing around in the direction of the shot as he pulled her in front of him as a shield.

"Let her go." Samuel spoke the words with such cutting calmness, even she shivered.

"He wants the professor," she yelled if the unfortunate were to occur and she was killed before relaying the information.

She didn't want to die. As she stared at her husband standing paces away, shadowed in moonlight, a smoking pistol at his side and another pointed at the cowardly man who used a woman as a shield, she knew she wanted life with Samuel. More than anything. More than her stories. More than the characters she had nurtured to life. She wanted Samuel. She wouldn't write another damn novel if it only meant growing old with him.

"We don't have the professor, so let her go."

She slowly became aware of the others standing behind Samuel. Evanshire and Sarah.

But Nathan was supposed to be in attendance that night. Nathan and Nora. Her eyes darted from side to side as she realized they were somewhere else. They must be assuming a different position while Samuel distracted her assailant. She had to keep talking. But what? What did she need to say?

She became aware of another noise then, and at first, she thought it might have been Nathan, approaching from behind. But the noise was greater than that. More complicated.

Feet. It was people running. Lots of people. The corridor flooded with light, and she blinked against it as footmen arrived carrying candelabras, holding them aloft for the guests that had followed.

Faces peered over Samuel's shoulders at the spectacle that was Penelope and her attacker. Her attacker uttered something then, and she felt the press of his mask against her shoulder. He was trying to hide. He was getting desperate. Dear God, she needed to say something. Anything.

She watched the faces fill in the space behind Samuel. So many eyes. So many exclamations of shock. Everyone was watching. Everyone was going to watch her die. Or worse, watch Samuel die.

"I'm Melanie Merkett!" The words ricocheted through the eerie silence of the corridor louder than any gunshot. "I'm Melanie Merkett. I wrote those novels. I'm her." She was blabbering, but she couldn't help it. She could only see Samuel now. His eyes so clear, so focused. Only on her.

Their audience erupted in a tidal wave of murmurs, whispers, and gasps. Her revelation spread like fire through a haystack, but she didn't care. She had to buy Nathan time for whatever it was they were about.

The attacker shifted her in his arms, and she came up solidly against his chest, one of his arms wrapping cleanly around her waist.

She froze.

She knew this man.

She knew him because she had danced with him before.

"Samuel!" she screeched. "Samuel, I know this man. I've danced with him. You need to ask Jane. Jane will know everyone I've—"

He twisted an arm around her neck, cutting off her air and her words, but she saw Samuel's pistol falter at her declaration, and she knew he'd understood enough.

"I'm going to kill you, you—"

The crash came from Penelope's right, splintering glass and splitting wood, and she closed her eyes, flooded with the realization that she had found enough words to give them time to act. Something hit them with the speed and impact of a runaway carriage. The wall met her opposite shoulder, her head cracking plaster as she slid to the floor. Bodies covered her. More than one. More than two.

Alec.

She hadn't accounted for Alec. Was it both of them? The brothers Black? She didn't open her eyes. She pressed into a ball, shrinking into the floor if only to survive.

She'd done her part. She'd used her talent for words to bide them time. That was enough. Now she needed to persevere. There was scrambling, shuffling, flesh hitting flesh. Gunshot.

And then the worst of all—

Silence.

CHAPTER 24

he point is not to win. The point is to never give up.
        From The Adventures of Miss Melanie Merkett,
Private Inquisitor

HE REACHED her within seconds but even that was too long.

"Penelope." He picked her up off the floor, pulled her into his arms, shook her when she didn't respond fast enough. "Penelope!"

"I'm fine, I'm fine." The words came out on top of each in breathy exhalation, but her hands finally gripped him in return. Her face came up, and he could finally see her eyes, her wobbly smile. "That was quite more adventurous than I had bargained for, Mr. Black."

He kissed her. He didn't care who saw. He didn't care that they had an audience. He needed to know she was real, alive. His. He kissed her mouth. He kissed her cheeks. He kissed her brow. Anything.

"Samuel, I'm all right. I promise. Just a few bruises, I'm sure." She pushed him away, and he only let her because her smile had grown less shaky. She looked about her. "Have you seen my reticule?"

"Your reticule? Why on earth do you need that in a moment like this?"

She pursed her lips at him. "My notebook's in it. You don't expect me to remember all of these details, do you?"

He didn't answer and instead helped her to her feet. Evanshire approached them, a hand pressed to his chest as he struggled to regain his breath.

"We lost him," he said before Samuel could ask.

Penelope looked sharply at him. "The man who attacked me? He got away?" And then when Samuel nodded, "But how?"

It was Evanshire who answered. "Bloody bastard had a gun. Damn near shot Nathan."

Penelope swung about in his arms, her gaze careening madly, but he stopped her with a hand to her cheek.

"He's fine. The bullet missed him." He shrugged, considered his words. "Uncle Alec took the bullet for him." Penelope's mouth dropped open, and he raised a hand to stop her. "In the shoulder. He took the bullet in the shoulder. He'll be fine as long as it doesn't become inflamed."

She continued to look about, and he finally brought her over to where Alec sagged dramatically against the wall as his wife held a handkerchief to his shoulder. He grinned up at Penelope.

"Do you know in all my years as a spy for the War Office I never took a bullet? You come into the family, and not even a year later, I'm getting bloody shot at."

"I was getting shot at. You stepped in the way," Nathan argued from where Nora surveyed the damage to Nathan's knuckles. Pieces of glass protruded from his hands, and Penelope turned to the doors on the opposite wall.

"Did you crash through those glass doors?"

Nathan pointed an accusing finger at Alec. "It was his idea."

"Eh, now, I took a bullet for you. Have you forgotten already?"

"Children!"

Both grown men grew utterly still at the single spoken word as Nora and Sarah hid their laughter. Penelope turned, and Samuel stepped back allowing her to see down the corridor at the source of the call.

Jane approached with his grandmother, leaning regally on young Jane's arm. Young Jane, too, tried to hide her smile.

"Your father is rolling over in his grave. The two of you playing at such games at your age." She swatted at Alec with her fan when she reached him. "Do you have any idea the gray hair you have caused me, young man?"

Alec snorted and swatted her fan away. "There's a lot of gray on your head, madam, that has nothing at all to do with me."

Lady Jane pursed her lips at him before turning to Penelope.

"Ah, Mrs. Black," she said, her lips spreading into a conspiratorial smile. "I would ask you where you get your ideas for your Melanie Merkett novels, but I think you've made that quite clear." She turned back to her sons without pause. "Come on then, you two. You've kept me up far too late as it is. When will you let your poor mother rest?"

Nathan took Young Jane's place as he helped Lady Jane back the way she'd come. "I'm sure that day will never come," he said.

Lady Jane snorted. "Don't make me contradict you, boy."

His mother touched his arm then, only to push him out of the way to get to Penelope.

"Are you all right, child?" she said, stepping in to take Penelope's hands into her own.

Standing there in the ruins of Brownlow's Egyptian mansion watching his mother tend to his wife, apprehension seized him as if it were a physical force attempting to rob him of air. Nora pulled down the collar of Penelope's costume to expose the bruising at her neck. A dangerous red clearly outlined fingers and palm against the pale white skin of her neck.

Samuel staggered. His legs turning against him as he took in the physical evidence of the attack on his wife.

His wife.

"Easy, mate," Uncle Alec said from beside him, and he felt his uncle take his arm.

He shook his head, but he couldn't clear the image from his mind. Alec prodded him.

"Eh, Samuel," he said, loud enough to pull Samuel's attention. His uncle's face creased into lines of worry. "It's hard. The first time. Hell, every time. But our women can take care of themselves." His gaze moved to Aunt Sarah, standing beside him with the bloody handkerchief still in her hand. "It's us who need to learn that."

Samuel heard his uncle. Knew the validity of his words. But still—

His mother pulled Penelope with her as the rest departed, heading for the quiet of their carriages and then home.

Home.

Had it only been that evening that he'd relished the word? Savored it? Felt the pulse of happiness that accompanied it?

And now.

Now his wife had been attacked.

He had only thought of himself as a threat. Thought of his anger. Thought of his origins. He had never considered—

God, what an idiot he was. He was a detective inspector for the police. His family had a legacy as spies. Of course, the danger was obvious.

But he hadn't seen it. Hadn't expected it.

Had never guessed the danger might come from the outside.

What had he done?

He'd married her. Thinking he could protect her with the respectability of marriage, but that was her very death sentence.

He strode after her departing figure, took her arm from his mother's grasp and led her out to their carriage despite his mother's protest that Penelope needed to see a doctor.

He would take care of her. He had to. This was all his fault.

"Samuel?" He heard the question in Penelope's voice as he put her in their carriage. "Samuel, what is it?"

He couldn't answer her, because it was everything.

$$* * *$$

"SAMUEL, YOU MUST SPEAK TO ME." She said the words again. For what was likely the twentieth or thirtieth time since they'd left the Brownlow estate. And like all of the other times, he didn't respond as they entered Stryden Place.

Mrs. Norton met them at the door, her expression impassive at her employer's obvious incensed state. "Summon a doctor, Mrs. Norton. Immediately."

"Mrs. Norton, there is no need for a—"

He didn't let her answer. He swept her off her feet and carried her up the flights of stairs to their bedchamber. He laid her on the bed without a word and set to undressing her. Not in the way he had before they had left, and his cold hands had her shrinking from his touch.

Finally, he froze and looked at her.

"Samuel, you must stop this," she said, her voice achingly flat, but what was worse was the way he looked at her. The absence of feeling. The utter emptiness in his gaze. It was as if her Samuel had left. Her beloved and loved Samuel. In his place was this creature. This creature with no warmth in his touch. No heat in his gaze. "Samuel, I am all right," she pressed. "This isn't your fault." For she knew exactly what he was thinking. Samuel would allow the fate of the world to fall at his feet if ever the need arose simply because of an event over which he'd had no control.

"You must see a doctor," he said, and his words held as much feeling as his touch.

For the first time, tears pricked at her throat. She tried to sit up. She tried to snatch away the hands that handled her with such unfeeling coldness. "Samuel, please stop. Talk to me." She reached his hands. The hands were attempting to untie her boots, but he wasn't looking at her. So focused was he on the task that he didn't see her. Didn't see what he was doing as he threw out his arm as if to brush off her words.

Only she had sat up. Sat too closely, and his arm struck her in the chest. She fell backwards. The sound of her head striking the wooden headboard of the bed split the silence of the room. She sat stunned, her eyes wide as her hand went to the place at the back of her skull that throbbed with the impact.

She stared at him. Her husband. This man she loved more than she thought was possible. This man who had just struck her with enough force to throw her against the wall. It was then she realized the depth of his fears. The reality of it. For he was capable of such anger. He was capable of inflicting such pain.

She knew that because she saw it in his eyes then as he stared her. His hands frozen. His whole body frozen. His face.

Oh God, his face. The horror. The horror at himself. The

horror at what he'd done. The horror at what he could do. It was all there on his face as he stared at her.

She pushed away from the headboard, scrambled to get off the bed as he backed up, his eyes never leaving her face.

"Samuel, it was an accident. You didn't know I was there. You were—"

He didn't hear her. Or he did, and he wouldn't listen. He was already at the door. Leaving. Running.

"Samuel!" Her voice was ragged, the tears that pricked at her engulfing her speech. "Samuel, please listen to me. It was an accident."

But he didn't listen. He left.

CHAPTER 25

When faced with unstoppable adversity, one must employ one's greatest weapon. Whatever that should be.

From The Adventures of Miss Melanie Merkett, Private Inquisitor

"I CAN'T BELIEVE I'm asking this of you."

She sat across from Sir Devlin Cross nearly a week later. Samuel had not spoken to her since the night of the Brownlow affair.

She wasn't even sure if he came home at night. If he were eating. If he bathed. If he changed his clothes. She'd been too ashamed to leave the house. To inquire of his well-being from her new family. Every time she closed her eyes, she saw his face. Saw the horror that lurked there. The horror at what he'd done.

He hadn't given her the chance to explain. To tell him it had been an accident. He hadn't done it intentionally. He hadn't meant it.

But more, he hadn't let her tell him it wasn't his fault. None of it. The attack at the Brownlow affair. The way he'd struck her. None of it was his fault.

But once, long ago, someone had done something to make him think only evil could come from him. And Samuel still allowed that someone to hold power over his future.

She thought she could bear it. She thought she could hide from it all and pretend someday it could work itself out.

Except...

That was when she'd sent for Sir Devlin Cross.

Penelope was wholly and completely, devastatingly famous. With her stunning revelation of her identity as the authoress of the Melanie Merkett novels, she could not so much as take a walk in the park without someone approaching her to tell her how much they enjoyed Miss Merkett and when was another story coming. She hated it. She hid more now than ever in her room in the back of the house, staring at pages that did not write themselves.

She couldn't bring herself to draw any more words. Her one and only talent. The one and only thing from which she drew pride suddenly stared at her in sullen judgement. One more word, and she would surely drown in celebrity. She couldn't do it.

Not now. Not when Samuel, her Samuel, was somewhere out there, hurting, believing in a lie. A lie she could conquer if only he would let her.

And so she had requested Sir Cross join her for tea. Well, Wickshire had suggested she enlist Cross' help. Of course, the earl would.

She squared her shoulders. "How did you deal with your sudden fame?"

Sir Cross stared at her with a familiar empty expression, but then he set down his teacup, and for the first time in their acquaintance, he appeared somewhat relatable.

301

"It's difficult, is it not? You wish to go about your day as you have always done, and yet something, or someone rather, is always in your way. It grows tiresome with stunning quickness."

"Yes, that's it exactly."

Cross nodded. "I know it may not seem like it, but I can assure you it will wear off. People forget about you, or perhaps, just the newness of you will fade with time. It always happens." The light in his eyes had dimmed somewhat at this.

"Is your own popularity dimming, sir?"

He waved a hand and laughed, but it sounded hollow. "No, not at all. My great discovery still draws in the admirers." He winked at her as if this would convince, but it really had the opposite effect.

She set down her own teacup. "Have you ever thought about, perhaps, applying yourself to your experiments?"

"You mean, focusing only on my endeavors?"

Penelope nodded. "You don't need worshipers to conduct your academic studies. Even Wickshire has proclaimed your aptitude a time or two." He had done no such thing, but Cross needn't know that.

He brightened somewhat at her words. "Has he truly said that?"

"Yes, of course." In for a penny.

Cross smiled, the gesture taking up the whole of his face. "Well, that is quite a thing to hear. You know, I've been working on this idea I've had, but I suppose I shall apply myself with more fortitude knowing Wickshire is interested."

Penelope grinned for the first time in days, anticipating the time when Cross would bring his findings to Wickshire. "That sounds splendid."

Footsteps sounded from the hall, short, clipped, and efficient. Penelope knew that tread and turned to the open door of the drawing room. Dread coiled in her stomach. Dread. Fear. Uncertainty.

She hadn't seen Samuel since that night. He couldn't know that Sir Cross was here. This couldn't be happening. Not like this.

Sir Cross stood as Samuel entered, but he needn't have bothered. Samuel took an involuntary step back at the sight of the man. His gaze darted to her, and she recoiled at the blank stare. So much like how he'd looked at her that night.

The opposite of love wasn't hate. She could handle his hate. It was his indifference which tore her in two.

"Mr. Black." Sir Cross bowed.

Samuel only nodded in response. "Sir Cross." His gaze never left her. "I'm sorry. I seem to have interrupted something."

"Samuel, I invited Sir Cross to tea to ask his advice on handling one's sudden notoriety." She held her chin at an uncomfortably high angle. She couldn't bear the suspicion that had entered Samuel's gaze, and more, she wouldn't tolerate it. "He was gracious enough to grant me an audience."

Samuel's expression did not change. He merely backed away toward the door. "Well, then I'd best leave you to it." He left without another word.

Penelope went after him only to be stopped by a hand on her arm. She looked back at the hand and then up at Cross.

"It won't help," he said, and the sincerity in his expression had her staying.

"But how can I convince him that this isn't his fault? That's he's—"

"A good man?" Sir Cross gave a self-deprecating laugh. "If you can figure that out, you might just be the smartest woman to walk the planet." He took a few steps towards the door, and she knew their tea was over. She felt a pang of regret at its sudden end, and she wondered if she had miscalculated Sir Devlin Cross. "You know," he said, turning back as he reached the door. "If he won't listen to reason, perhaps he'll read it. You are a novelist, aren't you?"

She nodded automatically but stopped. "Yes. Yes, I am a novelist."

Sir Cross bowed to her. "Then maybe it's time to employ your art in another fashion. Good day, Mrs. Black."

"Good day," she replied, but her mind had already returned to the pages waiting for her in her room at the back of the house.

* * *

IT WAS LATE when he entered the earl's study that night. He'd taken to spending his nights propped up in a chair or sprawled on a couch in the study rather than face Penelope. His wife. The wife he must now leave.

He had come to the conclusion shortly after that night. It was the only way he could be certain to keep her safe. He had to get her as far away from him as possible. Not only was he a danger to her, but his entire world was. How could he have been so stupid to miss it?

He poured a glass of the whiskey he had been using to dull the pain and went over to the vast mahogany desk, ready to take up his post for the night and ponder the problem of Penelope. He liked the desk. It nearly swallowed him up, and right then, he wanted nothing more than to disappear. By way of furniture or any other route. It didn't matter.

Something had to stop this pain in his heart before it consumed him.

He took a sip of his drink and leaned back in the chair, resting his head back until all he could see was the blackness of the ceiling. Mrs. Norton always left a single lamp lit, and the meager light did not reach as high as the ceiling. He swam in the darkness, letting it soothe the thing that could not be calmed.

Leaving Penelope would kill him.

For ten years he had denied the possibility that he could have her for his wife. At first, it was the mere business of police work. The all-consuming quality of it. The time it had taken for him to get the police force in place, push it along the legal avenues. And then working his way from constable to inspector. The police commissioner had been ready to install him as an inspector at the outset, but he'd refused. Like any man worth his salt, he wanted to earn it.

And earn it he did.

In time.

Time away from Penelope.

And in there, the danger had grown until he could no longer control it.

He had to get her away from him. He swallowed the last of his drink, surprised by how quickly the glass had emptied. The pain still throbbed in his chest, and he sat up, ready to refill the glass. To keep the ache at bay.

Except when he straightened, he realized something sat on the desk.

A stack of paper.

Pages.

Pages filled with neat, precise script.

And there, on the first page, words that struck him to the very bone.

FROM THE ADVENTURES of Miss Melanie Merkett

. . .

He stood, pushed himself away from the desk, and strode several paces before turning around. Peering at the desk as if he'd been seeing things. But no, it was still there.

Penelope's novel.

This is what she'd been working on in that little room in the back of the house. This was the reason for the ink stain on her cuffs, her fingers, her palms.

He had kissed those palms. Kissed those fingers. It tore at him. The sight of the pages, the memory of the taste of her. He turned and threw his empty glass before he could stop himself. It shattered much as the glass doors had shattered that night, and the sound pierced his soul.

He sucked in a breath, struggled to regain his balance.

When he looked back, the pages were still there.

There was only one reason her latest novel would be sitting at this desk. Penelope did nothing without a reason.

Without getting himself a new glass, he resumed his seat at the desk and began to read.

* * *

"What the bloody hell is this?"

She froze with the bar of lavender soap in her hand and looked up from her bath at her irate husband standing just inside the door of her dressing room, holding her latest Melanie Merkett novel aloft in his hand.

"Oh," she said, contemplating the bar of soap. "Do you really wish to do this now?"

His only answer was to glare at her.

"Well then." She set aside the bar of soap. "That, my dear husband, is my latest novel. I take it you read it."

"Yes, I bloody well read it." He shook the pages at her. "Do you know what you've done here?"

"Yes, and as it's my only copy, I would appreciate it if you showed it greater care until I can get it to my publisher."

He eyed the offending bundle of pages and set them aside if only to point at them accusingly.

"It's all a lie," he said.

She shrugged. "Of course it is. It's a novel."

He glowered with a great deal more angst and strode over to her, dropping to his knees beside her bath. He gripped the tub in his hands.

"That's not what I meant."

She couldn't help the smirk his angst boiled up in her. "Yes, I know, but I do so love how much it bothers."

He made to stand, but she closed a hand over his on the rim of the tub.

"Samuel, what I wrote in there is true. I changed the names and such, but the heart of it is true."

"That man, that hero—" He seemed to choke on that word. "That man is not me. I know you meant it to be, but it isn't."

"Of course, it's you, and it's the real you, Samuel. The one the whole world sees but you."

"It isn't. You're just mistaken. Deluded. Your love for me has clouded your vision. I'm not—"

She stood up, stopping his words as she knew it would. Soap and water streamed down her naked body, over her round breasts, through the dips and valleys of her stomach and thighs. She stepped from the tub but didn't conceal herself with a towel. She wanted him to see her.

"Samuel." She stopped in front of him but didn't reach for him. "Samuel, you're so caught up in the places where you could do harm that you cannot see all of the places where you do good. You are the hero in that novel. You are a hero as my husband." His face remained unchanged, stony and unyielding. "That night at the Brownlow ball you saved my life." He opened his mouth, but she cut him off with a raised hand. "I know you think you put me in danger. I know you think you hurt me. But can't you see that I would face danger without you? Only then you wouldn't be there to save me."

He shook his head. "Penelope, I—"

She flung a soapy hand towards the windows of the room and the city beyond. "Every woman who walks the streets of London faces danger. Theft, murder, or rape. Any of those things. If it weren't for you, I would face those dangers alone. But I mustn't face them alone, because I have you."

Now she did touch him. His face was streaked with sleeplessness, dark circles under his eyes and weariness in the lines along his forehead. She cupped his cheek, pushed the hair off his forehead.

"Samuel, I don't want to face that danger alone. I need you. I want you to be the hero you already are. My hero."

She knew the moment her words hit their mark, because his face relaxed into the palm of her hand.

"Penelope, I can't—"

"No." She pressed a single finger to his lips. "There is no more time for I can'ts."

He smiled weakly against her finger. "You're a very domineering woman, you know that?"

"I think that only suitable for a hero like you."

"Stop calling me that," he said, but his lips twitched with a smile. "It makes me sound like Sir Devlin Cross."

She laughed, stepped up on her tiptoes, and pressed her lips to his. "Or perhaps like Miss Melanie Merkett. I hear she's quite famous now as well."

His arms finally came around her, pressing her wet body firmly to his. He was dressed only in his shirtsleeves and trousers, and the muscled contours of his chest pressed into her breasts and stomach. Heat pulsed low in her belly, and she clung to his shoulders.

"Ah, Miss Merkett, I could never hope to reach such glorying heights." He trailed hot kisses along her cheeks, down to her jaw, and lower, dipping into the valley between her breasts.

She arched back in his arms. "Oh, I think you might manage it."

He released her so suddenly, she nearly fell backward into her forgotten bath.

"Not without a nap first," he said and strode from the room in the direction of their bed, leaving her laughing on the floor of her dressing room.

CHAPTER 26

*S*ometimes the end finds you.
  *From The Adventures of Miss Melanie Merkett,
Private Inquisitor*

"What time is it?"

"Time for you to eat something," she said, prodding his shoulder until he opened his eyes. "You've napped for quite long enough, Mr. Black."

He smiled before he even had his eyes fully open. "I doubt the validity of your words, Mrs. Black," he said and tugged her down on top of him.

She laughed but pulled free from his grasp. "I think not. It's nearly noon, and we've a villain to catch."

Samuel sat up, swiping sleep from his eyes. "Villain?"

She went about the room, picking up his discarded clothes as she went. "Now that I've gotten you to see things clearly, we still have the matter of the missing professor and poor Bobby Egemont. Or have you forgotten?"

He stuck his fingers through his hair. He was rumpled

and adorable sitting in their bed, his bare chest visible above the sheet that had pooled at his hips. "I have not forgotten, but what clues have we to go on from here?"

"You're forgetting that I knew my attacker."

His eyes finally opened with some degree of alertness. "Yes, you did say that, didn't you?"

"I did." She put his clothes down and made for the door. "Get dressed and come find me in the breakfast room. We have much to discuss."

"Pen." He stopped her at the door. "How do you know your attacker?"

She grinned. "At some point, I danced with him. I could tell by the way he held me. We only need to write down all of the names of the partners I can remember and then—"

He jumped out of the bed. "Cross check them with a list of the attendants at my grandfather's funeral."

She raised an eyebrow. "You think these cases are connected?"

He looked up from pulling on his trousers. "I've had a suspicion that something isn't quite right. I think we should start with the list of names together."

She nodded and tossed him his shirt. "After you've something to eat."

Only when she made it to the breakfast room, she found someone else eating instead.

"I beg your pardon."

The man looked up, and a jolt of recognition went through her. She knew this man, only she couldn't remember from where. She backed up toward the door only to stop when the man spoke.

"Good afternoon, Mrs. Black. I understand you've been looking for me," Professor Xavier Mesmer said.

"Good God." This came from Samuel who had come up behind her.

"As an academic, I cannot give a judgement on the goodness of any gods, singular or otherwise." The professor gave a smirk.

"You're so young." She had not meant to blurt out the words, but she couldn't stop them.

The professor only laughed. "I get that quite a bit, lassie."

"That's it!" she cried, stepping into the room. "You're the Scot from the inn in Oxenholme."

"I am at that. I'm sorry for the deception, but at the time, I couldn't be certain of your intent. However, after recent events, I've determined you seek to aid me in finding Bobby's killer." The professor's boyish face grew all too stern and jaded for such a young man. "I'm here to provide you with the information I've been able to gather so far."

Samuel moved into the room. "What information is that?"

The professor stood and leaned on the table. "I'm afraid my information may be as narrow as yours. I was approached by a solicitor offering me a great deal of money for my discovery in telescope technology. When I refused, he suggested that I would come to harm and left. I thought him a cheat and disregarded our meeting. I'm afraid because of this I cannot remember much about the man. I've tried over the past several months to recall anything about him but I cannot. Only that he called himself Jencks and purported to represent a man of great interest."

Samuel nodded. "Go on."

"It was shortly after that that someone broke into my rooms at the Astronomical Society. I do not keep any notes on my current research anywhere but on my person, so the thieves made off with nothing. But it was then that I realized my error in revealing the nature of my discovery. It was Bobby who devised the plan to lure them away from me. He boarded the research vessel bound north to get them off my tail long enough to allow me to board a ship for America. I never made it on the ship. I discovered Bobby's body in my rooms not a week after he departed. I moved his body to Wickshire's drawing room to enlist his help without exposing myself. I then fled to the Herschels as my only other allies here in England."

"I'm so sorry," she said. "I understand Mr. Egemont was a very good friend."

"He was, and I cannot live with the fact that I've done this to him. So when I discovered John Herschel had already headed for Portsmouth, I doubled back, determined to find the man who did this. I returned to my rooms at the Astronomical Society hoping to draw out the man."

"And?" Samuel prodded when the professor paused.

He looked at Penelope and then to Samuel as if deciding how best to proceed. "I watched the society from my rooms in the hotel opposite, hoping someone would appear that shouldn't be there."

"A man out of place. An obvious suspicion," Penelope said.

"Exactly. Miss Merkett would advise just such as that," he said with a proud smile. "So I waited. A man appeared more than two weeks ago. He went into the society and, according to the doorman, inquired if I had returned. The man was not a member of the society nor was he a guest of a member. He was dismissed without gaining any information. I waited until now to show myself here in the hopes of not drawing attention."

"Do you have a description of the man?" Samuel asked.

The professor shook his head. "The doorman was less than helpful, and from my position in the hotel, I could not see more than his clothes and hat. His back was to me the entire time until he returned to the carriage when his hat blocked his face."

"Damn," Samuel whispered, and Penelope laid a reassuring hand on his arm.

"However," the professor started, and both she and Samuel eyed him. "He rode in a carriage with a distinctive crest, so I followed him to see where he would go, hoping to ascertain the name of the family by his destination."

"Of course," Penelope said. "If he had a home here in London, as any titled gentlemen with a family crest on his carriage would suggest, you'd be able to determine the family and perhaps the man's identity." A thrill shot through her as the pieces fell together.

But the professor shook his head. "Only he didn't go home."

Penelope's hopes faltered, and Samuel interjected, "Then where did he go?"

Professor Mesmer looked between them once more as if deciding whether or not to reveal what he knew. Finally, he said, "He went to the War Office."

Penelope turned to her husband. "I'm going to need more pages."

ABOUT THE AUTHOR

Jessie decided to be a writer because there were too many lives she wanted to live to just pick one.

Taking her history degree dangerously, Jessie tells the stories of courageous heroines, the men who dared to love them, and the world that tried to defeat them.

Jessie makes her home in New Hampshire where she lives with her husband and two very opinionated Basset hounds. For more, visit her website at jessieclever.com.

Made in the USA
Las Vegas, NV
14 March 2023

69049915R00187